OASIS

Eilís Barrett

Gill Books

To Mom, the ultimate survivor

ACKNOWLEDGEMENTS

To my family, who are my everything. Thank you for being the most supportive, the most amazing, and the most likely to be there when everything gets a little too much. You are the best people I could possibly know.

To my oldest friends, Dearbhaile, Máire and Aóife Palin, for listening to every detail of this book's creation, from concept to reality, for the past three years. To Lily, thank you for not complaining when I disappeared for weeks at a time while writing this book and for always being so excited for me. And to Cath for being the coolest human and most fervent fan – thank you times random numbers.

To Serena Lawless for three years ago, when you were my first NaNoWriMo ML, for creating a kind, welcoming environment I wanted to come back to year after year, and for helping me build the confidence to take myself seriously as a writer. And now, for the 2 a.m. pep talks and endless support you weren't obliged to give, but did so anyway. You'll have a place in the acknowledgements of any book I write.

To Karen Cunningham, for believing in me from the word go, and for helping me set up my very first meeting with Gill Books.

To Conor Nagle and Catherine Gough: I didn't understand what the fuss over editors was until I met you two. Thank you to Conor for the million and one phone calls, and for the elated-puppy gifs; you're Epic. To Catherine, thank you for defending *Gilmore Girls* against the wrath of Conor and his horrible taste in TV, as well as for generally being a badass. To Teresa Daly, for being a real-life superhero, and to Emma Lynam, for making boring things fun, fun things hilarious, and for being an all-round magical narwhal princess. To Rachel Pierce, thank you for your insane attention to detail and for always being there if I needed you.

To my entire publishing family at Gill Books – you turned this first scary year in publishing into an adventure. Thank you.

And to all the readers – of Quincy's story and of others – thank you for making this community the kind of place I want to call home.

PROLOGUE

I have three memories of that day. Three memories of a life before reality, of life before desperation, before fear. I have three memories of the day everything changed.

One – I remember it like this: I'm seven years old and trapped in a white dress inside the school auditorium for the Quarterly Selection, where six faces appear on a huge screen at the front of the room, the Oasis President is talking on a recording in the background. He's dressed all in blue, the lights around him so harsh, he's almost painful to look at. He's talking about sacrifice, about how these six faces could be the six faces of people who are going to save our world, who are going to be the tool by which Oasis finds the Cure.

But I didn't care about the Cure back then. I didn't need it, no one in the Inner Sector did, and I was more concerned with the tightness of my dress than any sacrifice anyone else was making.

Two – I remember being pulled out of the auditorium by a tall female Officer, sent to bring me to my testing. My teachers had been explaining it for years. At some point during every child's seventh year they are taken to an off-campus facility to be tested for the X gene, the thing everyone feared.

I didn't understand back then what that actually meant.

I remember I wasn't scared. My parents were going to be at the facility, the Officer told me as we drove down elegant streets. I didn't listen to her; I didn't care what she was saying. Instead I watched the trees pass by, one at each corner, all of them the same colour, the same size, trimmed and beautiful and perfect. We pass my house, and I press my nose to the glass of the window. It looks exactly the same as the other ones, but I always thought it was the prettiest. The walls seemed just a little bit whiter, the garden just a little bit nicer.

We passed one of the billboards, the Oasis President's face inhumanly large on the enormous screen, and I smiled. I liked the OP. He had a slow, deep voice that made me feel calm, and blue eyes that looked like you could trust him with anything.

The Officer's car pulled up on the side of the street, and she escorted me into a huge building with lots of windows and the Oasis motto printed above the door: *Without Order, there can be no Prosperity – without Justice, there is no Peace.*

I didn't even know what the second principle of Oasis meant – Prosperity – but I liked the way it sounded. I liked the way the words rose and fell throughout the sentence, the way everyone could say it but everyone said it differently.

My parents were at the reception desk, and I went to them quietly. I didn't say anything, instead keeping my eyes trained on the nurse they were looking at. She was small and her hair was white blonde, and I didn't like her. Her smile was too wide. Her teeth were too big for her small face and she looked like she was pretending not to be angry.

She led us into a small room with white walls, urging me to sit up on top of the steel table. From a drawer in the corner of the room she pulled out an object no longer than her hand. I saw a tiny needle on the end as she came towards me, and I fidgeted slightly, afraid of its point.

The nurse smiled again, and my parents put their hands on my shoulders. To comfort me or to hold me down, I couldn't tell.

The pain only lasted a moment, and I didn't make a sound. I

glanced up at my parents, their faces stern as they watched the nurse carefully. I turned towards her, and I watched as she became very, very still.

All of a sudden the weight on my shoulders was gone.

She was saying something, something I couldn't quite hear over the sounds my mother was making.

I heard the words *X gene* and *Outer Sector* and *Cure* before my mother ran away. She moved towards the door so fast I could barely turn around before she was gone, and my father followed her and I tried to jump from the table but the nurse had hit a button on the wall and suddenly there were men in white suits and giant masks, and they looked like aliens and my heart was beating so rapidly and I tried to shout for my parents but I was being picked up and I kicked and I screamed – but it didn't matter.

With a drop of blood and the beep of a test they had discovered something integrally broken inside me, something so twisted, something so wrong, that they couldn't even look at me. And I knew as I was being pulled away, in the way you believe things as a child – wholeheartedly, undoubtably, heartbreakingly – that nothing would ever be the same again.

Three – I remember the Sector Wall had never been something I had even considered passing through, until I was. I remember that the other side was not like home. Everything was dark, and black and dirty. A stray dog ran across the road as the Officers drove us out, six children huddled in the back of a van, our heads banging against the sides with each bump in the road the van drove across.

I remember everyone else in the van was crying, but I wasn't.

I had been screaming. I screamed until my throat was on fire. But I hadn't cried.

I remember the van stopping and the back opening and the Officers pulling the girls out; the boys stayed in to be dropped off at the male Dorms.

I remember not knowing where that was.

I remember not knowing where *this* was.

The building was grey and there were noises I had never heard in the Inner Sector, howls and crying and shouting.

I remember shivering as I was pushed towards the entrance, and outside the high fence that surrounds the building another Officer stopping us, taking our names, handing us grey overalls and pushing us through the gate.

I remember the sound of the guards shouting at us, '*Move it, Dormants!*' The label felt heavy, like a physical presence, the weight of it hanging around my neck as I walked on.

And I remember, more clearly than any other memory I hold, the gates slamming shut behind me.

PART ONE

INSIDE

1

My last moment of freedom exists in the sliver of time just before the sun sets and the sirens sound for curfew. I grip my satchel, swinging it over my shoulder as I look out across the Celian City, the light from the Founding Towers radiating across the Inside, almost touching the Outer Sector.

Almost.

I have to turn around before the gates close, but I can't stop staring at it. This close, I can almost imagine what it would be like to live there, surrounded by so much light and beauty. I reach back into my mind for memories of before, when that was home, but as the image I'm seeking wells up in my mind, the final siren goes off in the distance and I am dragged back to reality.

The Wall behind me signifies the beginning and the end of Oasis, the utopian society we exist inside. It comprises the three rings of Oasis: the Outer Sector, the Inner Sector and the Celian City. But the Celian City is the only real paradise we have left. Out here, in the cold and dark of the Outer Sector, so far from the light of the City, I struggle to see the perfection.

But I know why I'm here. And that is why, no matter how much I want to, I can never enter the Celian City, never step foot inside its gates. At least, not the way I am now.

Hundreds of years ago, before Oasis was built, the Virus crept up inside us. While science leapt forward, curing the diseases that had plagued the old world for so long, something more sinister was waiting for its moment to strike.

When it finally did, we were defenseless.

Within months the Virus had dwindled the population, humanity teetering on the brink of extinction. Just as we thought all hope was lost, Oasis built the Peace Wall, a thirty-metre high circle of steel and stone around one of the largest cities in the old world, and the last safe haven for the Pure, those as yet unaffected by the Virus. The Wall kept the Pure safe long enough to let the Virus die out, but by then the world outside Oasis had burned itself to the ground, leaving only a wasteland behind. Suddenly Oasis was all humanity had left.

I let myself slide down the pile of debris I've perched on until I land on solid ground, steadying my feet underneath me as I begin my trek back to the Dorms. As I walk, I run my fingers along the Sector Wall that separates the Outer Sector from the Inner Sector and the Celian City, feeling the rough concrete tear at my fingertips. The pain holds me down, prevents these stories from drowning me as I attempt to keep moving forward, back to the Dorms.

For a hundred years after the genesis of Oasis, everything was perfect. The new world that Oasis had founded was everything everyone had dreamed of. But as Oasis developed, a new problem was already brewing, ready to take away everything Oasis had worked for. Oasis discovered the X gene, a genetic trait with the capability of reactivating the Virus. Fear bred panic, and panic bred chaos as the population tried to cope with the concept of the Virus's return, this time within the Wall.

Every citizen was tested, and over half the population tested positive for the X gene, which meant over half the population were ticking time-bombs, just waiting to go off and kill everyone in the process.

The X gene is dormant, a quiet, seemingly innocent trait that could go a lifetime without the appearance of any symptoms. But it only takes one person. One single person for the Virus to manifest itself inside, and the entire population would be wiped out in a matter of weeks.

Oasis's only option was segregation, to build a wall between those with the gene and those without it; between those who were Pure, and those who were not.

I am one of the Dormants, the infected people, those who threaten to destroy society simply by being alive. We wait in fear for symptoms to appear, a sign that the Virus has been resurrected. Paranoia controls our every movement, terrified of ourselves, terrified of each other, terrified of the blood in our veins. This Wall under my fingertips is the only thing keeping the Pure safe from people like me.

Oasis found it difficult to govern us from across the Sector Wall, so the Outer Sector began to crumble as the Inner Sector flourished. We became more and more distant from the heart of Oasis as fear of contagion grew, until all we knew of the Inside was the light of the Celian City shining across us.

I pull away from the Wall, snapping back to the present as I try to haul myself over another pile of scrap metal discarded by the factory on this street. I have to pick up my pace if I'm going to get back in time. There are few street lamps left along the streets of the Outside, most of them having shorted out years ago, and it's hard to keep my footing as I stumble over piles of rubble towards the Dorms.

Oasis is searching for the Cure. A way to suppress the X gene, to ensure the Virus never takes root, to ensure there will never be another contagion. They want to save us, but for now, while we pose such a threat to our society, we have to be segregated from the Pure, for their good and for our own.

I see the Dorms coming into view ahead of me and I break into a sprint. The sirens have stopped and I'm only metres from the gates as I see them start to close. The gravel beneath my worn boots crunches as I push myself forward. My heart is thumping crazily as I slip through the opening, just before the steel gates clang shut behind me.

'1712,' an Officer growls, and I freeze. I turn around slowly, afraid that if I move too fast he will see me as a threat.

'I'm sorry,' I say quietly, ducking my head. My heart rate should be slowing down, but it's speeding up.

He catches my upper arm in a vice-grip and I try not to flinch as he drags me towards the entrance to the Dorms.

'Move it, Dormant,' he grunts, giving me one last push towards the door.

I catch myself on the side of the building just before my head hits the concrete, and I scramble back to the door, ducking inside before he has a chance to change his mind.

The Dormants dream of the day that we'll be cured. The day that we finally get to live the life citizens of Oasis are supposed to live. But there are some Pure who think differently. There are some who believe we drain Oasis's resources while supplying them only with the limited services we can without danger of contagion. No one's really sure how the Virus is passed on, which leaves very little for us to contribute, and the Pures' resentment of the Dormants grows every day.

I hear the lock sliding shut in the door behind me, and the panic that always sets in at night comes in a tidal wave. I don't like small spaces, and I don't like being locked up, especially in here, but I know that it's worse outside the Dorm gates.

There are too many Dormants to be monitored, so their deaths aren't tracked the way the Pures' are and bodies pile up in the Outer Sector like flies on a summer day. I've known girls who refused to return at night, and the next day I'd have to walk by their bodies on my way to work.

Most children in the Outer Sector are parentless, either having left their families behind in the Inner Sector when they were removed from the Pure population, or orphaned from hard living. With no one to protect them, kids are quickly assimilated into gangs of bandits, robbing and stealing their way to survival, and too regularly the attacks end with blood pooling on the pavement.

We're left with three options: stay inside the Dorms, join a gang, or death.

I start walking towards the stairs, the hallway empty and quiet as I creep past closed doors, praying I won't meet anyone on the way. But everyone seems to be in bed already. The entire building is silent, and it makes my skin crawl.

Something must have happened today if they're this quiet. Sometimes, when we get too out of hand, the patrolling Officers have to take action. A vicious fight broke out between some girls six months ago, so bad the Officers had to step in, and the resulting chaos ended with four girls dead and six others severely injured. Now, if we get too out of hand, if the Officers get so much as irritated, silence reigns across the entire building.

As I make my slow ascent up the stairs, I almost trip over a girl asleep on the staircase. The power's been shut off and it's so dark in here that I didn't see her until my boot knocked into her knee.

She looks about thirteen or fourteen, so she must have transferred in from another Dorm. The really new ones are always the same, seven years old, confused, tear-stained, and completely unequipped to deal with the unspoken rules of the Dorms.

But this girl is as good as new. Sometimes the new girls think that it's safer out here, away from the others. But it's not. Some of the more malicious girls go hunting for stragglers at night, and being caught by them once means being on their hit-list forever.

I stop in front of the girl. I wonder if I should wake her, tell her how dangerous it is to be out here. Maybe I could tell her to go back in the communal sleeping area, to curl up in some corner and pretend to be invisible, tell her that it's the only way she's going to last six months in this place.

But I can't. I have to take my own advice and keep my head down. And besides, she should know better than to leave herself vulnerable, curled up out in the open like this.

I move on, pushing up the last flight of stairs to the sleeping quarters. It's overflowing, as usual. The Dorms weren't built for this many people, because Oasis didn't think there were ever going to be this many Dormants. They could never have foreseen how long it would take to find the Cure.

As I trip over outstretched feet and arms and find the little space on the floor in the corner I've claimed, my mind returns, as it always does, to the Cure.

I imagine what it would be like to take it, to finally be safe from my own body, to be Pure. What would happen if I was cured? Would I be taken back to the Inner Sector? Would I see my parents again? Would the Outer Sector be rebuilt, the slums replaced with houses, the crematoriums with hospitals?

Could I live a normal life again?

I lie down with my back to the wall, my eyes nervously scanning the room, watching the other girls stir in their sleep, bewitched by the images behind their eyes.

Normal life. I'm not sure I remember what that means anymore. It's been ten years since I've had anything remotely normal. Ten years since I was diagnosed as a Dormant. Ten years since my parents abandoned me here, seven years old, trembling with fear.

Fear is an understatement. Terror doesn't even begin to explain the way my heart raced and my gut twisted inside of me when I had to pull on the rough grey uniform of the Dormants and find a way to live this half-life. That first week was the worst. I was that girl asleep on the stairs, cowering in a corner in the hopes of being left alone. But I wasn't left alone.

I got into my first fight three days after arriving, when a girl with dark hair and blotchy skin tried to steal my food. I pushed her, knocking her to the ground. When I saw her move to get up, before I knew what I was doing, I smashed my boot into her face, the crunch of cartilage running up my spine, freezing my blood.

And when she lay there, coughing and spluttering around the blood pouring into her mouth, I didn't say anything.

No one touched me after that. No one tried to talk to me, and no one tried to steal from me. I did what I had to do to keep myself alive, and that's what I've been doing ever since. I keep my head down, I trust no one, and I wait.

Wait for the Cure, and for the day I can get out of this hell-hole.

2

I wake up before dawn, when the shadows hold the Outer Sector down like chains. I pull my sleeve over my hand and wipe the dirt from the window behind me, looking out at the Celian City. It's bright over there, like the dawn has already come, but it only makes the Outer Sector look darker in comparison.

I sit quietly, watching the sky turn pink, absorbed in my own thoughts. I always wake up before the other girls; I don't like being woken by their feet stomping by my head in the morning.

I don't like this place before everyone is awake, when the world is so quiet that the only thing I can hear are my own thoughts. I want to do something, anything. This unsettling stillness is unbearable.

o o o

An hour later, everyone is up and awake. I stay in the room long after everyone else is gone, staring at the holes in the plaster as I count down the minutes until I have to leave for work.

The room is finally cleared, and I stand up, replacing my knife in the pocket I have sewn into the inside of my uniform. I'm not allowed weapons at work, but the walk there and back is too dangerous to go without them, so I improvised.

Eventually I have to grit my teeth and face the rest of the day. As I'm jogging down the steps I hear a crash below me, and before I realise what I'm doing I've broken into a sprint, skidding to a halt at the door to the cafeteria.

I see the girl I found on the stairs last night being thrown against the wall, blood dripping down her chin. She pushes off the concrete, trying to slip by the girl with the black hair who seems so intent on fighting with her. I stop at the door and watch the fight play out. I can't afford to step forward. I can't afford to do anything but blink at them blankly, as if it doesn't touch me.

The girl with the black curls grabs the other girl by the hair, and as she reaches out I see the Brands on her arms: red, raised skin in the shape of triangles along her forearms, marking her as a criminal. By now, a crowd has gathered around them, swaying with their movements, vying to see, deathly silent. She yanks the girl towards her viciously and I want to look away, but I can't. The other girl, the one from the stairs, pushes away from her and finally builds up the courage to throw a punch.

It hits the girl in the face, grinding her teeth against her lip, causing blood to burst from her mouth as she releases a feral scream. The Branded girl launches herself forward, but just as she does so the crowd of girls jostles to see, moving as one and blocking my view. I take a step forward, standing on the tips of my toes to see over their heads, my heart pounding in my chest.

But when I see what's happened, I step back again quickly, my back hitting against the wall.

The Branded girl drops something as the other girl slumps to the floor, gasping for air as blood spurts from her neck. She is spasming on the ground as the Branded girl takes a step back, the insane smile on her face more like a snarl than a grin.

I look down at what she dropped, watching as a pen rolls across the floor, smearing blood as it goes. My legs feel weak beneath me, my stomach churning and my eyes squeezing shut as I try to keep myself from vomiting.

Someone has called an Officer from outside, and suddenly everyone takes several steps back as the guards come in through the double doors, guns aimed at our heads, bellowing at us, '*Don't move!*' They catch the Branded girl by the arm and drag her backwards, towards the door. Now, everyone is scrambling to get away from the centre of the action, not wanting to be targeted by the guards. A crowd of girls stampedes towards and then past me, pushing and shoving and running to get away. My satchel is knocked from my hand and my things fly across the floor, but the other girls ignore it, their fear of the Officers overtaking anything else.

I drop to my knees, forcing my eyes away from the girl bleeding out on the floor, and begin picking up the few items I actually own. I am so focused on keeping my vision straight and my hands from shaking that it takes me a moment to register the slim, pale fingers handing me the items too far for me to reach.

I jerk up my head and see a blonde head and the small frame of a little girl, her face blocked out by her hair. She looks up, her wide blue eyes staring at me, as if she's been caught doing something that she shouldn't. She couldn't be more than nine or ten, skinny and pale with thin lips and eyes too big for her face.

She must be new. I don't recognise her. The serial number on the shoulder of her uniform reads 3462, but I won't ask her her first name. There are rules you follow if you want to stay alive in here, and number one is don't let anyone get inside your head. Once you let them into your brain, you start learning things about them – their name, their history, the things that matter to them – and suddenly you're trying to keep two people safe in this place.

It doesn't work like that. You don't get to defend two people. You choose who matters most, and that's who's going to survive.

The only person I need to keep alive is myself.

'Will that girl be okay?' she asks, her voice small against the chattering backdrop of the other voices in the room, her eyes now carefully trained on the floor.

'It's a thirty-minute drive to the closest hospital,' I say, in lieu of something harsher, watching the Officers carry the dying girl out through the door.

She stares at me for a moment. 'What's your name?'

'Shut up,' I snap, snatching the last of my things from her hands. She looks a little shocked, but mutedly so, like I'm looking at her through a glass window, some nuance left out of her expression.

She stands up slowly, leaving me to scramble to my feet as she looks at me for a moment before turning and walking away, head down. I can see the knobs of her spine through the thin grey cotton of her uniform shirt, the shaking of her small hands as she walks by the pool of blood, the hollows in her cheeks screaming of either illness or abuse. But I have no reason to feel sorry for her, I remind myself. There are ten other girls in this room exactly like her, and I've never had it in me to feel anything for them.

I am snapped out of my thoughts when I remember the time. Propelling myself into motion, I grab my bag off the floor, swerving away from the pool of blood and towards the door. Towards work. Towards anywhere but here.

3

I remember ten years ago, seeing the Outer Sector for the first time, and thinking the air was dark.

The Outer Sector is dependent on the Inner Sector for most of its resources, but there's little we can contribute in return without threat of contamination. Over the years the Outer Sector has developed into the main factory sector in Oasis, producing mostly electricity and vehicles, among other things. But over time the heavy factory count has left a thick smog coating the sector, or the Black Fog, as the locals call it. A lot of the time, newly tested Dormants' weak lungs – bred on the clean, fresh air of the Inner Sector and Celian City – don't last more than a few weeks out here. But some of us are different. Some of us are strong. Sometimes, it's not just our minds that want to survive. It's our body, our blood and bones that press us forward, always gasping for one more breath, one more beat of our trembling hearts.

I stand at the corner of the main street, where hundreds of people jostle and push as they attempt to make their way to work. I take a deep breath, glancing up at the Oasis insignia printed on the wall of an apartment building in front of me. Three circles, each one bigger than the first, enveloping each other, like the layout of Oasis. They represent the Peace Wall, the Sector Wall and the Celian City.

My eyes catch on an X on the lower left-hand corner of the image, painted in red, but before I can see it clearly I'm swept along by the crowd, and I have to grit my teeth as I am surrounded. The crush of people on every side raises the hairs on the back of my neck as I feel each touch like insects crawling along my skin. I'm surrounded by hundreds and hundreds of Dormants, and all it would take would be for a single one of them to have an activated X gene, and we'd all be dead within days.

Every single person in the Outer Sector knows this. I can tell by the way they twitch, by the paranoid glances and the way they hunch their shoulders as they walk, as if they can protect themselves from the Virus simply by shielding their faces.

But they can't. The Virus, as much as we'd like to pretend it isn't, is part of us. It's in our blood and our bones, in the beat of our hearts and the swell of our chests as we breathe.

Years ago, people thought the Virus infected people. But that's not really true. Today we know that it's more than that. The Virus doesn't infect people, it *is* people.

The Virus is me, and I am the Virus.

○ ○ ○

I'm a block from work when I slam into the person in front of me, my breath catching in my throat. My head shoots up, along with everyone else's, and suddenly I'm looking at the OP, his smile broad and calm as he looks down on us from the broadcast screen, as if he can actually see each one of us.

'Citizens of Oasis,' he says, his voice so calm and warm that the entire crowd slows to a stop, faces upturned to their President. 'Every quarter, six individuals are chosen from among us, six Subjects who give up their lives in the search for the Cure.'

My heart slows down, and I flex my hands at my sides.

The Quarterly Selection is routine, and I'm more focused on

getting this over with so I can get to work than I am with the Subjects.

'To maintain a world like ours, sacrifices must be made. Sacrifices must be made to defeat the Virus, so we may live in complete peace, that our minds will be worried no more with thoughts of contagion, so we can press forward, into the bright future of Oasis.'

Beneath the image of his face on the screen, the Oasis motto is printed in block capitals, a stark black against the blue of the OP's suit, offset by the white wall behind him. *Without Order, there can be no Prosperity – without Justice, there is no Peace.*

I hear the people beside me, pressed in on all sides, take a deep breath, waiting for the faces to appear.

'Oasis, I give you this quarter's Subjects.'

The OP disappears, his face replaced by six others, first names and serial numbers listed beside them.

When we test positive for the X gene, our original surnames are stripped from us, replaced with a unique four-digit serial number, a much easier way to keep track of us.

My eyes drift over the faces now, the serial numbers blurring into the background.

A man, young, with dark hair and a firm set to his jaw.

A blank-looking young woman, her hair curling around her shoulders in thick red waves.

Another man, a little older than the first, dark-skinned and calm looking.

A young girl, my age, with sharp features and dark brown hair, cut sharply at her shoulders.

My heart stops. I take an involuntary step forward, bumping into people and not caring.

The girl. Green eyes blaze from her face, a look of indignation setting her features in a scowl.

I lose the ability to pull air into my lungs.

An indignant, dark-haired girl with green eyes and a sharp jaw – different, and yet so impossibly the same.

The name beside her picture feels like it's engraving itself into my bones, as if I can feel the drag of a knife writing that name through my flesh: Quincy.

I am the fourth Subject.

4

The room I work in at the Outer Sector power station is made of black glass, so that no light gets in to create a glare that could obscure the surveillance images. I can see nothing through the glass, but my supervisors, sitting beyond the glass, can see me, constantly watching to make sure I'm doing my job correctly.

Right now, the darkness offers protection. I sit in the quiet stillness of the surveillance room, waiting to wake up, to be notified of a mistake, for some kind of explanation. But it doesn't come, no matter how long I sit, and my heart won't slow down.

Subjects don't return. The OP said it himself. When people speak of the Subjects, they speak of sacrifice, of heroism, but never of return. The Subjects are chosen, they are sent to the Labs, and they are never seen again.

The hunt for the Cure is as harsh as it is incessant. The Virus has no mercy, so in the fight against it, we are left with no option but to be as ruthless as it was, as it *is*.

I can never know when I'm being watched at work, so I keep my fists tight and watch the monitors, attempting to keep my face blank of emotion.

But all I'm thinking is how I'm going to explain this to Aaron?

o o o

Hours later I am still watching the screens quietly. My shift is nearly over, and my eagerness to get out of this room is making the blood zing in my veins. This small, dark room feels like a prison now, panic breeding claustrophobia, and I can barely keep from walking out this instant. There are only forty minutes left in my shift, but it stretches out in front of me like a lifetime.

I force myself to sit still. The bank of screens in front of me shows the Celian City in all its glory, but I'm not here to admire it. I'm watching for the signs, the lights flashing on and off, dimming, any sign of damage to the outlets. I keep staring hard at the scene, as if I'll melt through the screen and into their world, a world that used to be mine as well.

The City of Light was built of celian – a clear, glass-like material so strong that nothing could shatter it, a substance created solely for the purpose of crafting the most beautiful, most impregnable city mankind had ever seen. But from the Outer Sector, the Celian City looks as if it's been built of diamonds, the perfect lines of the Founding Towers glittering in the sunlight. The city and its Towers were meant to symbolise what Oasis stood for, that beauty and strength could go hand-in-hand, that perfection wasn't impossible but was achievable, as long as each citizen adhered carefully to its principles.

The Founding Towers were built to represent a physical manifestation of the four pillars of Oasis: Order, Prosperity, Justice, Peace, each building named after the virtue it upholds. The Towers are so tall and so bright that you can see them from anywhere in Oasis, no matter how far you go or what time of day it is.

But all that light has to come from somewhere. The power station's Grid delivers over twenty-thousand megawatts to the Celian City every day, enough energy to power over two million homes in the Outer Sector. But in there, electricity runs everything. The lights are brighter, bigger and more elaborate. Light is everywhere in the Celian City, in every crack and crevice until there is no room for darkness, no room for the shadows that the rest of us live in. And all of that light comes at a price.

The system is so complex, and so delicate, it has to be highly monitored at all times. My job is to make sure that the Grid doesn't go down inside the Celian City. With everything powered by electricity, if it ever did, they'd be plunged into chaos. If that does happen, it's my job to make sure it's fixed as soon as humanly possible.

There is one person with my job in each power station, of which there are six across the Outer Sector. Each of us is assigned a section of either the Celian City or the Inner Sector to monitor. The Inner Sector is broken into four sections, North, South, East and West. The Celian City itself is broken into only two sections: East and West. Somewhere on the other side of the Outer Sector, someone else is watching a similar screen to mine, carefully monitoring for changes so that their side never loses power. Even though I've been doing this job for three years, when I stare at the city lights, I can still feel my heart rate picking up. It's the most beautiful thing I've ever seen. It's the most beautiful thing *anyone's* ever seen. It's like diamonds and gold have been melted together to create the kind of paradise people couldn't even imagine in the old world.

And now people exist inside of it. They live and breathe and work inside this bubble of light and power, and they take it for granted. The Celian City isn't like the Inner Sector – there are no houses or apartments – but it is where the most important, most powerful people in Oasis do business. It's where new laws are passed, where justice is served, it is the axis on which the entirety of Oasis spins.

And now I'm never going to see it. Not properly, not up close. I dreamt for so many years of the day I'd get to walk through the streets of the City of Light, but now, as a Subject, another sacrifice to the Cure, I'll never see it —

Without warning, I'm plunged into complete darkness. The monitors all switch off at the same time, and I'm so shocked I jump back, knocking over my chair in the process. All I can hear is my own heartbeat, like a sledgehammer in my chest, for an entire minute.

I have a sudden, hysterical sense that they're coming for me, that the scientists from the Cure Research Labs are going to break in here and drag me away, and that I'm powerless to stop them.

Then the monitors shudder as they come back to life, but as the screens power on, I no longer see the lights of the Celian City. Instead, written across a black screen in a white font, is a single sentence.

Without Secrets, there is no Peace.

Beneath it are three circles, each bigger than the first, enveloping each other, and beyond them, towards the bottom left of the screen, a small, insignificant x.

Except that it's not. My mind launches me back into the crush of the crowd this morning, reversing me back through my memories. Falling towards the power station, my heart in my throat, my image appearing on the broadcast as one of the Subjects, the Oasis broadcast, a small x just beneath the insignia.

Before I can process it, the screens go back to normal, showing panning shots of the Celian City. What the hell just happened?

My breath shudders out of my body, just as an Officer comes bursting through the Exit at my back. I lunge for the door unthinkingly; I just need to get out, to find out what's happening, to find out what that even was. Before I realise my mistake, the Officer's nightstick is cracking into my ribcage, sending me crashing into the wall.

I look up long enough to see it coming towards me again, just before the Officer's arm is caught from behind him, and suddenly the weapon is across the room, the Officer shoved up against the door.

'Would you like to explain to me,' a furious voice growls, 'why you were assaulting a girl at her place of work?'

Aaron.

'Sir, she was trying to attack me.' The Officer grunts, his arm twisted up behind his back.

Aaron looks back at me briefly, and I shake my head minutely, trying to breathe around the pain in my ribs.

He tightens his hold on the Officer's arm, making him grunt in pain again, before leaning in to whisper something in his ear.

'No sir,' the Officer mumbles, agony in his voice.

Aaron drops the Officer's arm, pushing him towards the door as he lets him go.

'Tell your supervisor she'll be hearing from me,' Aaron says, pushing the officer out the door and slamming it shut behind him.

I watch his shoulders go up and down as he takes a deep breath, calming himself before he turns to me.

'Are you okay?' He offers his hand to help me up.

I stand up gingerly, my side aching.

'I'm fine,' I lie, gritting my teeth against the pain.

'Good.' Aaron nods. He blinks at me for a moment, resetting himself. I can see the change in his eyes, the sides of his mouth tilting up as he looks at me.

'Hi.' He smiles like it's the first time he's seen me, like it's okay, like there isn't already a bruise blooming across my side.

'Hi.' I try to smile back, try to mirror the look in his blue eyes. He leans forward, placing his hand on my cheek as he presses his lips gently to mine.

I try to enjoy it, try to savour his warmth, but there are too many voices in the back of my head, screaming of Infection, of the Virus, of killing the only boy I have ever loved because I was too stupid and too selfish to pull away.

So I do pull away, and I try to pretend I don't see the disappointment in his eyes.

'Ready?' he asks, squeezing my fingers briefly, as if I must give him some form of consolation.

I glance back at the monitors, running smoothly, and for a moment I wonder if I imagined the whole thing. But I blink and the small red x is printed on the inside of my eyelids, a different sort of brand, sending a shiver up my spine.

'Ready,' I whisper.

5

Does he know?

I should tell him.

I scan my ID as we pass through registration, but the ranking marks on Aaron's blue uniform get him a free pass. Seven black stripes across his upper left arm, placed above seven matching black marks inked into his skin.

We walk out of the huge grey building in silence, and neither of us says anything as we pass through the gates of the power station. It isn't until we're back on the streets of the Outer Sector that Aaron speaks.

'You sure you're okay?' He looks down at me, concern in his eyes. His golden hair catches the sunlight as he bends his head towards me, and my breath feels like a weight within my chest.

I should tell him. Right now. It would be the perfect moment. I could say it, and he would fix it, because Aaron fixes everything.

I look forward, at the streets of the Outer Sector, darkening as the sun sinks below the wall of buildings on all sides, and though the lack of light blurs the filth of the streets, when I close my eyes it's still the same place. I can hear people fighting, there's a child crying somewhere in the distance, and the whole place smells like rot and decay.

Aaron is still looking at me, a question on his face.

'Tell me what you're thinking,' he says. He's leading me back towards the Dorms, where it's safer, but down these streets he's hyper-observant, just waiting for something bad to happen.

'I just–' I take a deep breath, trying to let the tightness in my chest go, but I can't. 'I just can't wait until they find the Cure.'

The lie makes my stomach churn.

Aaron gives me a sharp look. I shouldn't have said that.

Nine months ago, when I met Aaron for the first time, he never meant to get involved with me. None of this was supposed to happen. Aaron came to the Dorms looking for recruits for a new programme they were setting up, training Dormant kids to be Officers, so the Outer Sector could start policing itself. He had interviews with every girl at the Dorms, but he interviewed me twice.

Later he told me that I never stood a chance. The programme was seeking out athletically talented OS kids, ones they wouldn't have to train as extensively. I'm five foot three and slight, not exactly a soldier in the making. But somehow I had caught his attention, and even after the interviews were finished, he kept coming back to see me.

But I'm still Dormant, and he's still Pure.

We are forced into hiding, our relationship an illegality. Eventually they'll find out. We both know it. You can't keep something like this a secret forever. Our only hope is that by the time they do find out, I'll already have been Cured. But still, I hate it. The sneaking and the hiding and the lying; loving him and never really getting to be with him. But any time I tried to convince Aaron that this was a bad idea, he said he couldn't live without me.

So instead, we pretend the Virus doesn't exist. We pretend I'm not Dormant, and he's not Pure. We pretend that the thick, solid line drawn between the Pure and the Dormant doesn't exist, that we are the same, and while I'm with him, it feels like that.

But Oasis reminds us. When he must remain a safe distance from me on the street. When I can't meet Aaron's father because he can't know about us. When Aaron has to go home at night, back to the Inner Sector where he belongs. When Officers hit me with nightsticks for walking towards them too fast, but treat Aaron like royalty the minute he walks in the door, all because I have the X gene and he does not.

I hate the Virus. I hate the divide it causes between me and the boy I love.

'I need to tell you something,' Aaron says.

I can see the Dorms ahead of us.

'What?'

'They're training kids in the Outer West Sector and they need some people who've already been through the programme to give them a hand.'

My heart drops.

'And you're going with them?'

'I have to.' He shrugs. 'They need me.'

I need you, I think, trying to stop myself from crying.

'Hey,' he says. He glances around, pulling me into a dark alley. He continues pulling me until he stops between two dumpsters, glancing back to make sure no one can see us. But the streets have quietened down since rush hour, and this alley doesn't lead anywhere.

He goes still for a moment, taking my face between his hands. 'I love you,' he says quietly. 'And I'll be back in a week or two, don't worry.'

He kisses me, soft and hard at once, his hands in my hair and the heat of his body soaking in to me. I put my hands on his chest to push him away, afraid. Of the Virus, of Infecting him, of every nightmare I've had about us becoming a reality. He catches my hand with one of his own, pressing my palm flat against his chest.

'Shh,' he whispers. 'Stop worrying.'

Aaron is like the Celian City. He's golden and beautiful and perfect, the kind of perfect you don't think exists until you see it, standing there asking you for something and you can't bring yourself to say no. He has warm-toned skin and golden hair and eyes that are too blue to be real and high cheekbones and a straight nose and he's just too perfect.

I have to remind myself that I'm lucky. He's an Officer of the Seventh Tier, the highest level Officer there is, an Elite, and he's beautiful and kind and good to me, and if he has to leave every now and again because he has an important job, then so what? He's still my Aaron.

'Are you okay now?' he says, pulling back enough to look at me. 'All the worries gone?'

'Yes.' I nod, and smile and smile and smile until he smiles back in a way that makes me know he believes me.

His phone buzzes in his back pocket and he doesn't even need to check it to know what it is.

'I need to go.'

'It's fine,' I tell him, pressing a kiss to his lips. 'Go.'

'Thank you.' He kisses me back quickly, then walks away. Disappearing back into the main street, falling back in to the push and pull of the crowd that makes way for him, leaving me behind.

I press my back harder against the grubby walls, squeezing my eyes closed and balling my hands into fists as I attempt to gain control over my emotions. There is this indescribable feeling that bubbles up inside me as he walks away – like I can't catch my breath, like gravity is suddenly trying to drive me into the earth, like the world drains of colour the minute he's gone – and I wonder if I'll ever feel okay when he leaves.

6

Not long after, I pull myself up on top of the scrap pile left over from the factory, my eyes fixed on the Celian City as I sit down. I try to breathe deeply, to calm my shaking hands as I look out over the city I've been in love with for so many years. The four Founding Towers look stark and elegant against the night sky, promising so much. But we are still here, and they are still there, and it seems their promises don't extend as far as these forgotten shadows we reside within.

I've done this so many times. Sat up here for so many hours, thinking, wondering what my future will be like.

Now I'm not even sure I'll have a future.

I've been eligible to be chosen in forty Quarterly Selections in my lifetime, and somewhere along the way I decided it would never be me on that list, until suddenly I was.

I pull my knees up to my chest as my mind drifts back to my picture on the broadcast on Main Street. There aren't any mirrors in the Dorms, so the only image I've seen of myself in the past ten years have been glimpses of my distorted reflection in windowpanes and in the monitors at the power station.

The picture printed on the broadcast must be from six months ago. Every year ID photos are taken by the power station to keep track of the workers. That must be where they got the photo. I never even got to see it.

My breath shudders out of me as I think of the message written across the monitor, and I wrap my arms around my knees, feeling suddenly cold. Someone must have hacked the server. Maybe one of the Branded, angry at their sentence? But still, how could they? The mainframe was built by the Celian City's top technical security experts, and the technology you'd need to even try to hack it isn't available in the Outer Sector.

So who, then? Someone from the Inner Sector? And what did the message mean, anyway? *Without Secrets, there is no Peace.* I recognise that it's taken from the Oasis motto, but I don't understand what it could possibly mean, and why someone would twist it like that.

I feel ill. I try to focus on the Celian City, try to imagine Aaron living, existing inside of it, but then I remember he's not.

I remember he left.

Then I remember that soon I will leave, to go to the Labs.

I feel like someone's strangling me.

Oasis, the Celian City, the Cure: these were the things I lived for. These were the things that kept me moving, breathing, living, no matter what. These were the things that meant everything to me.

But how am I supposed to live for something I'm not even going to survive long enough to see?

7

When I return to work the next day, there are Officers everywhere. The power-cut was across the entire building, and now the supervisors are watching everyone, sure that it must have come from the inside. You can smell the fear in the air as you walk through the clear glass doors. Even here, in the power station, celian is too expensive to use.

I am assigned an Officer at registration, who follows me in to the room where I work. She places her hands behind her back and looks straight ahead, her eyes dead, and yet I know she's watching me like a hawk.

Everyone knows the Officers are afraid of the Virus. They are sent to work in the Outer Sector as punishment for misdemeanours, or to toughen them up if they seem lacking. They're afraid of Infection, afraid of being so close to us, afraid that we will activate the Virus and they'll die alongside our horrible, stinking bodies.

But I don't blame them.

As I stare at the surveillance monitors, I catch a glimpse of my reflection in the screen and stare at myself. I look at my eyes, and I know they're green but I can't see that from the monitor. I try to piece together an image between the memory of the photo on the broadcast and this distorted version, but I can't.

And even if I could, what would I look like then? Would I look like a girl with a secret? The kind of girl who didn't tell the boy she loves that she was being taken away? The kind of girl carrying a gene that could wipe out humanity, and is still reluctant to do the one thing she could to help?

I am a Subject. I say it to myself again, staring at my twisted reflection. I am a Subject.

I turn away, and stare into the light of the Celian City instead.

The glistening beauty of the Celian City as the sun begins to set is almost putting me to sleep when it happens again.

I grip the desk with my hands, which I can't see in the pitch-black of the room. I hear the Officer behind me inhale sharply, the metallic click of her gun as she raises it, but there's nothing to fire at.

Suddenly the screens come alive, blinding me.

Without Light, there are no Prisoners. 10/12/0000

o o o

The entire building is on lockdown.

Once the servers restarted and the lights came back on, the supervisors closed the gates and locked the doors until they can figure out who's doing this.

But I don't think it's someone inside the building.

The Officers have moved all the workers on to the main floor, where they build generators for the off-Grid buildings, and everyone looks terrified and confused. The Officers line the walls, and the one guarding me an hour ago is talking quietly to the head supervisor at the front of the room.

All of the workers stand shoulder-to-shoulder in the middle of the room, something we were taught to do during training, and wait with bated breath to see what happens next. Will they interrogate us individually? Surely that would take too long. But if they don't, how will they figure out what happened?

Eventually the supervisors turn to us, and the head supervisor nods. For a second I think she nodded at me, but I brush it off, until one of the Officers starts walking directly towards me. Without a word the male Officer, almost a foot taller than me, pulls me from the centre of the crowd, bumping against several other workers as he drags me towards the front of the room. I don't dare to pull against his grip, but when he stops me in front of the supervisor, a tall, slim woman with greying hair, I begin to wonder if I should just run.

'Explain to me what happened this morning.' Her voice is gravelly and emotionless.

For a moment my mind goes blank, and all I can think about is my knife pressed against my hip in the hidden pocket I've sewn into my grey trousers, and I feel suddenly paranoid that they can see it.

But eventually my brain catches up with the request, and I begin fumbling with the seam of my uniform as I speak.

'The building lost power and the monitors shut off.'

'How?' she snaps.

'I don't know.'

'Were you involved in the loss of power?'

I glance up, and her eyes are trained so intently on me, I wonder if it matters what I say to her. She looks like she's already made up her mind.

'No, of course not! I have no idea how it happened.'

'Do you know who was involved?'

'No,' I say, but there's something in the back of my mind, something I can't quite put my finger on, that makes me think I might have an idea.

'And what about the message?' she says.

I'm surprised she even mentioned it.

'I—' my throat suddenly feels tight. 'I don't know.'

'What did it say?'

'I don't remember.'

'Yes, you do.' Behind her calm expression her brown eyes are like stone.

'Without light, there are no prisoners,' I choke out.

'Take her away,' the supervisor orders, glaring at me. Two Officers

34

immediately catch my arms, and I look up at them in terror.

'What?! I didn't do anything wrong!'

The supervisor eyes me calmly. 'You quoted a terrorist slogan. You're under suspicion of being a threat to Oasis and its citizens. You will be contained until evidence is provided otherwise.'

'*I didn't do anything*!' I scream, pulling my arms free of the Officers. Another one jumps forward, trying to grab me from the front, but before I know what I'm doing my fist is connecting with her face, and she's sent reeling into a table. She bounces back faster than I expected, launching herself at my waist, sending us both crashing to the floor.

I can feel the other Officers dragging at me, trying to pull me away, but I'm more concerned with this Officer's fist cracking into the side of my face. I take her arm, twisting my hips as I launch her over to the left, using the momentum to land on top of her, my elbow connecting with her right cheek before I'm pulled away by two of her colleagues.

One of the Officers pushes me back against a wall, flipping me around and smashing my face against the wall as he handcuffs me.

'*Get off me*!' I scream, just before I feel a sharp pain in my neck, and the world fades to black.

8

I wake up to the sound of slamming doors and someone shouting, and I sit up so fast I hit my head against the bars above me. I blink at the white-washed room in confusion as I'm overwhelmed with the sense of wrongness all around me.

And then I remember. The lights cutting out, the message, the lockdown, the fight, and then … nothing.

They must have used some kind of sedative to stop me from fighting back.

I look down at my bleeding knuckles, and my stomach drops. What have I done? Even if I'm proven innocent of the power cuts, I assaulted an Officer of Oasis. I'm guilty of that much at the very least.

I look around the small containment zone as I try to steady my breathing, wondering how much longer they'll keep me here before shipping me off to a prison somewhere. Three of the walls are plain grey concrete, but one is made of celian. It's two-way, not like at the power station, which means the inmates can watch the Officers watching them.

But there's no one here.

Just as I think that, someone storms into the hall beyond my containment zone, all blue eyes and blazing rage.

Aaron.

I can't hear him from inside the glass, but I can see him ordering another Officer to open the door, and when he does Aaron is inside immediately, closing the door behind him.

His shoulders rise and fall as he turns towards me, barely containing the anger that I can feel rolling off him, and I take the smallest step back.

'What the hell did you think you were doing?'

'Aaron, I—'

'They're telling me you've been arrested for suspected treason and assault. Not only that, they're telling me that you're a Subject. Do you know what that means?'

'Aaron, please, just let me explain—'

'*DO YOU KNOW WHAT THAT MEANS?*'

I cringe at the sound of his voice.

'Yes,' I whisper, trembling all over. 'I know what it means.'

He turns away from me, running his hand through his hair, and I'm not the only one shaking.

'You're going to get yourself killed,' he says, his voice unsteady. 'Do you realise that? Do you realise that you're playing with your *life*?'

'Aaron, I'm sorry. I don't know what happened.'

'About what, Quincy? The Selection, or you attacking an Officer? Because the first one I can understand, but what in the name of Oasis possessed you to attack an Officer?' The revulsion in his voice is as evident as it is absolute, and my chest squeezes tightly, tears springing to my eyes.

He pushes a breath out through his nostrils, closing his eyes as he realises his mistake.

'Listen, I'm sorry for shouting, but I don't know what I'm supposed to do with you.' He runs his hands over his face in frustration.

I sit down on the bunk-bed that's pushed up against the wall, leaning my elbows against my knees as I try to think straight.

'It's not like there's anything they can do to me, Aaron. I've already been Selected – there isn't anything else they can do.'

'They're pushing up your transfer date,' he says, his voice dead.

'What?'

'They're transferring you next week.'

'How is that possible? They can't do that, they have to give me one month's notice.'

'Not if you're a public menace.'

'A public *menace*?'

'You attacked an Officer of Oasis for no reason.' Aaron isn't even looking at me anymore.

'They were going to throw me in containment for something I didn't do!' I argue, but my anger is lost in my fear.

'I'm going to fight this, Quincy, but there's only so much I can do.' He looks at me now, but the disappointment in his eyes makes me wish he didn't.

'Aaron.' I stand up, reaching for him, and I don't know which of us I'm trying to comfort.

'Don't,' he says, pulling his hand away from me. 'I don't know what I'm supposed to do with you anymore.' He closes his eyes briefly, then motions for the Officer to let him out, and leaves without another word.

I fall back onto the bed, my head in my hands, my heart racing, and I can't breathe. The only thing I can think about is that look on his face, that I've seen on so many people's faces, so many hundreds of people have looked at me like that, but Aaron never did, not ever for a second.

He looked disgusted.

9

I'm pacing. And seething. I feel it like oil beneath my skin, thick and black and ugly, and I'm too exhausted to try and stop it from sinking deeper.

How *dare* they? How dare they try to take everything from me? How dare they turn him against me?

This was not my choice. I didn't want this life, I didn't want to be a Subject, I didn't want any of this.

But I never had a choice.

I pound my fist against the celian window, screaming at the top of my lungs.

When he left, I couldn't hold it together. I was watching my life fall apart, piece by unwilling piece, until I was left with nothing.

But eventually pain turned to anger, and anger to rage, until all I could think about was getting out. Out of everything. I'm done. I am done with this cell, with my useless job, with the Dorms, the Outer Sector.

I slam on the celian wall and scream until my throat is raw, but no one shows their face.

Aaron is gone, and no one can hear me.

○ ○ ○

'Up,' a gruff voice announces, dragging me from the corner and pushing me towards the door.

I stumble forward, trying to regain my balance as I blink the sleep from my eyes. I must have fallen asleep at some point, but I can't remember it.

'What's going on?' I ask, putting my hands up between me and the Officer.

'You're being released,' he says. 'Give me your hands.'

I do, slowly, watching him suspiciously as he takes them. A pair of automatic handcuffs snap across my wrists, adjusting to the size of my arms as they tighten, and he takes a step back.

'I thought you were releasing me!' I tug my hands back, twisting them as if I can pull myself free.

'Protocol,' he says. 'Now let's go.' He jerks his gun in the direction of the exit, a silent reminder he's the one in control.

I swallow, trying to push back the memories of my dream, and take a tentative step towards the door. My eyes sweep the hallway, looking for him, for Aaron, but I can't see him anywhere.

'What are you waiting for?' the Officer growls, pushing me forward.

I don't know why, but I was sure he would be here. I was sure he'd turn up, no matter how angry he was. But there's no one in this hallway, or the next, or on the stairs leading up into the main building. When I'm being processed, I scan my ID card when I'm told to, and the Officer attending to the records presses her lips together as she watches me from behind her desk. Her dark eyes flick over my dirty Dorm uniform as she hands me my personal items, her lip drawn back in a sneer.

I pull the plastic bag towards me, but my cuffed wrists won't allow me to do anymore. I hold my hands up towards the Officer behind me, but he just shakes his head, pushing my hands away.

'Not so fast,' he says. The Officer behind the counter hands him a small black box. He catches my left arm, pushing up the sleeve of my uniform to reveal my bare shoulder.

'What are you doing?' I ask, my voice trembling, but he doesn't respond.

From the black box he removes a small metal object, flicking a button on the side. The end of the object begins to glow red. I tug at the Officer's grip, my heart like a kick drum in my chest.

'What are you doing?'

Again he doesn't respond, and suddenly the skin on my shoulder is burning, the smell of scaring flesh entering my nose as a scream is torn from my lungs. I drag at his hold, but he's too strong, and his arm is wrapped around my waist, holding me in place.

Finally he releases me, and I fall forward, my knees cracking against the tiled floor as tears run down my face. I scramble backwards, and I can't catch my breath or steady my hands and adrenaline feels like knives up my rib cage and they're just standing there, watching me, indifferent.

He slams shut the lid on the black box with his left hand, passing it back to the Officer behind the desk.

'You were Branded as a public menace.'

'Public menace?' I can hear the hysteria rising in my voice. I lean my hand behind me, my fingers trembling as I touch the mark, hissing as pain rips across my neck and down my arm.

'It's just protocol.' He shrugs, his body language nonchalant, but I can see the gleam in his eyes, the vicious satisfaction lurking there.

I pull myself against the wall, stumbling towards the door.

'You forgot—' he starts, but I'm already gone. I'm already out and down the steps and running through the streets. Tears burn my eyes and I try to blink them away, but there's always more waiting to fall. There's always one last punch, waiting to land.

10

Two hours later, I find myself where I always find myself: sitting on a pile of scrap a quarter mile from the Dorms, watching the Celian City, the world I always wanted.

But it doesn't feel like that anymore.

I tear the sleeve off my uniform, struggling to rip the fabric without my knife. When I was unconscious they found the knife hidden within the secret pocket in my jacket, and held it as evidence.

If it wasn't for Aaron, I wouldn't have been released at all.

I finally manage to rip the sleeve from my uniform, pulling it away from the blistering flesh of my shoulder. The mark is angry and red and swollen, and tears spring into my eyes as the cold air hits it.

I have five days left until I'm transferred to the testing facilities. Five days left to find a way out of this mess. I'm scrambling for ideas, trying to find a way to fix this without ruining everything else in the process, but I'm not sure if I have anything left to ruin. Aaron is gone, and I can't tell if he's coming back. I can't tell if I'm worth coming back for anymore.

I hear something moving behind me and I jerk around, my eyes immediately searching for something to use as a weapon.

But it's only a child. The girl from the Dorms with the too-big eyes and the stupidity to help me with my bag.

'What are you doing here?' I growl, pushing myself up into a half-squat.

'I was looking for you.'

'Why?'

'Because I know what happened,' she says calmly, climbing the pile of rubble.

'What do you mean?' I try to cover up the Brand, but I've already ripped the sleeve off, and there's nothing I can do.

Once you're Branded, the Officers see you as a target. I thought I could cover it up, hide it from them, but if this girl plans on ratting on me, I'll be dead before they have the chance to ship me out to the Labs.

'I know what happened at the power station today,' she says, sitting down beside me. I nudge backwards on the heap, a jutting piece of scrap metal digging into my back as I go.

'How—'

'Everyone was talking about it. The power cuts, the messages, all of it.'

'I don't know what you're talking about.'

'The message that they put up on the screen? I know what it means.'

My blood freezes in my veins.

'You're insane,' I say, because she has to be. Like that girl with the dark hair who stabbed the new girl the other day. It happens all the time. We all go a little bit crazy out here. You watch the smoke and the filth and the desperation all around you, and eventually it gets inside your head, too.

'No I'm not. I knew it was gonna happen.' Her blue eyes are steady and unwavering and eerily calm as she speaks, never breaking eye contact, not even for a second. 'I've been waiting for it.'

'What are you talking about?' I try to sound like I'm ridiculing her, but my voice comes out quiet and shaky.

'My father told me it was gonna happen, that the ones on the Outside would get in eventually.'

'Outside what?'

'Outside the Wall,' she says quietly.

'There's nothing outside the Peace Wall.' My mouth says the words before I'm sure I believe them.

'How do you know? How do you know there isn't loads of stuff outside the Wall? The Wall is there so we can't see, so we can't know what's happening Outside.'

I go quiet.

'Without light, there are no prisoners. That's what they said, isn't it?'

I swallow.

'They're going to cut the power from the Outside. It's the fence that's keeping us in. Once the electricity is cut, we can get out. You can get out, before you're taken to the Labs.'

I stand up, suddenly shocked back into reality. This girl is crazy.

'No,' I say, sliding down the pile of rubble past her, my heart pounding. 'That's not going to happen.'

She leaps up and follows me, even as I start winding down the streets, back towards the Dorms.

'Quincy, listen—'

'Stop,' I say, turning on her. 'Don't you dare. You do not know me. I do not know you. End of story.'

She drops her head to the side, as if she can't understand my frustration with her. I refuse to say anything, but I can feel the silence between us like a physical weight.

'10/12/0000, the code at the bottom of the screen? That's a time and date. The tenth of the twelfth, midnight.'

'How do you even know that that's true? It could have meant anything.'

'Because my father knew. He told me how to get out when the time came, if he wasn't there to help me.'

I glance down at her for a millisecond, her small face finally turned away from me. Sometimes memories are more painful than reality.

I grind my teeth, trying to figure out a solution as I walk.

'The supervisor told us it was terrorists,' I say, but even my own voice sounds weak.

'They also said you were a terrorist, right?'

I look at her sharply, and she points at my arm. I reflexively move to cover it up, but I can't – it's too painful.

'They're lying to you. They've been lying to you your whole life. We need to get out now, or we'll never get the chance again.'

'There is no *we*,' I say, stopping in the middle of the road. The Dorms are right ahead of us, and the gates are going to shut in a matter of minutes. 'I don't know what kind of crazy conspiracy theorist your father was, but he's probably in a mental asylum somewhere now, so you need to forget what he told you. Someone is breaking into the mainframe to scare people; there is no "Outside". Now leave me alone, okay?'

I begin walking away, but before I get out of ear shot, she shouts back to me.

'He's not in an asylum, he's dead. They killed him because he knew, and they're coming for me next.'

11

I sit up suddenly in the middle of the night, my blood pumping as I try to get a bearing on my surroundings. My breathing slows as I look around the room, everything familiar, everything exactly the same as always.

But something inside me drops.

I dreamt I had escaped. Or at least, I dreamt I wasn't here anymore. I dreamt of open fields and blue skies and clean air and someplace warm to go at night. I dreamt of other people, smiling people, none of them Dormant or Pure, just people. Happy people.

I shudder and fall back against the wall behind me. It's damp, and there's mould on the walls and the window doesn't close properly, and suddenly all of these tiny imperfections are smothering me.

I tighten my fists in the blanket thrown over my knees, trying to tell myself it's a stupid idea. I have no way of leaving, no one does, and even if I did, I wouldn't survive a day outside. The girl is crazy, and everything she said was a lie. But my mind is turning it into possibilities that don't exist.

What if she isn't, and it's all true, and I end up dying in here because I was too afraid to go out there?

I grind my teeth, banging my head on the wall behind me, trying to stop the tears that are threatening to fall. I'm being stupid. I'm getting upset over something I shouldn't have been thinking of in the first place. But there's this voice in the back of my head saying things I wouldn't dare to say out loud.

Like, maybe it'd be worth it. Because maybe leaving and dying out there is better than staying and dying in here, at some undisclosed location in the Labs, just another Subject dying for the sake of the Cure.

12

I turn up to the power station the next day in a stained and ill-fitting uniform jacket. After ripping up the only spare shirt I have to use as a bandage for my burn, I had to come to work in an old uniform I grew out of, all because I stupidly tore the sleeve off the other one after I was Branded.

I walk up to the entrance, pulling out my ID card to scan it at the gate. Before I can do that, an Officer stops me. He holds out his hand, and thinking it's just a routine check, I hand it over.

'Please step to the side,' he says, gesturing for me to move away from the gate to stop blocking the other workers from getting in.

Something feels off suddenly, and I can hear my heart thudding in my ears as I move out of the way.

He lays his hand on top of my right shoulder, catching the fabric badge with my serial number printed on it, and tears it off.

'What are you doing?' My voice comes out a shocked half shout.

'Your services are no longer required,' he says in a monotone voice. 'Your ID card is being confiscated.' He throws both the ID card and the serial number badge in the bin, the only two forms of identification we are given.

'What?' My voice sounds high-pitched and scratchy, and I can't tell if it's from all the screaming when I was taken to containment, or if it's the fear I feel pooling in my chest.

'Branded citizens are not authorised past this point.'

I fall back a step.

Somehow, in the middle of all the confusion, I forgot about the second part of being Branded – the part where you're stripped of your rights, your job, your ID.

'Please vacate the premises, or I'll be forced to call security,' the Officer says, and suddenly the cold edge to his voice makes me want to scream.

I turn on my heel, trying not to touch anyone as I walk by the other workers, but as always, every step I take is another invitation to bump into someone, make contact with someone, the fear of Infection rising with each touch.

My heart is pounding in my ears as I walk away, and the emotions I felt in the containment centre return with a vengeance.

I want out.

But this time, maybe I have a way.

Aaron is gone, I've been stripped of my job, and I have less than a week to live before I'm shipped out to the Labs.

I have nothing left to lose.

If what that girl was saying is true, it's my last shot at having some kind of life. At staying alive.

And if not? Then I guess I'm not leaving anything behind, anyway.

o o o

Without an ID card to procure food, I end up sitting on the scrap heap, listening to my stomach growl at me. Hours pass, but all I can do is wait.

The girl said the tenth day of the tenth month, which means, if she's telling the truth, the power will be cut tomorrow at midnight. She'll walk by the scrap heap on her way back to the Dorms, so I sit with my back to the Celian City for the first time, not waiting for the future, or for the Cure, but for a way to escape.

When she finally turns up, I'm almost asleep. I haven't been able to sleep the last few nights, and last night, with the Brand burning into me, I didn't even close my eyes.

She climbs the pile and sits down beside me without a word. She pulls a roll of bread from the satchel slung around her shoulders, and hands it to me.

For a moment I just stare at it, but she nudges me forward.

'Eat. They took your ID, didn't they?'

I look at her infuriatingly blank face, trying to understand what she's thinking. I nod slowly, ripping a chunk from the bread and biting into it.

My stomach growls again as I swallow, and I realise how hungry I am.

'That's what they did to my father. They Branded him, they starved him, and then they killed him once it was easy to cover up.'

Part of me still doesn't want to believe it. How could Oasis be so cruel? And yet the burn on my left shoulder speaks of just how cruel they can be.

I don't know how to pose my next question, so I sit for a long time, chewing the hard bread and staring at the lights of the Celian City.

'Are you ... are you coming?'

'Yes,' she says, not asking where I mean.

'How do you know it's going to be worth it? You don't know what's going to be out there. What if it's just like they said? What if it's a wasteland?'

She turns, looking at me for a long moment.

'And this isn't?'

My chin drops to my chest automatically, and I see my life in a kaleidoscope of memories, wheeling into each other. After I was dropped into the Outer Sector, I had to learn how to survive in a world I didn't know or understand. The rules were different here, and yet no one would explain them to me. At home, there was always enough food. Here, if you didn't fight for it, you'd go hungry. At home, I had my own bed in my own room, with soft, warm blankets. Here, we slept on the floor, the dry spots regularly fought over, sometimes to the point of blood, and the thin blankets gave little defence against the dropping temperatures.

The people acted differently, too. Suddenly people were something dangerous, something to be feared. I had to learn which ones to avoid, which ones were safe, and which ones would hurt me. The Officers, a symbol of peace and safety back in the Inner Sector, were different out here. They had short tempers and were more likely to punish you than smile at you. The whole place was a cesspit of violence and fear.

But then there was Aaron. He was worth all of this, wasn't he? He was worth the pain and the fear and the hunger. He was worth everything … until … until he looked at me like I wasn't worth anything at all.

Something in my gut whispers that he's not coming back. That he's done with me, of course he is. Nine months I knew him. Nine months I had the privilege of seeing him, hearing him, holding him. But perfection doesn't last forever, and Aaron was perfect. He was too perfect, and now he's leaving. And if Aaron's leaving, so am I.

I finish the bread with Bea at my side, and I can feel the reluctance in both of us to return to the Dorms.

'How old are you?'

'Thirteen,' she says, her chin rising slightly.

'Thirteen?' I ask, confused, looking at her. She doesn't look thirteen. She looks ten.

I can see it in her face that she realises what I'm thinking, and her expression sours for a moment and I almost laugh.

She reminds me of myself. Young and small and always a little bitter, always ready to bite, green eyes flashing the moment someone spoke to me.

But then the expression melts, replaced with that same vaguely bland look she's had since I met her.

'My name is Beatrice,' she says, as if trying to change the subject. I freeze a little, but she continues on, ignoring me completely. 'But you can call me Bea. My sister couldn't pronounce Beatrice when she was little, so she started calling me Bea.'

'You have a sister?'

'Yes. Her name's Sophia.'

'Does she ... is she Pure?'

Bea looks down at her hands. 'No. She was tested a few years after me, and we were placed in the same Dorms for a while. They moved me a few weeks ago.'

I go silent for a moment.

'I'm going to find her,' she says. '7425. That's her serial number. If Oasis can use the serial numbers to track us, I'll find a way to use them to find her.'

'But why are you leaving then?'

'I need help,' she says. 'Those people who hacked the mainframe?

They know how to do things like that. They can help me find her.'

I don't point out the flaws in her plan. Like how she's supposed to get back in, or how she even knows there really is anyone outside. But I'm escaping too, I remind myself. She's not the only one risking everything for a tiny sliver of hope that things might get better.

Eventually we pack up and go back to the Dorms, waiting for tomorrow. My heart is in my throat, my blood like fire in my veins. This feels like fear, but not. Like the moment between one breath and the next. Like the thing in my chest, pushing and expanding within me when I saw Aaron in the distance, like a beacon of light.

And maybe Aaron was hope all along. Maybe Aaron was the hope of something better that would never come. And maybe I've found a new hope, and if it will not come to me, I will go to it.

13

Oasis has three lines of defence: the Peace Wall, the fence, and the patrols. Just beyond the Outer Sector there's a thick line of trees with a stretch of open ground beyond it that's heavily patrolled by Officers. The fence is a fifteen-metre high electrical contraption, the top lined with barbed wire and sensors to detect any attempt at breaking in.

If you manage to get past the fence, you're faced with the Peace Wall. It's thirty metres of steel and stone, several metres in width, and completely indestructible. But there are drains every couple of hundred yards, covered with iron grates. If we could figure out a way to get past the grates, we'd be able to slip out through the drains and out into whatever exists beyond.

We have to build our plan quickly. With less than twenty-four hours until the power is cut, we have to figure out a way to get past the guards, out of the Dorms, past the patrols, past the fence, through the Wall – all of it sounds impossible, all of it has to be figured out fast.

The only tools we need are wire-cutters and a screwdriver, and Bea says she knows a way to get them. She works in the crematorium, and she says she's seen a toolbox inside the building. I try not to think about working there, or about why she works there, because citizens are only elected as crematorium workers as a punishment. I wonder what she could have done to have been given that job, but I can't be slowed down by useless details.

Bea leaves for work after the sirens go off in the morning, but with nowhere to go, my job is to scope out the perfect place to leave from. I spend the day wandering the border of the Outer Sector, my nerves on edge. Since I was seven years old, the Outer Sector has been all I've known. And no matter what it's done to me, there are memories here, clinging to the walls. And in every good memory, there's Aaron's blue eyes, his perfect smile, his golden hair falling in waves across his forehead.

I haven't heard anything from him since the containment centre. But with only a few days between now and me being carted off to the Labs, I can't afford to wait for him any longer.

That's when I see it. I've come full circle, going deep into the Outer Sector and walking back out. On the way out, with the Dorms in view and far from any Officer patrol stations, there is a drain. I feel fireworks going off in my chest, dizzying excitement mixing with crippling fear.

This is it.

○ ○ ○

When Bea returns hours later, we meet in the hallway and she slips the tools into my hand. Now that we have everything we need, there's nothing left to do but wait until dark.

My heart's been racing in my chest since I woke up, and I can't stop myself from fidgeting. Beatrice puts her back against the wall opposite to me, and I do the same, and we stare at each other as people file back into the Dorms, loud and boisterous and then slowly, slowly getting quieter and quieter as they slip off to sleep one by one, but Bea and I never break eye contact. Not once. Not for a second.

In Oasis, clocks are everywhere. In the streets and at the power station and in every room of every building, ticking the seconds away to the next place you need to be, the next thing you need to do. I glance at the clock above the door and watch the seconds tick by, waiting.

Eventually I nod to Bea, and we stand up slowly, moving towards the stairs.

Nobody at the Dorms is a light sleeper. If they were, they wouldn't get any sleep at all, so there's little chance of waking anyone, but I still carry my boots in my hand, afraid they'll make too much sound on the wooden floors.

Bea is standing at the top of the stairs, a terrified look on her face, as if she's suddenly realised we're actually doing this. For a split-second I think I should leave her behind. She's going to slow me down, trip me up, get us caught. But when I look into her eyes I see the desperation in them, not fear of escape, but fear of living here for the rest of her life, and I can't convince myself that she deserves to be free of this place any less than I do.

So I move past her, and I don't nod or encourage because I can't and I shouldn't and I won't because it's dangerous, and I am pulling and tugging and struggling on the inside to get away from this place where everything is summed up in terms of how dangerous it is.

There is a window in the hallway, and I push it open slowly. It creaks under the pressure I put on it, but eventually slides open, the cold night air slapping me in the face.

Leaning out of the window I place my boots gently onto the fire escape outside, then slide myself through as quietly as I can. Suddenly I am outside, and the sky is black-blue and speckled with droplets of light, and the moon is huge but hiding behind clouds in fits and starts, and I am at once nervous and intoxicated by this semblance of freedom.

The air is damp and cold, and I wait in the half-light for Bea to slip through the window behind me, silently nodding her around the side of the building's fire escape. They loop around each floor of the building, rickety mesh things that are barely held to the wall of the Dorms, but all of the downstairs exits are so tightly locked up it would take hours for us to even get out into the yard.

I pull the window back towards me, cringing at every squeak it emits. I quickly scan below for Officers who might catch us moving around up here, but there are none in sight, so I follow Bea around the corner. I find her staring down two storeys to the laundry bin beneath her, and something about the way she stands there, white-knuckled hands gripping the railing, makes me think she's guessed what I intend to do.

I swing a leg over the rail and catch her arm, pulling her over to me until her ear is by my mouth.

'If you want to turn back, do it now,' I whisper.

Her wide eyes stare at me, and she shakes her head firmly.

Bringing my other leg over the railing, I grip the side with my toes.

'Wait thirty seconds before you follow me down,' I tell her, before releasing my hold on the side and falling.

My breath is knocked from my lungs as I land, and it takes me a minute to get my bearings before I swing myself over the side of the bin and onto the safety of the gravel. Seconds later I hear Bea land after me, scrambling to find her footing.

I reach into the clothes and search for her hand, feeling around until I am met by thin, cold fingers. I pull her out after me, and we crouch beside each other at the north-west corner of the Dorms.

I pull on one of my boots, tying it as fast as I can so we can keep moving.

'What now?' Bea whispers, looking nervously around her. She didn't bring enough clothes, and her shoulders are huddled over from the cold.

I pull on the other boot and begin tying up the laces with enough force to cut off the blood circulation to my feet. I rest my trembling fingers on my over-tight boots. I don't answer her, instead whispering for her to stay low and be quiet, grabbing her arm as I pull her around the back of the building and around to the other side of the Dorms. We push our backs up against the wall, and we wait and we wait and we wait until it's the right moment, and then we run.

I catch Bea's hand, and we're not stupid enough to run for the open gate, but instead I start pulling myself up over the fence, which isn't much taller than me, and I can hear Bea following, her laboured breaths mixing with the night air.

We land on the other side of the fence, and something comes loose inside me. The real freedom was never in the lack of walls, but the lack of regard for them. It wasn't the Wall that was holding me back, it was the fear I had for the people inside it, and now that that's gone?

We are indestructible.

14

We loop around the Dorms, staying as far away as possible from the guards' line of sight. But quickly we find the stretch of forestry that runs along between the Wall and the Outer Sector streets, running as quietly as we can as we speed across the damp earth.

Bea is lagging behind, and I grab her hand, tugging at her to go faster. After several minutes of running, I start to slow down, moving closer to the Wall as I watch for the escape route I chose.

Finally I pull up, stopping Bea along with me, and I crouch at the edge of the tree line. There are light posts along the fence for the patrolling Officers, and I stare at them, waiting for the power to cut out.

A minute passes, and nothing happens. Another comes after that, and another, and still, nothing.

My stomach drops. I'm an idiot. Stupid, stupid, stupid, naive hope.

Panic starts welling up inside me, and I glance over my shoulder, my heart in my throat as I consider running back to the Dorms, but before I can move, the lights die. I freeze, my heart hammering in my chest.

It worked! It *worked*!

I move forward cautiously, my eyes scanning the area around me for movement, but I don't see anything. If Bea could figure out the code, then others must have too. I know – like you know when someone's watching you even when you can't see them – that there are others like me. Moving like shadows through the dark, invisible, out there somewhere in Oasis, risking their lives for this nebulous hope of something better.

I jump when I hear a shout go up in the distance, probably an Officer wondering why the lights are dead, but the voice is too far away for me to have to worry about it.

I sling Bea's bag across my body and hold up a finger to Bea, telling her to stay put, and then I kneel in front of the fence. Ripping a piece of grass from the ground beneath me, I throw it at the wire, making sure it's dead. Nothing happens.

I pull the wire-cutters that Bea stole from her bag, and with a steadying breath I start cutting through the fence, one link at a time. I work methodically and steadily until I've cut a hole in it big enough for a person to squeeze through.

I push myself through the gap. The sharp ends of the wire cut into my skin, but I can barely feel it. There are a few metres between the fence and the Wall, but my sight isn't set on the Wall, it's on what's built into it. The drainage system passes pipes from the Celian City, the Inner Sector and even the Outer Sector out to here, releasing the waste outside through small grates built into the Wall.

Crouching down, I pull Bea's screwdriver from the bag and start unscrewing the bolts in the grate. They are old and rusty, and I push and pull for a long time with no movement, but eventually I feel the smallest give, and keep pushing until the screw comes out, rolling along the grass. I switch sides, unscrewing the other bolt faster.

Before I can free the grate from the clip at the back, though, I hear a sound.

'Freeze!'

I spin around, adrenaline shooting into my bloodstream as my eyes fall on an Officer, his hand wrapped over Beatrice's mouth, her eyes like saucers above his hand as his gun locks onto my head.

'Don't move,' he says, slower this time.

I drop the screwdriver from my hand, my mind scrambling to keep up with the situation in front of me.

I should have left her behind.

I should have left her behind!

I'm not sure who I'm more angry at: her for making me bring her, or me for agreeing to it.

'Step back inside,' he says. 'Slowly.'

I start moving towards the fence, taking tiny steps, trying to buy myself time to think. I could try to run at him and attack him, but he'd shoot me before I'd get anywhere near him. I could just run, but he'd shoot me then, too.

I step up to the fence, not willing to touch it, afraid that the electricity will come back on.

'Crawl back through,' the Officer growls. But as he says it, a figure steps out of the trees, and there's a loud bang and the Officer is on the ground and Bea is running backwards, stumbling into the figure behind her, who catches her by the arm and drags her forward.

Aaron.

I swear I can feel my heart stop. I can't stop staring at the dead officer, bleeding out at his feet.

'What are you doing here?' The words fall from my mouth before I can stop them.

'What am I doing here? *What am I doing here*?'

I flinch at the anger in his voice.

'How many stupid mistakes am I supposed to dig you out of?' he asks, sounding bewildered. He's gesturing with the gun he killed the Officer with still in his hand, and I shy away from it every time it lands on me for a second.

'I got a call from the Warden before midnight, saying you and another girl had disappeared from the Dorms. She asked me did I have anything to do with it. *Me!* And now you're asking me what *I'm* doing here?' He is shaking Bea for emphasis, who is staring at me, pleading with her eyes for me to do something, terror written across her face.

'Aaron,' I whisper.

'What are you trying to do?' he asks, his voice dropped in pitch. 'Is this revenge? Are you trying to punish me for something?'

'Aaron, stop. You can come with me. Please.'

'Come with you? Are you insane?' His eyes are so wide I'm afraid they're going to pop out of his head, and there's a vein standing out in his neck. 'Get back in here, right now.'

'Aaron, this isn't everything. This can't be everything. There's more outside those walls. I can't stay in this place anymore.' My voice sounds desperate and verging on hysteria and broken. I am caught in that perpetual moment just before an elastic band snaps, just before it all falls apart.

'You hate Oasis because it is the edge of your world,' he says, his voice like the first cracks in a dam as the water seeps out and you wait for everything to come crashing down. 'But when you look past it, you will regret it.' There is something seething and desperate behind his teeth, but he won't let it out. Nothing is let out, nothing is free in here, and I can feel it draining the blood from my veins a drop at a time.

I can't take it anymore.

'You,' I say, and I step forward, reaching for him through the fence, and I feel myself unravelling, breaking down cell by cell as I am pulled towards him. But I can't let him decide this for me. 'You are my everything, Aaron. But that's …' I take a deep shuddering breath as I pull my fingers free, '… that's not good enough anymore.'

'There's nothing for you out there!' he shouts. 'It's a machine, don't you understand? It's a machine that runs on flesh and blood and bone. It will eat you alive and spit you right back out at my feet.'

Tears are pouring down my face as I pull back.

'If I die out there, it's better than being their lab rat,' I breathe. 'I have to stop belonging to people.'

I shake my head, taking a step back, away from him.

'Come back,' he whispers, the sound like breaking glass.

'No.'

'What?' He blinks.

'No,' I whisper. Not when I'm this close. Not when freedom is on the other side of that wall, so close I can feel it.

'Quincy,' he says, using a voice I've never heard him use before. 'Get inside, right now.'

'No.' I start shaking my head, backing up.

Then he does what I never thought he would do. He aims the gun at Bea's head, and the look in his eyes is as cold as it is deadly.

'I said. *Get. Back. Inside.*'

My hands are shaking, and I feel dizzy.

'No,' I breathe.

'LAST CHANCE, QUINCY,' he roars, suddenly alive and on fire and savage.

Bea looks at me. She looks at me and she knows he's going to kill her if I don't stop him, and her eyes are too big for her face and she's too skinny and too strange, like something caught between this world and the next, and I should save her.

I should sacrifice myself, and she could live.

But I don't know her. She isn't my problem.

'No,' I say once more, my voice quivering.

The sound of the shot going off will never stop ringing in my ears.

She drops to the ground and he lunges, coming after me, and I only spare her the smallest second, the tiniest sliver of a moment to watch her body crumple, and then I yank off the grate and I dive through, grabbing the screwdriver as I go. I wriggle through that narrow space, eyes fixed on the exit at the other end, body fighting towards the gap. It's all I can see, the black on the other side, punctuated by the stars. Finally I reach it, push my head out, my shoulders. I'm on a narrow ledge, two metres off the ground. Without thinking, without breathing, bag slung across my body, I jump. And all that there is left is to run

run

run

run.

PART TWO

BEYOND

1

If this is freedom, I don't want it anymore.

Branches tear into my arms as I sprint through the trees, my breath coming in short gasps as I try to put as much space between me and the Wall as possible. The forest is eating me alive, tormenting me with his shape, turning the shadows caught between the gaps in the trees into his form. It's his limbs that I keep tripping over, his hands clawing at me from every side, his voice I keep hearing. I can feel him watching me from behind every corner, and fear won't let me slow down, even for a moment, but I know he's not here.

He's back there, with her body.

When I can't run any longer I collapse, face-down in the dirt, bleeding into the cold earth beneath me. It's still dark, though it feels like I've been out here running forever. Every noise I hear sounds like patrols and shouts and whistles and gunshots, but it's always just the wind playing tricks with my mind as I stand on the edge of sanity.

What is happening to me?

I can't get up, I can't move, I can't do anything but lie here, my brain unable to process what's going on.

I see her falling, see his finger pulling the trigger, see her hitting the ground too hard, see his face, the way it twisted as he looked at me, as if to say, *This is your fault, I never wanted to do this.*

I didn't think he'd do it. Not really. I didn't think he was capable of that kind of heartlessness, no matter how furious he was. I was wrong.

I keep asking myself who it was that shot her, because it wasn't Aaron. It couldn't have been Aaron, not really. The boy I fell in love with wouldn't do something like that. The boy who cared about me when no one else would wouldn't do that.

My fingers dig into the dirt beneath me, and I try to push up, push away from the ground, but I can't. My muscles shake and I fall straight back down, and my breath is knocked from my lungs.

I don't want to fight back. I'm too weak, and I'm sick of fighting. I'm sick of getting thrown to the ground and telling myself that if I try one more time, everything will be fine.

It's not fine.

It's never going to be fine again.

Aaron is gone. I refuse to believe that monstrous thing that shot a girl in cold blood could be Aaron. Not my Aaron. My Aaron was good. My Aaron was beautiful.

I loved my Aaron.

And now he's gone, as dead as Beatrice, and I lie in the dirt and wait for the sunlight to find its way to me, and I cry for the loss of the only thing I ever loved that loved me back.

My life has been one punch after another, and I'm tired.

I am so, so tired.

Hours pass like that, lying in the dirt, crying, because there's nothing else to do. But eventually it comes, that voice in my head that won't let me give up, won't let me give in, won't let me lie here. And I feel it again like I felt it those first weeks at the Dorms – the pull, deep within me, the fabric of my flesh and blood, always wanting more.

Always wanting *life*.

I pull my feet up under me and I push off the ground, taking a single step forward. I watch my feet beneath me, step after step after step, and I find myself moving.

I slip more than once on the icy ground as the sun begins to warm the surface of the frozen earth, but I lift myself up again and I push on, because I have to, because I can't afford not to.

Hope is not something that is smothered easily, and it's what has kept me alive all these years. In Oasis I always had hope for the Cure, that someday I would be Pure, and that Aaron and I could be together, really be together. And now that that is gone, and Aaron and Oasis and the Wall are miles behind me, I have to find something new to hope for, something to keep me alive.

So I have hope that there is something beyond danger and stagnation revolving, something other than fear and betrayal, something more. I hope that I can find it, and that I can be happy.

I think of Aaron. I wonder if he's looking for me, if he's worried about me, if he misses me, but it doesn't matter anymore. None of that matters. I left Oasis to save myself. I left to find something better. I left to be free, no matter what the cost, and from now on, that is all that matters.

2

Time doesn't make any sense. There are times when the light fades around me, but I am so buried in this forest I'm not sure what is day and what is night.

I walk until I can't walk any further, and then I sleep, just to wake up and start walking again.

There is pain in my bones, my muscles and the wounds on my arms and legs, but that doesn't matter. My lips are cracked and bleeding, I can feel the blisters forming and bursting inside my boots, but that is not what I think about.

 I think of the fresh air passing in and out of my lungs, of the silence surrounding me for the first time in my life. I think of freedom, and how I have it, for this moment, even if it's short. At least I get to feel that freedom for however long I have left.

It is not what I thought freedom would feel like, but it is freedom, and I surround myself with it, breathing it in with every inhalation.

It's getting cold. The light snow showers from before I left have stopped, leaving behind bitter, steady winds that keep me awake at night. I press forward blindly, hunger and thirst my only driving force. It doesn't rain, but my thin grey uniform is little defence against the harsh wind, and sometimes I think I'm going to die from the cold alone.

But I don't. My body keeps fighting, even when my mind cannot, and I live. On and on, each breath a small miracle.

3

The last moments of the escape come back to me in flashes. Getting through the drainage grate, leaping across the ditch between the wall and the no-man's-land beyond it. I almost made it across, but had to scramble up the bank before my feet landed on solid ground. Once I got my footing I took off, terrified of hearing the stomp of their boots behind me, terrified of being hunted down and caught and brought back there.

A short distance from the ditch I was faced with a wall of trees, so dense at first that I couldn't even run, only push my way through slowly. But all the panic was still there, all of the adrenaline, urging me to run, to flee, to put as much distance between me and Oasis as possible.

And now the sun is rising, and it looks different out here. I've lost my direction and ended up outside the tree line, overlooking a river as light bleeds across the never-ending expanse of the Outside.

The sun out here, with no Celian City to contend with, looks brighter. My knees buckle underneath me, and I stare at the dawn until my eyes grow sore, and then I stare at my hands.

It's beautiful, but I don't deserve it. I shouldn't be here, not alone. There are so many mistakes that I made. If I had told Aaron sooner, if I hadn't got into a fight at the power station, if I had made Bea stay, or made Aaron release her, or went back when he told me to.

My stomach growls at me, and it's such a stupid, insignificant human need, and the laugh that escapes me is dry and humourless and I can't tell if I'm angry anymore, or just broken.

I move down to the river, climbing down a steep bank, and I drink without thinking if the water is clean. I have to find something to eat. I can already feel my hands starting to shake, my blood-sugar levels dropping dangerously low. But all I see is grass and trees and rocks. I don't know how to find anything out here, and even if I did, how would I know if it was food?

I pull myself back onto my feet, and face the forest. This is what I wanted. I was the one who decided to leave, and I'm the one who's going to have to deal with that decision.

o o o

Hours pass, and the sun is high in the sky before I find something. Above my head is a small cluster of branches, like a bush growing on the limb of a tree. I pull the strap of the bag over my head, leaving it against the base of the tree as I pull myself up, higher and higher, until the plant is at eye level. Among the branches are small, white, almost translucent berries and when I pick one, it's soft between my fingers. I carefully place it in my mouth, biting down tentatively. It tastes sweet and sour at the same time, and it's not the nicest thing I've ever eaten, but nothing else happens.

After several more moments of feeling nothing at all, I climb down the tree to collect my bag to fill it with the berries. I didn't think I'd find anything. I thought I'd starve. Thoughts start running through my head as I climb back down, fistfuls of the berries rolling around inside my satchel.

I sit down at the base of the tree and start eating. I'm dizzy from hunger, and within minutes I've eaten all of the berries. I lean my head backwards, staring up at the sky. For the first time since I escaped I feel something like calm. I've found food and water and I'm still alive.

Maybe I can do this. Maybe I can survive. Maybe that moment at the Wall wasn't the end.

Maybe this is only the beginning.

4

I don't remember falling asleep, but I wake up forcefully, rolling onto my side as I throw up, my entire body heaving. I puke until there's nothing left inside me, and then I open my eyes.

The world is a blur, colours and light blending together, and I can't focus and I can't see. I pull my knees up under me, trying to stand up, but I lose my balance before I'm even on my feet and fall over, cracking my head against the base of the tree.

I try to breathe, but my breaths are gasps I have to fight for. I pull my blurry hand up towards my face, but I can't make a fist. I'm shaking, my entire body is shaking, and the pain shooting up through my abdomen has me curling up on the forest floor, strangled sounds coming from between gritted teeth.

My body convulses as I retch again, rolling over onto my side as I squeeze my eyes closed, trying to block out the world.

The Virus. It hits me like a fist to the gut. It's been so long since anyone's seen an outbreak that I don't even know what to look for. I don't know what the symptoms are other than what everyone knows: that it's fast, that it's brutal, and that no matter what you do, you're going to end up dead.

5

I don't know how long I spend lying there, dry heaving against the earth as I try to grasp on to anything, anything at all that will make it stop, make the pain stop. Slowly my vision comes back, the blur of the forest gradually taking shape as the nausea slows. My throat is dry and burning, and all I can think about is water.

I need to drink something or I'm going to die.

I don't know where I am, or where the river is, but I start crawling towards the light on my left, out of the forest. Eventually I gain enough strength to pull myself to my feet and using the trees around me to steady myself, I make my slow journey towards the tree line.

When I see the river, I almost cry.

I try to speed up, but my stomach cramps and I have to stop and breathe for several seconds, tensing against the pain. When I can move again I go slowly, one shaky step at a time, and then shuffle down the bank towards the clear water, the sunlight making the surface shimmer.

I kneel down, as close to the edge as I can get, and reach my shaking hands into the water. It's so cold that once my fingers touch the surface I yelp and pull my hands back out, just as the unsteady pebbles at my feet slip and my feet go out from under me.

I am in the water, and it is like ice trying to pull me under as I frantically try to get a foothold at the bottom of the stream, but I am too weak, and the current is too strong. I am pushed downstream in a stupefied frenzy, and the water is in my eyes and in my mouth and in my lungs, and

I

can't

breathe.

The water is painfully cold, making my muscles lock as I desperately try to get my head above the surface. But I can't. I don't know how to swim, and my legs won't work, and all I can feel is my lungs screaming and the water is everywhere, and I am sinking. My body goes numb, and something tells me I knew this was going to happen all along.

How long did I expect to survive?

I see Aaron's face, golden-lit, blue-eyed and smug. He smiles as my body shuts down, as I pull at the water and continue sinking, sinking, sinking.

My eyes are closing, and I'm ready to die with that image printed inside my head when I feel something clawing at my shoulders, and I blink up at the boy with dark hair who's swimming above my head, pulling on me too hard, and I wonder why he's looking at me so desperately, but then—

Nothing.

6

Pain is in every fibre of me. I wake up slowly, but I immediately want to fall back to sleep, just to get away from the agony. There is burning in my lungs and throat, a searing pain in my left elbow, and I feel like I've been beaten all over.

My eyes flutter open and my mind is trying to grasp something, anything to make sense of what is going on. There is light coming through the walls of a small room, and it takes my sluggish brain several seconds to realise I'm lying inside some kind of tent.

I hear voices. Someone is standing outside the tent, or several someones, and I'm struggling onto my hands and knees, my heart thundering in my chest. But a wave of dizziness hits me before I can get to my feet, and I fall back against my elbows, the world spinning around me. I try to blink away the fuzziness in my vision, but my body is rebelling against me.

I can hear the voices getting closer, turning into whispers, and my breath catches in my throat. I glance around desperately, and then notice my bag thrown in the corner of the tent, along with the grey fabric of my uniform. I lunge across the distance, flipping my satchel open and pulling out the screwdriver just as a boy not much older than me walks in, taking a small step back at the sight of me.

I try to stand up, the screwdriver gripped so tightly in my trembling hand that my knuckles are white, but I stumble backwards, the ground dipping beneath me.

'Careful,' he says, lunging to catch me by the elbow before I take the entire tent down with me.

'Get away from me,' I growl, pointing the screwdriver at him. He takes a hesitant step backwards, eyes on the screwdriver, not me.

Good. I'm glad. It's good that he's scared. Aaron always said that if someone was scared of you, it meant you didn't have to be scared of them.

At the thought of Aaron my stomach turns, memories washing over me in a tidal wave, turning dizziness to nausea in a split-second. The boy must see it on my face because he takes another huge step back, giving me access to the opening of the tent.

I barely make it out before I vomit. There's nothing in my stomach but river water and bile, burning its way up my oesophagus as I retch, my entire body heaving with the effort. Hot tears burn my eyes as the spasms slowly die down, leaving me exhausted and disgusted, stumbling backwards.

'Careful,' he says again, gentler this time. I glance up, and finally something clicks in my brain as it all floods back – the water surrounding me, dragging me down, and the small, traitorous part of me that swelled with relief because I wouldn't have to fight anymore.

And the boy who saved me, who looked so frantic underneath the water, his dark hair billowing around him as he tried to claw me upwards, towards air and light and this. My gaze flicks around me, to the darkness closing in on top of us as the sun sets, the cold of the air around us almost as bitter as the cold of that rushing water, and some dark, hopeless part of me asks a question that I cannot ignore: would it have been easier if he had just left me there?

I try to straighten up, to find my balance, but the world starts tipping again. My head feels heavy and I lean backwards, like the ground is pulling me greedily down towards it.

'You need to lie down,' he says calmly.

'Stay the hell away from me,' I hiss, but he's nowhere near me.

I don't want to lie down, not when I can see people moving in the distance and my brain is full of so many questions it feels like my head is going to explode. But I don't know if I have a choice. My body is shutting down of its own accord, so before I collapse onto the ground, I move towards the tent, trying not to look vulnerable as I pass him.

The minute I'm inside the tent I start shaking, and I don't know if it's fear or cold or exhaustion. I crawl under the blanket that's left on the floor and before I can make a decision about what I should do next, I'm asleep, the screwdriver still gripped in my hand.

7

I wake to warmth on my face, and sit up to see the dawn rising along with me. A brief glance around my surroundings only confuses me further. I can't make sense of these disjointed buildings, making a muddle of what's left of my sanity. Eventually, my eyes land on something familiar, a blonde head and square shoulders, turned towards the sun. There is contemplation in those hands, clasped behind his back.

Aaron.

He is wearing a suit, a grey suit, finely tailored, and like everything else Aaron has ever worn, it fits him perfectly. I can't help admiring him from where I sit.

He turns around, and I immediately notice his shirt and tie are the same grey as his suit, but he is walking towards me now, and I don't have time to ask myself why that bothers me so much.

'Quincy,' he says, stretching out a hand to me to pull me up. Once I am standing, he utters my name again, a single, quiet, deeply intoned and horribly disappointed, 'Quincy'.

Although his hand is still in mine, his eyes are bonded to the ground beneath us, his bottom lip held between his teeth like he's trying to work up the courage to say something difficult.

'Aaron,' I say, not in the way he said my name, and not in an angry way.

I am begging.

'Quincy,' he says again, this time like he's starting something.

'Aaron, look at me.' Panic appears inside of me, something savage and primal, screaming at me unintelligibly.

'Quincy. You are not. Allowed. To. Leave. Me.' He grinds out the words, his teeth grating off each other as he stares at the ground like he's trying to intimidate it.

'Aaron, look at me!' I wail, and now panic has me by the throat, has crawled inside my stomach and is burning me alive from the inside out. '*LOOK AT ME!*' I scream.

He does. His eyes are grey, and I remember.

Aaron never wears grey.

o o o

My blood is on fire.

Someone is screaming, but I can't concentrate on anything but the crushing pain in my chest and my veins like searing wires within me, contorting my limp body in agony.

Someone is talking to me, trying to get me to drink, but I vomit the minute it passes my lips.

I fall back into the darkness.

o o o

I'm drowning again, but the water is turning red. There are cuts on my arms, and they colour the river until I can't see anything but Aaron, a single, clear image staring at me, mocking me through the water.

o o o

I gasp awake, sitting up straight, and I feel like I'm drowning all over again. My head swims, and I throw out my hands for something to steady me and find a hand, an arm, a dark-haired boy staring at me.

'You had a fever,' he says, urging me to lie back down. 'You need to rest.'

'Where–' Oh. I remember everything again, but backwards: the boy with the dark hair, drowning, leaving Oasis, Bea getting shot, Aaron, escaping the Dorms.

'I'm not dead,' I say, slowly, because I'm not entirely sure.

'You're not dead,' he says, and there's something at the corners of his mouth like he wants to smile but he refuses to.

'I thought. I thought it had activated,' I say quietly. I know by the way his expression changes that he knows what I'm talking about.

'It's okay,' he says. His eyes are dark, too, a deep, intense brown that makes me feel dizzy. 'It was just a fever.'

I nod, relieved.

'What's your name?' he asks softly.

My rules pop into my head, but a fierce kind of rebellion follows straight after it. I don't care. I left Oasis behind, and my rules along with it.

'Quincy,' I tell him, watching for a reaction, as if there's going to be one.

'I'm Kole.' His voice is more gentle than it was before, and I don't trust it. I sit farther back in the tent, desperately trying to put some distance between us.

I can tell by the way he's watching me that he notices what I'm doing. He bites his lip like he's trying to decide how to calm a feral animal, his dark eyebrows drawn down over his eyes.

'Do you think you could eat something?' he asks, averting his eyes. I don't know why, but the act makes me feel a little less uncomfortable, less monitored.

I nod slowly and he stands up, unfolding himself, and I realise how tall he is, though he looked small while he was talking to me, his knees drawn up under his chin.

He's gone for several minutes and the longer he's gone, the more frantic I get. What is he doing? Who else is out there? Why is he taking so long?

But before I can do anything, he steps inside the tent again, holding a small tin in his left hand. He hands it to me silently, and the warmth of the tin immediately starts seeping into my frigid fingers. It's cold in the tent, despite the blankets across my legs, and I'm glad of the heat.

Before he can pull his hands away, I see it: his knuckles are crisscrossed with many overlapping scars. He catches my eye, and I don't know what he sees in my face, but he pulls his hands away from me so quickly the tin almost falls as it's passed over. He stuffs his hands deep in his pockets.

The silence lasts for several minutes, and he doesn't move as I eat the soup, drinking it down ravenously.

I look at him now, with his jet-black hair falling across his forehead, and his long limbs bundled together like he's trying to make himself small, and somehow I can't differentiate between the him that is here in front of me right now and the image in my head.

The image of him screaming at me underwater, even though I couldn't hear him.

'When I pulled you out, I thought ...' he says out of the blue, almost to himself.

'... that I was dead.' I fill in the blank he's not willing to fill in himself. There's a harshness to my voice that I didn't mean to be there, but I can't help feeling distrustful of him.

Why would he risk jumping in the river for someone he doesn't even know?

'You weren't breathing,' he says, getting to his feet. I try to get up too, because he is too tall when I am sitting down, but my head starts spinning again.

'You're still weak.' He hunkers down beside me, picking up the soup container where I left it down and standing back up. 'Get some rest,' he says, his voice devoid of emotion, and then he's gone.

8

I must have fallen back to sleep because when I wake up the sun is getting low again. I sit up, bringing a hand up to my forehead gingerly. The headache has eased some, but I still feel the fog over my brain, like a mist cast over my thoughts, obscuring them.

I hear quiet voices outside the tent, and I move forward tentatively on my hands and knees, listening. They couldn't be more than a metre or two from the tent because for the most part I can hear everything they're saying.

'It's not worth the risk,' I hear someone say, the voice distinctly female.

'Clarke, she's just a kid!' a man's voice replies, and there's a sinking feeling in the pit of my stomach.

'A kid who we know absolutely nothing about, Mark.'

'We all need to calm down a little,' Kole's voice slips in, and even through the lining of the tent I can hear the way he's using his voice to draw them in. 'We've dealt with situations like this before.'

'Not like this kid. She could be an undercover Officer for all we know.' The girl, whoever she is, uses the term 'kid' as an insult.

'Do you really think she could be working for Oasis, Clarke?' Kole asks, his voice laced with dark amusement. 'She was almost dead when we found her. She's not a threat.'

'You don't know that.'

I hear someone moving away, but I can still hear the others, the leaves beneath their feet crunching as they fidget from one foot to the other.

'She's just scared.' The unfamiliar male voice says, so gentle I can barely hear it.

'I know,' Kole says, releasing a long, exhausted sigh.

There's a long silence, and the sound of footsteps walking away from the tent. After another moment, I hear someone approaching, their footsteps light against the grass.

'Is she coming?' a girl's voice says, concern bleeding into her voice, though I'm not sure for whom.

'I don't know,' Kole says. 'I don't know what I'm supposed to do.'

'What are your instincts?'

A pause.

'She's just a girl,' he says, and I feel strange, listening to them talk about me. 'She's terrified out of her mind, and she's just as likely to be a threat as anyone we've taken in.'

'So we bring her with us.'

'It's not that simple. Ever since the attack, everyone's been on edge. They don't trust her, and they shouldn't have to, but if I side with her, they'll see it as a betrayal.'

'Kole, they may be scared, but they trust you. They're not going to feel betrayed if you do for this girl what you did for all of them.'

'I don't know,' he murmurs, then growls in frustration. 'It was never this complicated when Rob was here.'

'I know,' the girl murmurs.

I move away from the walls of the tent. I can't listen to them plan my life anymore. They never thought to ask if I wanted to go with them, wherever that even is.

But then I think of the days I spent in the forest. Almost killing myself with those berries, starving and cold and then almost drowning, and I wonder if I have a choice. If I stay out here, I'm not going to survive more than a few more days.

I think of dying out here, alone, the forest slowly eating me alive, and I shudder.

I can't go back to that. I can't do that again. I *can't*.

9

'How are you feeling?' a soft voice murmurs, as someone steps inside the tent.

I am woken from my daze by a blonde girl, coming towards me with another can of soup. She's tall and thin, with high cheekbones and long eyelashes and the palest blue eyes I've ever seen. I wonder if that's what Bea would have looked like if she'd lived to be that age. My heart twists, and I glance down at the food in her hands to distract myself.

'I'm fine,' I say, a little too sharply. The girl just smiles at her hands as she sits down on the floor of the tent, a short distance from where I'm kneeling.

'Can you eat?' she asks. I nod, my eyes following her every movement. She pushes the can over to me on the floor, and I keep watching her as I eat.

'My name's Lacey.'

'Quincy,' I murmur.

Back in Oasis, every day on the way to work I passed the same buildings. Over and over again, twice a day every day for two years. I remember there was this dog, halfway between the Dorms and the power station, with mangy brown-grey fur and a bite gone from one ear, tied to a fence with a chain, and he looked like he was just about dead every single time I passed him. He was leery and territorial, but always too exhausted to try to attack me. I remember he always barked at me twice. Two sharp barks and that was it.

And that's what I sound like, barking my name at Lacey like a senile old dog, half searingly aggressive, half just plain terrified.

'We have to leave soon,' she says gently, and she's doing that thing that Kole did, keeping her eyes on the floor as if she's trying not to provoke me.

I don't say anything.

'I don't know what you were planning on doing, but you're welcome to come with us if you want.'

I laugh, and I'm not sure if I'm laughing at her suggesting I had something better planned to do out here or at her acting as if I'm welcome.

'You don't have to pretend you want me here,' I snap, placing the tin down beside me. Lacey looks shocked, pulling her head away from me slightly as she finally makes eye contact.

'Quincy, I—'

'Stop, okay? I heard Kole talking to those other people outside, and I get it. I'm too much of a risk.'

'Quincy, everyone has a rough time in the beginning.' She looks away again, like she's gathering her thoughts, then looks back at me, an intensity in her eyes I didn't expect.

'We're vulnerable right now, okay? I don't know what Kolc told you, but we were attacked last week. That's why we're on the move. People don't like being out here in the open where we can't defend ourselves. Some people are going to take some convincing, but that doesn't mean you shouldn't come with us.'

'You were attacked? What do you mean? By who?'

She looks down at her hands again.

'A team of Officers attacked us nine days ago. It was in the middle of the night, and we didn't see them coming. It was a scout group, not a full squad, but we lost twelve people. Two Officers got away, so we had to leave before they could alert anyone and start tracking us.'

My head is reeling with this information, and I can't catch up with it quickly enough to say anything. What she's telling me is that Oasis knows there are people out here, not only knows it but comes out here and attacks them physically. Suddenly everything I've spent my whole life believing isn't true, and it feels like the ground that was beneath my feet a moment ago has disappeared.

I don't want to believe her. I want to tell her she's crazy, but she's here, and that's proof enough. Oasis told me she didn't exist either, that outside the walls of Oasis life had ceased to be. And here she is. Heart beating, lungs breathing, just as alive as me.

Without fully understanding it, something shifts inside me, a murmur of the anger I felt in the containment centre. I feel myself respond to her words, every muscle tensing, joints locking, my throat swelling.

'I'm sorry,' I manage to get out, and there is too much. Too much fear and too much anger and too much guilt and too much everything with nowhere to put it, and suddenly the inside of this tent is too small and its flimsy walls are too close.

I push past her, moving towards the opening of the tent, needing to be out, to be outside. I haven't worked up the courage to leave the tent since I woke up that first time, afraid of what might be waiting for me outside, but being cramped in there with my thoughts suddenly becomes so much worse than anything I might have to face out here.

The river, the one that almost claimed me only days ago, flows serenely along beside the camp. The camp itself is almost as serene, with about a dozen people milling around, talking and laughing quietly, but they all look up when I burst from the tent.

'Quincy, are you okay?' Lacey comes up behind me, leaving her hand on my shoulder. I shrug away from her.

I'm pulled back in time, to things I've been trying to push away, push down. To Bea calling me by my name, and me snapping at her, telling her she didn't know me.

Lacey doesn't know me either. None of these people knows me.

The only person who ever knew me was Aaron, and now I've lost him, too. *And now I've lost him, too.* The words burn themselves into my heart, and I find I can't breathe, can't move, can't exist. Not like this.

Not without him.

Human beings are not supposed to be alone. We are not supposed to be known to no one, cared for by no one, loved by no one. I lived so long on my own. For nine years I was the only one looking out for me, the only one who cared if I woke up in the morning, went to bed at night unharmed. And then Aaron came along. Perfect, beautiful Aaron, holding the answers to everything. In Aaron's arms the world made sense for the first time in years. I could see the pain of the Dormant, I could watch agony in the faces of those newly assigned to the Outer Sector, and I could cope, because there was Aaron, which meant there was hope. For a new life. A better life.

And now he's gone. Not only physically gone, but gone every way that mattered. Gone is the gentle boy who wouldn't hurt me, even as every other one of his kind did. Gone is the trust that linked me to him. Gone is the boy I fell in love with, the one who looked nothing like the monster I saw that night, his hands gripping that gun like a life-line.

The worst thing is, I can't decide who betrayed whom – if it was me, who was willing to leave Oasis without him, or if it was him, so desperate to have me back he murdered an innocent girl.

But no. It was my fault. Because the old Aaron never would have done that. *I* was the one who broke his trust. *I* was the one who ruined everything by getting arrested. And it was *me* who decided to leave, to run from Oasis without ever telling him anything.

I didn't pull the trigger, but I might as well have.

All of this is raging on inside me, and my breathing is so short and so fast I can feel myself growing lightheaded, and everyone is just standing there.

Watching me fall apart. Watching the crazy girl grow ever crazier.

And the forest is there, and it might kill me, but at least it's there. At least I won't drive it away, so I run to it, and I run blindly for as long as my weakened body will carry me, until I fall hard on my knees, and I cry until there's nothing left inside me.

But it doesn't make it better. It doesn't bring her back and it doesn't make him here, and none of it makes the hole in my chest any less wide, or any less painful.

10

Eventually, someone comes to find me, and it's a strange and unfamiliar feeling that wells up in my chest at the sight of her.

Lacey approaches slowly, tentatively, one foot carefully placed in front of the other, eyes wide as she watches me. I only glance up once when I hear her coming, then look back down at my hands. I feel stupid, but the feelings are all still there. I've just bottled them up for long enough to stop crying.

She sits down, a bit away from me, and crosses her legs. She cringes a little at the coldness of the ground, but I hadn't even noticed. I don't know what I'm expecting her to say, but whatever it is I'm tensed, waiting for it. Waiting for some kind of blow to fall, but it doesn't.

She doesn't say anything at all.

She just watches me, breathing gently, her stare neither disinterested nor invasive. She's just there.

'What?' I snap, and then I release a deep breath. I need to calm down.

'Nothing.' She shrugs.

'Why are you here?' I demand, and I just sound tired now.

'It's dangerous to be out here alone,' she says, as if that's an explanation.

'It's dangerous to be with other people, too.' I try to contain the anger in my voice, because it's not aimed at her. Not really. I was never angry at the Dormants, I am one, so how could I be? But I am angry at the Virus. I am angry that it makes my stomach clench in fear, that every touch, every breath shared is a constantly rising risk of Infection.

'What do you mean?' she asks.

'You're not … are you Pure?' My voice is shaky. If she is, if all of those people are and they find out I'm Dormant, they'll kill me before I have a chance to run.

She looks down at her hands. 'No. But it doesn't matter out here.'

'How could it not matter? It always matters.'

She looks at me strangely for a moment, like she can't believe I haven't caught on.

'Think about it, Quincy. There were hundreds of thousands of you in the Outer Sector, and you were never Infected. There are a handful of us out here. What are the chances of it being one of us, one of a couple of dozen, to activate it first?'

I go silent. I understand what she's trying to say, but it sounds more like an excuse than an explanation. The Virus is everywhere, in everything, and it's going to get us eventually, either in there or out here.

'What good is it worrying?' she says, like she can read my mind. 'We can't do anything about it. If they do find the Cure, which is unlikely, it's back in Oasis. You gave up on the Cure the moment you stepped outside the Wall.'

My heart stops in my chest. I hadn't thought of it like that. I had been so caught up in fear of the Labs, fear of the Officers, fear of being a Branded person, that I hadn't thought of all I was giving up. Aaron, yes, I had considered. But the Cure hadn't crossed my mind.

For a long time everything is quiet, and all I can hear is the wind rustling in the trees and the river in the distance. The bitter curl of winter is in the air, the frigid air singing past my bare skin, making me shiver.

'I'm not wearing my uniform,' I say, pretending to be casual. I noticed this fact a long time ago, but I need something to fill this bruising silence.

'You were pulled out of a freezing river, if you've forgotten,' she says, smiling gently.

'I haven't forgotten.'

But I'm trying to, is what I don't say. Every time I think about it I can feel the water crushing my lungs, the complete lack of control as my body was swept downstream. And I remember Kole, and the way his eyes sought out mine, made contact, trying to keep me from giving up. He shouldn't have cared. It shouldn't have mattered to him, but it did, in too desperate a way, and I can still feel my heart pause when I think about it.

My hand drifts to the Brand on my shoulder, and my eyes snap to Lacey.

'Don't tell them,' I whisper, my eyes wide with fear.

She blinks at me slowly.

'I won't, ' she says, shaking her head. 'And I want you to know you can come, if you want to,' Lacey says, firmly. 'I'm not saying everybody's going to be happy about it or it's going to be easy. I'm saying you have as much a right to a second chance as anyone.'

And I think no. I think thank you, and I think no, I don't. I think, you don't know me, you don't know who I am or where I've been or what I've done. You don't know the things I'm responsible for, I think, but I don't say any of those things.

I take a deep breath, too deep and too shaky.

'I have so many questions,' I tell her. 'About everything. I don't know who you people are. And how did you get out here? And where are you going and what are you doing and since when are there Officers out here and attacking people and what the hell is going on?'

'We have answers to all of those questions,' she says, too calm, making me seem even more crazy sitting beside her. 'And we have so much we want to ask you. But we can't stay here much longer. We need to get moving. We're less than a hundred and sixty kilometres from Oasis, and out here in the open, that's just too dangerous. If you really want answers, then you need to come with us.'

I hold her stare for a beat, two, three, four, and then look away. Rip a blade of grass from root to tip. Nod slowly. Keep my eyes drilled to the ground.

'Good,' she says, and I can hear her smiling, and she sounds like she knew I was going to agree all along, but she's pleased to hear me say it anyway.

She gives me a hand up from the ground, and I take it after hesitating for only a second, and we brush ourselves off and start walking, slowly, silently, back towards the camp.

And I wonder how people like this exist out here. I wonder how I never knew about them before. I wonder who hacked the messaging system at the power station, and if they're in this group. I wonder where Aaron is now, if he misses me, if he regrets what he did. I wonder about Bea's father. I wonder what he knew, who he knew. I wonder if I knew what he did, would I be better prepared to deal with this mess, this maze of unregulated territory full of people who shouldn't exist?

But I never let myself really think of Beatrice. My mind shies away from her memory, swerving around it like the pool of blood on the floor of the Dorms that first day I saw her. And I do it because I need to keep moving, keep pushing forward, keep breathing, and I know if I think of her I won't be able to do any of those things, not even for a moment.

11

When we got back to the camp, Lacey gave me a pile of warm clothes to change into before we left. She offered to help me change, but I insisted I could do it myself.

Half the group left to go ahead of us this morning, Clarke leading the way, and the camp felt relatively quiet when we returned, with only thirty people left behind. Kole wants us to follow them as soon as possible, and everyone but me is ready to go.

It turns out it's harder to get changed than I expected. Most of the clothes are mismatches, worn and ill-fitting, and my balance is off, making it hard to get my legs through the too-big trousers. When I have the top pulled over my head, and a warm hoodie over that, I have to sit down for a moment to regain my equilibrium.

After a few minutes I walk outside, breathing in the fresh, chilled air. I didn't notice it before, maybe because I was too scared, but this place is beautiful. It's somehow brighter, greener, more alive than anything ever was inside Oasis, even with winter rolling in.

'Eat something,' Kole says, thrusting more soup into my hands as he walks past, startling me.

I'm beginning to think this is all they eat.

Kole didn't make eye contact with me, and hasn't since I overheard his conversation with Clarke. Almost everyone just ignores me, acts like I'm not even here. The only exceptions are tall, broad-shouldered Mark, who throws me a sympathetic smile every now and again, and Lacey, who won't stray far from my side, as if I need a bodyguard. The rest of them just look at me with irritation, because I'm slowing them down.

And I am slow. Everything feels sluggish. All the energy that forced me on when I was escaping has drained from my body, leaving me exhausted.

I drink the last of the soup, and Lacey takes the can from me, washing it in the river before placing it in her backpack. Everyone is finished eating now, and by the time Lacey makes her way back up the bank, we are all on our feet.

'Okay,' she says, smiling at us once her pack is securely strapped on. 'Ready!'

We start walking at a brisk pace, and despite my recuperation over the past few days, I'm finding it hard to keep up with them. Kole is at the front of the group, making his way through the forest with a careful eye, practically twitching as he waits for something to jump out at us.

'Why does he look so edgy?' I ask Lacey quietly, pulling my sweaty hair from the back of my neck in annoyance.

'He's just nervous. It's not safe to be out here in the open. We're too vulnerable.'

'But why is he the only one acting like that?' I watch Mark talking to him up ahead, and while Kole is obviously responding, his eyes never leave the surrounding area.

She shrugs. 'He's our leader. It's kind of his job.'

'What?' I look over at her to make sure she's serious. But her blue eyes are sincere when she looks back at me, her hands tucked beneath the straps of her pack. 'But he's the same age as us!'

'He's nineteen, but yes, lots of people react like that at first. The guy who was there before him said that if he ever died, Kole was to take over, and ...' Lacey trails off, shrugging again.

'He died.' I nod. Of course.

'And he's okay with it? Being a leader?' I ask, hoping Lacey doesn't notice how many questions I'm asking about him. I just can't get that image out of my head, the dark-haired boy at the bottom of the river. He could have been the last thing I ever saw.

'It's hard.' She shrugs again, trying to sound light. 'Everything's hard. But he's a good leader. He cares about the group.'

There's a pause in the conversation, and I listen to the crunch of footsteps on the frozen ground until I work up the courage to ask another question.

'How did he die?' I ask, fiddling with the straps of the pack Lacey gave me, which is cutting into my shoulders. Inside, safely stowed away, is Bea's bag, which Lacey gave back to me this morning.

'Rob? In a raid earlier this year. It was a smaller attack, and we didn't lose many, but when we lost Rob ... it was hard. Hard for everyone, but especially for Kole.'

'Were they close?'

'Close enough for Rob to trust Kole with the group.'

'And what about you? Did you know him well?'

'Not as close as some,' she says. 'But Rob was a special person. Everyone misses him.' Her voice gets tight, and she says no more.

I wonder how they do this. Get ambushed, lose their friends, their mothers and fathers and children and siblings, and they just have to pull themselves up and keep moving, because if they don't, it's only going to get worse.

I take a shaky breath.

'You okay?' Lacey asks, glancing sidelong at me.

'I'm fine,' I murmur.

I just need to get through today. Lacey said it should only take a few hours to complete our journey, and then I can figure out what's going on in my head. Then I can try to make sense of this mess, and how I keep seeing faces between the trees that aren't there.

I just need to get through today.

12

We step out into the clearing, and my eyes travel up the tall building looming above us, three stories high with half the windows smashed in and ivy crawling across every inch of it.

It looks dead.

It looks hollow.

It looks like its eyes have been ripped from its face.

A gangly teenage boy bounds out of its mouth, jumping around like a hyperactive rabbit.

'MARK!' he yells, full-body slamming into Mark before dragging himself away almost immediately, pointing at the house and talking so fast his mouth looks like a blur.

The sun is setting, and Lacey leans over to me in the half-light.

'That's Walter, Mark's younger brother,' she explains.

Kole claps Walter on the back, and Walter turns his beaming smile on Kole.

I drop back a step as the group starts filing into the building, Kole, Walter and Mark up ahead, talking rapidly, heads bent together. I stand at the door, my boot on the threshold as I run my eyes across the interior.

The front door leads into a wide, grey room, the roof hung low over a strangely three-legged table, one corner leaning towards the floor. I take a tentative step inside the door, eyes flicking around the room, not sure what to expect. There are four doors, but two of the interior doors are missing, hinges hanging loose against the wall. The room I'm standing in now seems to be some kind of kitchen, judging by the dented stove in the corner.

I watch Kole step over a ceramic sink that somehow ended up smashed to pieces on the floor, running his hands through his hair as he surveys the place with a calm expression.

I'm staring at his reaction to this place, at once panicky and in control, when Lacey appears behind me.

'How are you?' she asks.

'Fine,' I say, pulling back a step.

Just as the words are out of my mouth, Kole whispers something to Mark, who runs upstairs and comes back a few minutes later, the rest of the group on his heels. Walter's smiling face stands out against the grim expressions of almost everyone else filing into the room.

Once everyone is here, Kole starts talking, and though he never raises his voice, I can hear him perfectly from the other end of the room. The room drops into silence the moment he starts speaking.

'I need everyone to settle down as quickly as possible, and then we can eat. Walter, take half the group and start setting up the second floor for tonight. Everyone else, take all the supplies to the top floor and unpack.'

People start nodding, and everybody starts moving towards the door at the back of the room. Kole motions Lacey over beside him and I hang back, unsure who to follow. Kole whispers something to Lacey, and I can't hear what they're saying, but Lacey looks serious. She nods once, and moves back towards me.

Kole slings two backpacks over his shoulders and begins moving supplies upstairs with the others.

'What did he want?' I ask cautiously.

'Aw, nothing, he just asked me to show you to your room,' she says brightly, but she won't make eye contact with me. I nod cautiously, but instead of leading me towards the hall with everyone else, she turns to the right, taking the smaller door that no one else has touched.

She pushes it open to reveal a tiny room with one small window in the corner, letting in dappled light through the branches of a tree outside. It's completely bare, with a concrete floor and the same grey walls as the kitchen.

Understanding hits me like a punch in the teeth.

'Ah,' I say under my breath. They don't trust me enough to let me sleep in the same room as everyone else. It's both sensible and ridiculous, because if I really wanted to kill them, it wouldn't take much to climb a single flight of stairs to where they all sleep.

'I know it doesn't look like much, but we'll get in blankets and things and it'll look great. I'm so jealous; it's impossible to sleep when everyone around you is snoring.' Lacey laughs, but she's talking too fast and there's a slight note of panic in her voice. But I don't care that they're segregating me.

'Don't worry,' I say without looking at Lacey, 'I've been quarantined my whole life.'

Lacey mumbles something quickly about helping Kole move the

supplies before disappearing out the door, desperate to get away.

I close my eyes, just for a second, and breathe. I can almost feel the Dorms surrounding me again, hear the clatter of girls all around me, the floor moving underneath me as they clomp around, rushing to get down before the Officers have to enforce the curfew.

I shiver, leaning my back against the cold concrete wall. I need to pull myself together. I don't trust anyone here, and they're making it perfectly clear that they don't trust me either, so I need to make a plan. I slide down the wall, running my hands over my face as I try to decide what to do.

First off, I need to get information from them. I can't leave without getting some answers. And once I have them, I need to find a way to survive outside on my own. If I depend on these people for food and shelter, they own me. Oasis taught me that much.

I drag in a steadying breath, feeling a little more sane now that I have a plan.

Get answers, find a way to survive and get away from this place.

It's that simple, and that complicated.

13

Within minutes of getting into the house we're called back into the kitchen, and I push myself up off the ground to follow the others. There's a table pushed up against the far wall, but everyone sits down on the floor without a word. Walter and Mark are sitting towards the opposite end of the room, their backs to the table as they talk to a pretty, dark-skinned girl and Lacey, who hasn't said a word to me since she showed me my room.

My eyes are on Lacey as I sit down, just as everyone goes quiet. I look up, startled by the abrupt silence, and see Kole standing on the table, a smile across his face.

My eyes widen at the sight of him. He trusts that table a lot more than I do.

'Okay, so the last group won't be here until tomorrow, but for tonight we've made it this far in one piece. I want you to all count that as a victory. You did well.' He keeps smiling, and I keep watching the wood beneath his feet. 'Now, I'm sure you're all hungry, so let's eat!' He claps his hands together, grinning down at everyone, and they all whoop in response.

He jumps down from the table like a cat, not making a sound as he lands, and a few people who hung back in the kitchen start bringing in food. The food isn't anything special, but there is a sense of celebration in the air, and I wonder at how he can do that. He turned the night on its head, and the frowns and creases between eyebrows that everyone was wearing earlier disappear, replaced with smiles and laughter as the room grows steadily louder.

'How are you feeling?' His voice comes from behind me, and I jump. 'Sorry. I didn't mean to startle you.'

'No, it's fine.' I turn to face him. In the short time since I saw him last he's changed into a T-shirt, this time too loose, and a pair of worn out jeans, and he's crouched beside me, his arms hung across his knees. 'I'm feeling fine,' I say.

'Exhausted?' he asks, running his hand through his hair. He seems nervous.

'No,' I say, sitting back a little so I can get a better look at him. There's a thick band of leather around his left wrist, and several thinner ones on his right.

'Get something to eat,' he urges, looking around the room. 'There's going to be a lot of work to do tomorrow.'

'Yeah, okay.' I blink at him for a second. 'Are you okay? You seem tired.'

He looks taken aback, as if no one has ever asked him that before.

'I'm … fine. I just haven't been sleeping very well.' He looks surprised at himself for answering honestly.

'It must be hard,' I say to him, 'being the leader. Do you mind it?'

He cocks his head to one side and looks at me for a long moment. 'It doesn't matter what I want,' he says quietly. 'What matters is the group.' Another long look that I can't look away from. 'Thank you, though,' he says stiltedly. 'For asking.'

Neither of us moves for a long moment, but then Lacey calls me from her spot in the corner.

'I'm gonna go see what she wants.'

'Of course.'

'Okay.'

I start walking over to Lacey, and when I look back, he's gone.

o o o

I end up sitting silently throughout the entire meal, my back to the wall as I watch Lacey, Mark, Walter and Clarke chatting together. The dynamic is strange, as if Lacey has been adopted into their little family but Clarke hasn't. They have no lack of warmth towards her, but there is a boundary between her and the others that isn't there with the boys and Lacey.

I wonder who is responsible for that.

I eat slowly, considering my options. I don't know if I should approach Kole tonight or wait until tomorrow. I don't know if I have the energy for an interrogation tonight, but I'm worried I won't get the chance to talk to him if I wait.

'This tastes like roadkill.' Clarke pokes at a piece of meat that's floating in her soup. From what I can tell, the food is just meat, some kind of pale vegetable and a lot of water.

I look down at my own tin can, watching it curiously. It doesn't taste that bad to me.

'It's rabbit,' Lacey says.

'Kole told me it was deer,' Mark says slowly, looking into his can with wide eyes.

'He told me it was chicken.' Walter winks, and when Clarke punches him in the arm he just laughs. 'What did he tell you it was?' he asks, nodding towards me, a slow grin spreading across his face.

I sit up a little straighter from where I was slouched against the wall.

'He didn't say anything to me.'

'She's a bright one,' Clarke murmurs, raising her eyebrows at me. I stare at her, feeling myself bristling. She holds my stare without flinching, cocking her head to the side in a challenge.

'Give her a break, Clarke, she's new,' Mark says under his breath, as if I won't hear.

'I hadn't noticed,' Clarke says sarcastically, rolling her eyes as she stands up. 'I'm finished.' She picks up her can and walks away without looking back.

Lacey and the boys both stand up and move to go after her.

'You coming?' Walter asks me, pausing at the door.

'I'll be there in a minute.'

'Okay.' He shrugs, and then he's gone.

I keep my place against the wall as I watch everyone slowly file out, until I'm the last one in the room. I stand up, my already empty tin gripped in my hand, and I start walking towards the kitchen, hoping Kole is still there, when I hear raised voices in the other room.

'… can't keep doing this!' a man's voice says.

I stop, leaning my back against the wall by the door so they won't realise I'm listening.

'They've spent the last week in the woods, I needed to do something before they lost hope.' That voice is definitely Kole.

'And you thought the best idea would be to use up supplies that we don't have to spare?'

'We have food, Don.'

'How much?' the man demands gruffly. 'It's January, Kole. There's nothing growing, it's not exactly easy trying to hunt out there, and anything we do find is so skinny it's barely worth the bullets it takes to kill it.'

'We'll get by. We always get by.' Kole sounds like an elastic band pulled too tight.

'We're barely surviving the winter, Kole. If you don't change something, we're not going to survive another.'

I hear loud footsteps stomping away and a door slamming, and then silence.

I wait five seconds, then I step out into plain view. Kole jerks around to face me, his expression only shocked for the tiniest second, before he masks it with a stiff calm.

'Quincy,' he says slowly. 'You should be in bed.'

'Lacey said you had answers for me,' I say, setting my tin down against the wall. I'm as exhausted as he is, and I want to get this over with so I can go to bed.

He closes his eyes, inhales slowly and runs his hands over his face.

'I really can't take this tonight.'

'I want answers,' I say, and I have to stop myself from raising my voice.

'Can't we do this tomorrow?'

'No.' I fold my arms in front of my chest.

He runs his hand through his hair, breathing out. He looks at me, looks at the door behind him, back to me, his eyes narrowing as he considers his options.

'What do you want to know?'

'How did you get out here? Are there more of you? How long have you been out here? How are there Officers outside the Wall? Why isn't everyone dead?' Every time I try to pause so he can answer, another question pops into my head, just as urgent as the last one.

He laughs a slow, dead laugh.

'That's a lot of questions,' he says, tapping his knuckles against the lopsided table.

'Nothing out here makes any sense. Of course I have a lot of questions,' I snap.

'I'm not answering them all tonight. But I'll tell you this much: there are more of us, the Officers are outside of the Wall because Oasis sends them here, and I don't know why we're not all dead. We probably should be.'

'You didn't answer—'

'Stop,' he says, standing up. He towers over me as his lips compress into a hard line, his dark eyes sharper than they were before. 'No more. Not tonight.'

I go to say something, then close my mouth tight. There's no point.

'Get some sleep, Quincy. I'll see you tomorrow.'

And he must trust me more than the others, because he turns his back to me and then he walks out the door without another word.

14

I wake up, and for a moment I'm so disoriented I can't process what's going on around me. Everything is blurry, and I'm so cold, my bones stiff from the icy temperature. I try to inhale, but all that enters my lungs is water, and that's when it clicks.

I'm underwater.

I can see the surface, the sun glistening above, the blur of trees leaning across the bank, and my arms and legs thrash, trying to push me up, but my body is a dead weight and I start sinking faster.

I try to hold my breath, but my body keeps inhaling, pulling more and more river water into my lungs as my body spasms.

And that's when I see her. She's under the water with me, but she doesn't seem bothered by it, a cold smile stuck on her small face. Bea floats above me, and her skin is icy blue, her white lips curled upwards beneath empty eye-sockets.

My legs pump faster, my heart crawling into my mouth as I try to push away from her, but the faster I move away, the faster she comes towards me, pale fingers stretched out in front of her. I try to move my lips, form an apology, a scream, anything, but I can't move.

I am frozen in time, horror searing through me as my body shuts down.

My muscles have stopped working entirely, just as her small hand grips my arm, sending knives of ice through my bloodstream. My heart stops as the black holes where her eyes should be suck me in, dragging me deeper.

15

I am screaming.

It's the first thing that I realise, before I realise where I am, before I realise that the sound of thunder above me is people moving upstairs, before I realise I've thrown myself across the room so hard my head has cracked against the wall. I slide down the wall, pushing myself into the corner as I swallow another scream. I'm shaking so violently that it's making the panic well up inside me even faster, and I stuff my hands between my knees to stop them from trembling, so I don't have to watch myself fall apart.

The door flies open, slamming against the wall as someone storms in, but I don't pick my head up from my knees as I pull farther into the corner.

'What the hell—?!'

'Get *out*!' I shout, and my voice is making strange choking sounds and I need them *out out out*.

'What happened?' the voice asks, gentler now, and I recognise it as Kole's.

I jump from my spot on the floor, dragging my arm across my eyes and stepping up to him, toe to toe, as adrenaline finally kicks in, making me feel braver than I actually am.

'I said, *get out*,' I growl, and the unsteadiness in my voice isn't fear or anger, but something deadly caught between the two. He looks slightly taken aback, then his eyes narrow as he studies my face, trying to read something that's not there. '*Now*,' I snarl.

He holds up his hands in surrender, taking a step back without taking his eyes off me. I watch him walk through the door backwards and pull it closed behind him. Then I am on the floor again, and I am coming undone, the hinges of my joints pulling apart as I tremble into a mess on the floor, just clothes and tears and this unstoppable shaking.

What is happening to me?

o o o

The voices outside my room are incessant.

'She's lost it,' someone says.

'We can't afford to house mental patients, Kole.'

'She's a danger to us all.'

'She's obviously insane.'

'I thought someone was being murdered.'

'I thought we were being attacked again.'

'We can't keep her here any longer.'

It goes on and on until I feel like I actually am losing my mind, and to make it worse, I don't hear anyone arguing with them. I want out of here, but I need more time. If they kick me out, I won't survive to the end of the week.

Suddenly I'm struck by the insanity of it all. That we are here, far from Oasis, far from any kind of normalcy, and they are demanding answers but refusing to ask questions to my face. It feels like Oasis rules still apply here, but the lines are less distinctly drawn.

They wear no Officer uniforms, but they act like they should have authority over me.

I drag open the door separating my room from the kitchen, and a dozen shocked faces turn in my direction.

'What?' I ask, and my voice comes out strong, but on the inside I feel like I'm unravelling. 'If you have something to say, tell me.'

No one says a word, but several eyes meet across the table.

I try to rein in my anger, to push it down like I always do, but before I can stop myself, I snap, 'If you want answers, this is the only way you're going to get them.'

Clarke shoulders her way to the front of the crowd.

'We don't know you,' she says, as if that needs to be said. 'We don't know who you are or why you're here. We don't trust people like you.'

'People like what?' I snap, but she doesn't back down.

She steps around the table until she's face-to-face with me. 'People like you. People from the Inside. How do we know you're not one of them?'

'*I nearly died out there!*' I yell. 'Why would I put myself through that?'

'We don't know you,' Clarke hisses again, as if that's an argument, as if that's reason enough for anything.

'Clarke, calm down,' Kole says, stepping forward, and we both look towards him. 'Quincy, we need to know we can trust you.'

'You need to know that you can trust me? What about me? I don't know anything about you people. Are you Pure? Are you Dormant? Are you Infected?'

Kole's eyes widen, as if that's a new idea. He seems to think about his answer carefully.

'Infection status isn't a consideration out here,' he says slowly, making pointed eye contact, as if he's trying to pass on some deeper message.

Whatever it is, I'm not receiving it, because all that comes out of my mouth is a choked, '*What?*'

'There isn't any proof that the gene even can be activated, so we choose not to terrorise ourselves with the idea of it.'

'The *idea of it?*' I splutter. 'The Virus almost wiped out the *entire population*. How can you just ignore it?'

'Have you ever seen an outbreak, Quincy? When you were inside Oasis, did you see anything at all that suggested that the X gene could activate the Virus?'

'But the scientists—'

'Anything that *wasn't* fed to you by Oasis?' he interrupts, and my mouth snaps shut. This is too much. That Oasis was killing off people from outside the Wall I could imagine, but *this*? The amount of fear, of *work* that surrounds keeping the X gene from activating …

'There's no point,' he says. 'We've all been over this a million times. Even if we did know for sure, there's nothing we could do to stop it if it did activate. We have to keep living, Quincy.'

His words punch holes in my chest, resonating with that voice in my head, always pushing me forward. *We have to keep living.* That, at least, I can understand.

'How did you escape?' Mark says, and my head snaps around in his direction. I can tell, by the way he's looking at me, what he really means.

How did someone like you escape Oasis?

I imagine them pulling me from the river, soaking wet, ice cold and unconscious, and it's not hard to believe I might not seem capable of escaping the fortress of Oasis.

I clench my jaw.

'I had help,' I say, and it's harder to get out than I would have expected. 'Someone hacked the mainframe and left a message. There was a girl back in the Dorms, she knew what it meant. She knew of something, or some*one*, who was getting past the firewalls and leaving messages in monitors all over Oasis. They cut the power in the middle of the night. The rest was …' I think of Bea, of the sound of the gun, of the boy holding that gun '… easy.' I swallow.

'What happened to the girl?' Lacey asks quietly.

I immediately seize up, my jaw clamping shut. Understanding floods their faces, but before the silence can linger too long, I notice Kole, his eyes hungry as they roam my face, looking for something more than I'm telling him.

'You know who hacked the mainframe,' I say. Not a question, but a statement, my stomach plummeting as I speak.

I can see him holding his breath. 'I don't know who did it.' He exhales. 'But I've heard … rumours.'

'What kind of rumours?' I ask, wary.

'That they have power,' Clarke says. 'That they have people on the Inside. That they're planning something.'

My eyes fly back to Kole, and he answers my question before I can ask it.

'A war,' he says.

I can't drag my eyes from his face.

'They call themselves Genesis. Supposedly, they believe that those with the X gene are not a threat.'

'And you don't?'

'We don't have proof of either side. What we do know is that sometime last year, people started escaping Oasis, and they were able to because of Genesis. They leave messages in maps and broadcasts, create gaps in patrols and short out the power to the fence so people can escape. They don't seem to fear Oasis in the least. We know that they have the resources and know-how to hack the most highly secure networks in Oasis. But we don't know important stuff, like who they are, or where they stay – that's why we haven't been able to find them, and presumably why Oasis hasn't found them yet either.'

'But what are they trying to do?' I ask, my mind's eye still seeing the logo, and the x.

'No one's really sure, but it's clear they hate Oasis. They're trying to pick it apart from the inside out,' Kole says.

'But from what people have said, they have everything – running water, electricity, food, invisibility. Wherever they are, it sounds good,' Mark says, a warble of longing in his voice.

'Rumours,' Clarke says, shaking her head dismissively. 'We can't be sure of anything.'

'Except that they mean business,' Kole says, sitting forward.

'So then why not try to find them? If they're the ones with all the answers, why not try to track them down?'

'One, that's impossible,' Clarke says, a vague layer of disgust still soaking her every word. 'If Oasis hasn't found them, there's no hope of us ever tracking them down.'

'And two,' Mark cuts in, 'there are others we're waiting on before we go further away.'

'A lot of people still have family inside Oasis,' Kole says, running his hands through his dark hair as he leans his elbows against the table. He sounds exhausted. 'We can't just leave them behind.'

'You're planning on waiting for them?' I say, borrowing a little of Clarke's disgust, along with my own disbelief.

'Yes,' Kole says firmly. 'Our plan is to gather everyone together and then we'll set out to find a place far from here where we can settle safely. We never wanted to fight Oasis, we just want safety from it. We need to get as far away as we can, and then we can start rebuilding. A roof over our heads, food, a proper bed to sleep in – we can have all of that once everyone is here, and we find someplace safe.'

I look at him doubtfully. It all sounds a little too romantic to me. I prefer the idea of picking Oasis apart – that I can understand.

'But doesn't it make more sense to focus on finding allies, finding these hackers and fighting with them to undo everything?'

'We don't even know if Genesis exists,' Kole says impatiently, 'and we certainly don't know if it's anything like we're imagining. Plus, like Clarke said, no one can find them. We're not giving up on our people Inside just for some slight hope of finding a rebellion no one's even sure is real.'

I sit back in my chair, chewing on my lip. I wonder if that's what I should do, once I get what I need. If I found Genesis, maybe they could help find the Cure.

Unlike these people, who seem to have forgotten about it.

Kole looks out the window. 'We need to get moving. The daylight won't last long.' He pushes his chair back, and they all follow suit.

'Lacey, do you want to get Quincy set up with something while we're gone?' Kole murmurs.

'Sure.' She brightens, turning towards me. 'I was just about to start fixing up some of the clothes. Do you know how to sew?'

'A little.' I think of the hidden pockets in my uniform.

'Wonderful!'

'Okay then,' Kole says. 'We'll be back in a few hours. Clarke and Walter, come with me. Mark, stay here and make sure everything runs okay with the repairs.'

He gives Mark a pointed look, and I get the feeling that he's leaving him here to watch me. But I don't care. I remind myself I'm here for a purpose, and these people have nothing to do with it.

Kole and the others move out quickly, leaving the kitchen cold and alien, and I get the sense that the brief respite from their distrust is over as Mark watches me from the other side of the room.

'The supplies are upstairs,' Lacey informs me. 'You ready?'

'Yes.' I nod. My mind is whirring with everything I've just learned. I'm ready. Ready to get answers, find a way to survive and get out.

16

I hiss, jerking my hand away as I stab myself with the needle for the hundredth time. I've been on the third floor for three days, only going downstairs for meals and to sleep. Lacey spends most of her days helping downstairs, but she visits me from time to time and helps with the boring work I'm doing: sewing until I'm seeing double.

Lacey sits across from me now, her fingers fast and nimble as she patches up a pair of trousers. She's a chatterbox, and when she's up here there's a never-ending stream of words coming from her mouth, most of which I try to ignore. But somewhere along the way, her story of a strange berry she discovered one day while out foraging has drifted towards Clarke, and I suddenly tune back in.

'What did you say?'

'I said that it's because it's her family's, that's why she won't let anyone call her by anything else.'

'Her name?'

'Yeah. I asked her once what her first name was and she wouldn't tell me. She said it didn't matter anymore.'

It reminds me of the day I was stripped of my last name, Emerson, and had it replaced by a serial number. And later, when even the serial number was too much of a privilege and had to be taken along with my job. The thought makes my blood boil all over again, but there's no point getting angry.

I feel like I'm banging my head off a brick wall. I've been trying to get to Kole again, to ask him more questions, but he's out hunting all day, and comes in so late he can barely walk in a straight line.

Whoever it was that I overheard arguing with Kole about rations was right. We're being fed two small portions of food every day, barely enough to keep us going. A large group goes out every morning to hunt, and every night they come back empty-handed. They have a small store of canned foods on the third floor, but it's dwindling quickly as the days pass. No one will tell me where they got the food, or how they can get more, but I keep asking anyway. I even tried to talk to Kole about it last night, but he just held up his hand and told me he couldn't deal with it right now.

I need to be studying them, to learn from them, to figure out how they survive out here, how to hunt, what to eat, but they won't let me get close enough. I finish repairing the ripped knee of the trousers I was sewing, breaking the thread with my teeth and throwing it down on the floor beside me with a grunt.

Three days. I've been here for three days, and all I've learned is how to fix clothes. I stand up, throwing my supplies onto the floor. Enough.

I jog down the stairs, ignoring the way the unstable wooden structure moves under my feet, and then I'm outside. I can see them walking towards the tree line, six men and two women. The only ones I really know are Mark and Kole, but I notice Clarke on the outskirts of the group, fixing a knife at her hip as she walks.

I move up beside them, slipping into the group without a word, my heart racing in my chest.

'What the hell are you doing?' Kole asks, looking down at me with wild eyes.

'I'm coming with you,' I say firmly, sounding more confident than I feel.

'What is she doing here?' the middle-aged man standing beside Kole practically hisses at me. I remember Lacey telling me his name is Jonas.

I lean across Kole, looking straight at Jonas.

'I'm coming with you,' I say, my voice clear and unbending.

He blinks at me several times and then looks away, angry.

'Kole?' Mark asks quietly, unsure what to do.

Kole is still watching me, sizing me up. 'Why do you want to come?' he asks.

'I want to learn.'

He narrows his eyes, sensing something more behind my words, but he's wrong. He's wrong and at the same time he's not, but I keep my face completely blank as I look up at him. I see him thinking, then I see him deciding.

'Fine, she can come,' he says. 'But you better not get in our way.'

'No problem.'

He nods. 'Then let's go.'

We start moving again, all nine of us, heading into the wilderness.

17

The forest is cold as we trudge through the underbrush. Kole has split us into three groups of three so we can cover more ground. The first group is made up of me, Kole and Clarke. The second, which heads north, includes Mark, Walter and a boy I haven't met yet, and the third is Jonas, his wife, Meredith, and an unfamiliar man they call Don. I know Kole put me with him because the other groups don't want me. I try not to let it get to me, that it's going to take time, but I can't help feeling frustrated. I haven't done anything to them. I haven't made a single move against them, yet they're still treating me like the enemy.

I kick a branch underfoot, and Kole glares at me.

'Quiet,' he hisses.

'It's not like there's anything out here,' I fire back.

'Well there won't be if you keep tramping around the forest like an elephant.' He catches my arm and pushes me down to avoid a low-hanging branch. 'Are you trying to make as much noise as possible, or does it just coming naturally to you?'

'Shut up,' I growl, shaking his hand off me. 'And I'm being as quiet as I can.'

He barks out a disparaging laugh, just as Clarke comes up behind us.

'You both need to shut the hell up, or we're going to starve to death, got it?' she says, her eyes boring holes through us.

'Got it,' we both say at the same time.

We glance at each other as Clarke walks away, and Kole's face suggests that if I was anyone else, he'd be smiling right now.

∘ ∘ ∘

'Don't. Move.'

Kole's voice is the smallest whisper, his hand laid against my arm to stop me. My eyes take in our surroundings, trying to spot what's made him pause. I see the tiniest movement ahead, no more than six metres in front of us.

Kole pulls his gun from his backpack, a long rifle of some sort, and his movements are as smooth as water. He rests the gun against his shoulder, taking careful aim as I hold my breath, afraid my heart is beating so fast it will alert the creature.

Out of nowhere, something flies through the trees, and I hear it, a thump and then a crash, the animal is down, but when I look back at Kole, he hasn't fired.

I look at him in confusion, then we hear a loud whoop go up in the forest and Clarke jumps out in front of us, a wide smile spread across her face.

'I told you it would work!' she says elatedly, holding a roughly hewn bow above her head.

'You didn't,' Kole breathes, eyes wide in awe.

'I did,' she says. 'I did!' And then she takes off towards the animal.

'What was that?' I ask, turning to him. My heart is still thundering in my chest, and I have to resist the urge to lean against the tree beside us.

'She shot it with a bow,' he says. 'I said it would never work, but it did.'

'What did? The bow? What?' I feel like an idiot, lagging behind, not understanding a single thing that's going on around me.

'She's been making that bow for weeks. Trying to find a new way to hunt that would save bullets. I never thought it would actually work. We've tried before, to make something similar, but we could never generate enough power to kill anything. But she wouldn't let it go.' He shakes his head. 'And she finally got it to work.'

We start following Clarke's path through the thick foliage, my mind scrambling to keep up. Maybe this changes something. Maybe if there's food, if people are properly fed for the first time, then they'll calm down. Maybe, with the threat of hunger taken away, they'll tell me more about Genesis. Or at least let me learn enough to find them myself.

We find Clarke standing victorious above the body of a huge deer, a grin plastered across her face, her dark curls a halo above her head. Kole smiles at Clarke, and then at me, and I think, This is the chance I've been waiting for, and I smile back.

18

It takes hours for us to get back to the house. First we have to track down the rest of the group, and it quickly becomes clear that dragging the buck on ropes isn't going to work. It's incredibly heavy and slows us down to a stumble. When we find the others, Kole and Mark pull out knives the length of my forearm and set to work chopping the still warm body of the buck into chunks, so we can carry it home.

My stomach is turning at the sight of the blood soaking into the ground, but I won't let myself look away. I hold my ground and grind my teeth, and I try to ignore Clarke's grin from across the clearing, the look in her eyes at once quiet and vicious. Once the entire thing is in pieces, Kole starts delegating parts for people to carry.

I surreptitiously glance away, heaving in a deep breath as I try to calm down. I've never seen anything like this, never seen so much blood in one place, and I want to vomit at the sight of it.

Meredith comes to stand beside me, and offers me something in the palm of her hand. She's tall and lithe, with long, dark hair that's beginning to grey at the roots, matching the startling grey of her eyes. She nudges me with her elbow, a small smile on her lips.

'For your hair,' she whispers, winking at me. In her palm lies a thin strip of leather and I take it gratefully, using it to tie my hair away from my face. The cold air that hits my cheeks and neck immediately calms me.

'Thank you,' I say, surprised at my own sincerity.

She smiles at me and takes a single step back, as if she's about to leave, but at the last second she steps closer.

'It's hard in the beginning,' she whispers. 'It'll get easier, I promise.'

I nod numbly. She smiles again before stepping up to Kole, who hands her a haunch of meat, which she takes as if it weighs nothing.

I'm left a little rocked, unsure what to feel about her approach, which is so different from how I've been treated up to now. I don't get the chance to think about it much, though, because a moment after Meredith walks away, I hear a whistle at my back and whip around to find Clarke standing directly behind me, the deer's head in her hands.

Its blank eyes stare at me, and I take a stumbling step backwards as she cackles.

'Sure you don't want to hold it?'

'Clarke.' Kole's voice is deadly from behind me, but I won't turn around. I won't turn away from the dead thing's eyes and Clarke's sharp mouth turned up in a snarl. 'Drop it,' he growls, and I'm not sure if he means the head or harassing me, but I'd be glad for either one right now.

She rolls her eyes and throws it at my feet, stomping away like a petulant child.

I step aside, trying to stop the bile rising in my throat. My heart is pounding in my chest so fast that I start to feel lightheaded, and it's not just my reaction to the bloody head. It's my reaction to Clarke. To that look in her eyes, like if she could just slit my throat and get me out of the way, she would happily do it.

As I turn around I notice Kole staring at me, an inexplicable emotion on his face. I give him a questioning look and he looks away from me. He picks up one of the front legs and holds it out to me. My piece of the kill. Heavier than some of the other cuts, but a lot less gruesome.

'Thank you,' I say, nodding at him. I understand the gesture, and I appreciate it, even if he's just trying to make up for Clarke's malice.

'We better get moving,' he orders, heaving the last piece over his shoulder. I fall into line behind him, watching as blood soaks into his T-shirt.

o o o

The sun is beginning to set when we arrive at the clearing, the newly boarded-up windows of the house coming into view first. That's Mark's handiwork, an attempt to keep the heat from leaving the house. I release a heavy sigh at the sight of the place, my pace picking up as I anticipate finally being able to put down the piece of meat somewhere.

Someone comes out of the building, and when they see us or, more importantly, when they see what we're carrying, they run back inside, calling people out excitedly. Within seconds we're swarmed, and the noise of voices shouting questions and calling out in delight at the sight of real food is deafening after the silence of our trudge through the forest.

We eat well that night, and I was right: the glares from the rest of the group turn into smiles, maybe not purposefully aimed at me, but there all the same. But still, Clarke sits in the back of my mind, and I can't stop thinking about what she did out there, and why. I run through all of her reactions so far, and I don't understand it. I don't understand how she could hate me so much when I haven't done anything to her.

I make eye contact with her from across the room, and she sneers at me, and my stomach drops. If I don't do something about her quickly, she's going to turn them against me.

19

I do not sleep.

I roll onto my side and stare at the door of my room. Everyone else is already asleep, but I feel ridiculous just lying here, waiting for dawn. Eventually the restlessness becomes too painful and I stand up, pushing away from the floor and letting the blankets fall from around me. I thought having a room to myself would be bliss, after all those years sleeping in a web of too-close bodies. But it doesn't really work like that. Sometimes the smallness of the room just makes me feel claustrophobic.

I need up and I need out. I need to not be in this tiny room. I need space.

I lay my hand on the door knob, my heart loud in my ears as I twist it slowly. I step out soundlessly and creep into the kitchen. Running my fingers across the rough concrete wall, I examine the kitchen, cold and empty as the moonlight breaks in through the gaps in the board that cover the window. The sink on the floor was removed that first day, and I stand where it used to be, feeling the house sleep around me.

During the day it feels electric, so much desperation packed into four walls makes the place stifling, but at least it feels alive. At night, it feels dead. It feels like it must have felt before we arrived here, abandoned and gutted and lifeless.

I hear something moving and I freeze, my entire body going deathly still as I listen. If Clarke finds me in the kitchen this late, she's going to wake the entire house and they're going to throw me back out into the forest, with no hope of survival.

Before I have a chance to run back into my room, the door creaks open, and Kole steps into the room. He stares at me blankly for several seconds, and I watch him slowly come back from inside his own head.

'Why are you up so late? You should be in bed,' he says, slightly bewildered.

'Why are you awake?' I ask. 'Shouldn't you be asleep too?'

He blinks at me. 'I can't,' he says slowly, slipping further into the room. 'I can't get to sleep.'

'Why?'

'Has anyone ever told you you're like a child?' he asks, sounding frustrated. 'You won't stop asking questions.'

'You're avoiding my question,' I observe. I cross my arms in front of my chest, the oversized T-shirt and sweatpants doing little to keep me warm against the freezing air.

'Yes, I am,' he says, shrugging, not offering any kind of explanation. He's wearing a dark grey woollen sweater, and abruptly he pulls it over his head, revealing a black T-shirt underneath, and throws it across the table at me.

I catch it in the air, and give him a questioning look.

'Take it,' he says.

'But—'

'You're cold, I'm not. Take the damn sweater.'

I pull back a little, caught off-guard by the hard edge in his voice. He rubs his temples, closing his eyes as he pulls in a deep breath.

'Do you want something to drink?' he asks, not looking at me as he pulls things from a wooden box in the corner.

'Sure,' I say quietly, more to appease him than because I'm actually thirsty.

Mark has been working around the clock since we got here. He's been teaching some of the others how to make things from wood, like he can. The lopsided table has been given a fourth leg, and now it can actually stand reliably. Even the box that Kole was pulling things out of a moment ago is one of Mark's creations. The stove that we found in the building actually works, and the fire from dinner is still burning as Kole places a steel kettle atop it, before going back to the box.

I watch Kole move around, preparing some kind of drink at the stove, and it's the first time since I met him that I have looked at him, really looked at him. His hair isn't actually black, just such a dark brown that it looks black, and as he leans forward it falls into his equally dark eyes. He is tall, but comfortable in his height, his movement fluid in a way I've only ever seen from Aaron. And though there is power in his shoulders, and pride in the way he walks, there's something … off about him. There is no balance in him. Even the few smiles I have seen on his face are crooked, tipped to one side and uneven.

'What?' he says, watching me inquisitively as he moves around the kitchen, head cocked to the side.

'Nothing.' I shake my head.

He watches me for a second more, and a muscle in his face twitches, making me think of Aaron again, the way he could tell what I was thinking even when I didn't know myself.

'Okay,' he says, and he seems to be relaxing in a way I haven't seen from him before. 'Give me a second.'

He pours water from a container on the ground into the kettle, pulling out a small box with an old Oasis label on it. I wonder at how fast these people have set up their lives in this new place.

'Where'd you come from?' I ask, but he frowns at me. 'In Oasis, I mean.'

'Again with the questions,' he groans.

'You can't expect me to just sit here, completely clueless.'

'I can't?' he asks, and I'm distracted by the almost-smile on his face. I don't know where all of this is coming from.

'No,' I tell him.

The kettle whistles.

'Did you have any family?' he asks, ignoring the high-pitched sound.

'Dead,' I say, and it's out before I can even think about it. But it's easier this way.

I don't actually know what happened to my parents after they put me in the Outer Sector, and I'm not in the mood for being asked questions I don't have any answers for.

'I'm sorry,' he says, sliding a cup of hot liquid towards me.

'An actual cup?' I ask, putting my hand to my heart in mock surprise.

'An actual cup!' he mock-enthuses, sitting down with his own across from me. We're sitting on chairs with wobbly legs and drinking out of actual cups with actual chips gone out of them, but it feels different suddenly. Like the world outside doesn't exist.

'So what now?' he asks.

'What do you mean?'

'What's next for you? Are you staying here?' He takes a sip of his drink.

'I'm staying, for a while at least.' I try to make myself sound sure, to make myself sound like I don't wake up every morning wondering when they're going to kick me out.

'Okay.' He nods. 'What then?'

'I don't know …' I pause, wondering how much I should tell him. 'I think I need to find my own way.' I wonder if I should be talking to him now, this late, when I'm this tired. I don't know what I'm saying.

'And this isn't?'

'Falling in a river and being saved isn't something that you do, it's something that happens to you.' I stare into my cup, swirling the greenish liquid around, half afraid to drink it. 'I just want to stop reacting. Eventually you have to figure out how to make your own decisions, instead of letting everyone make them for you.' The minute it's out of my mouth I regret it. I'm saying too much. I need to shut up before I get myself in trouble.

I glance up at him, and he's watching me with an emotion I can't name. It's like he's fascinated.

'I know what you mean,' he says after a while. 'I got to that place in my life a few years ago.'

'And?'

'And? And it gets better. And you'll figure it out. And if you didn't have to figure it out, if it were easy, if it were natural, if you were just you, well then it wouldn't be worth it. It's only worth it if you have to fight for it.'

'Huh. What I would give for that to not be true,' I mutter, looking into my cup again.

'That's what everyone thinks at first.'

There's a brief silence, and I'm thinking over what I've said, trying to figure out why I couldn't stop talking.

'Drink it,' he says after a moment, nudging my cup with his empty one.

I lift it to my lips slowly, taking a tentative sip. It's warm and it tastes strange and I keep swirling it around in my mouth. I take another sip.

'You like it?' he asks, and the smile on the corners of his mouth is warmer than before.

'I think so.' I drink down the rest of it, and that warm sunny feeling comes back. I decide that I do like it. I like the feeling of it running down my throat.

'Well then, that's another thing.'

'What?'

'You like nettle tea. That's another thing you know about yourself. Collect them up and figure yourself out.'

I laugh quietly, trying not to wake anyone upstairs, but I like the idea. Compiling a mental notebook of facts about myself. Maybe if I do that for long enough, I won't feel so unsure. Maybe freedom is in knowing who you are, so no one can try to make you think you're someone else.

Maybe that's it. As simple as that.

'What did you do?' he asks quietly, like the question just slipped out without him realising.

'What do you mean?'

'You're Branded.'

I feel my heart stop. I feel my insides turn to sand and pour into my feet. I feel my throat shut tight and my heart refuse to restart.

'What?' I hiss, and there are so many things in my voice I can't count them. Anger and fear and hate and pain and something raw, like an open wound.

'I saw it when you tied up your hair while we were out hunting. The neck of your shirt fell down and I saw it.'

All of the sunshine is gone from my insides. I can't breathe, and I can't speak, and I stand up and I try to do something, anything, but I can't.

He keeps talking, like he can't stop, like he's too exhausted, too stupid to stop.

'You're from the Outer Sector. They don't Brand people in the Celian City, so you must be from the Outer Sector. So what did you do?'

'*Go to hell,*' I say.

'What?' Now it's his turn to look shocked. He's leaning across the table, so close that I can feel his breath on my face, and I feel my heart, every pump of it pushing the rage faster through my system.

'*Go. To. Hell,*' I spit, and I turn on my heel and I tear open the door to my room and I slam it behind me, ignoring the voice in my head warning me that I'm going to wake everyone.

I feel dizzy with fear and anger and fear and fear and fear and oh my God.

I do not sleep.

20

I hear people begin to wake upstairs, but I don't move. My back is to the wall and I'm facing the door with my knees pulled up against my chest as I try to figure out a solution. I can't let Kole tell the others what he saw, or how I reacted. It's not like they wanted me here in the first place, and if they find out I'm Branded, they'll never let me stay. The Branded are known only as cruel, insane, violent monsters, and if the group found out, it would only confirm what they had suspected from the beginning: that I'm dangerous. My heart pounds in my ears as my mind scrambles to come up with an excuse, an explanation.

But it doesn't matter what I say. The Branded are reviled the same way the Pure are glorified, and that's never going to change.

No one comes near the door. I hear people talking outside, Kole's voice rising above the others as he starts delegating work for the day, most of it centred around the house now that the threat of starvation has temporarily disappeared.

I push myself up off the ground, squaring my shoulders as I walk out into the kitchen, pretending nothing happened.

And nothing seems to have happened.

Nobody stares at me, nobody points or starts shouting. They continue moving around the building as usual, and a few of them even make brief, unaggressive eye contact with me.

I feel a sense of relief so strong I begin to feel lightheaded, and lean my hand against the table for support.

Kole is talking to a group of men in the corner, and when I pass he doesn't look up. He acts like he doesn't see me, and maybe he doesn't.

Maybe I can pretend last night didn't even happen.

Lacey finds me a few minutes later, two containers in her hands.

'I'm going foraging with a few of the others,' she says. 'Do you want to come?'

I nod mechanically, and she nods back, moving away and gathering a few others. The lack of warmth in her voice startles me, and I wonder if Kole told her, even if he didn't tell the others.

I take a deep breath, and try to convince myself it'll be okay even if he did, but I know that's a lie.

o o o

There are four people in our foraging group: me, Lacey, Meredith and Walter. We don't push as deep into the forest as we did the day we went hunting, and we don't have to stay quiet either.

Walter makes a joke about the berries not running away, and nobody laughs.

I lag behind, because I am the only one here with no idea what they are doing. They search slowly, not passing a single bush without investigating.

'If you see this,' Lacey says, pointing to a green shoot growing at the base of a tree, 'dig it up. We can eat the root.'

I nod solemnly and begin looking for it under the dense greenery.

'Hey,' I say after a few moments of quiet searching. 'If I found white berries, up in a tree, what should I, uh, what should I do with that?'

Lacey and Meredith both turn to me with wide eyes.

'You mean mistletoe? Don't go near it. If you eat that stuff, you'll be sick.'

I nod slowly, trying to pretend I don't already know that from first-hand experience.

'You didn't ... you didn't eat some, did you?' Lacey asks nervously, looking around to see if she can locate the plant.

'No, no, no. Of course not,' I say, heat crawling up my neck. 'I just saw it a while back, and I was wondering, that's all.' Eventually the group starts to spread out, trying to cover more ground as the sun rises higher in the sky. I'm just walking around aimlessly, not trusting myself to pick the right stuff, when Lacey calls me over to where she's hunkered by the base of a tree.

'Help me pick these,' she says, pulling tiny white flowers up by their roots.

'What are they?'

'Wood sorrel.'

'They don't really ...'

'Look like much?' She laughs. 'I know, but they're edible, okay?'

I smile a weak smile back at her. The old warmth is there in her voice again and he didn't tell her and it's going to be okay.

'Hey, Lacey?' I ask after a while. 'What's Clarke's deal?'

Her pale hands pause on the root of a flower she's placing inside the container.

'What do you mean?' she asks, but her voice sounds like she already knows.

'She seems angry at me. I don't know what I've done wrong.' I keep my focus firmly on what my hands are doing.

Lacey finishes putting the flower gently into the container and turns to look at me.

'Everyone's under a lot of stress right now, and Clarke's always been a bit wound up.'

'But it's more than wound up, Lacey. She hates me.'

'She doesn't hate you, I promise. She's just a little intense. It'll ease up. You just need to give her time to get used to you.'

Time for her to get used to me, or time for me to get used to her attacking me?

'Would you please tell me what's going on today?' I ask, changing the subject.

'What do you mean?'

'Everyone's been acting weird. They seem, I don't know, upset or something.'

'Oh,' she says.

I brace myself for the answer, but when it comes, it's not what I'm expecting.

'Do you remember I told you there was another group? You were sick at the time, so maybe you don't. Anyway, they were supposed to join us here a while ago, but there's no sign of them.'

'But … how is that possible? I thought you had to run before the Officers found you.'

'Yeah, well Jay thought he could raid the Officers while we knew where they were, after the attack. He just wanted blood after what happened and no one could talk him out of it.' She sounds exhausted.

'Who's Jay?' I ask quietly.

'He's just another one of us. But he's reckless and angry, and I think he might have got himself killed.' Lacey's voice whispers to a halt, and I find myself reaching out to her. My hand touches her shoulder gently, and she looks up at me with tear-filled eyes.

'I know you've been having a rough time, Quincy, but I'm glad you're here.' She places her hand over mine.

I pull my hand back.

'Uh, thanks,' I say, my throat feeling tight. 'I think we've got them all.' I gesture to the flowers as I stand up, trying to pull myself together.

I'm letting these people get to me too much. I need a break.

'I'm gonna just head back now and see what's going on at the house,' I tell Lacey. She starts to say something, but I just walk away.

I need to pull myself together.

21

'I want to help you find the other group,' I tell him, walking up to Kole, who's talking to Mark in the kitchen.

'What?' He looks at me. He looks edgy, and I can't tell if it's because of me or something else.

'I'm coming with you. To find the second group. I want to come.'

'You can't,' he says dismissively, but I won't let him turn away from me.

'I can help.'

'How?' he asks, and when he looks at me he seems more tired than anything else.

'You're searching for a group of people, Kole, not performing surgery. I don't need experience.'

Kole turns to Mark for a moment, says something too quietly for me to hear, and Mark nods, walking away.

'What did you say to him?' I ask.

'You can't come because we might meet Officers, and besides, we're tracking them, not just mindlessly stumbling into the forest and hoping we'll see them somewhere.'

He turns away from me, passing through the kitchen and up the stairs. I follow him, ignoring his obvious attempt to shut down the conversation.

'I can hold my own against an Officer,' I argue. 'I escaped Oasis the same as everyone else.'

'How many Officers have you actually fought?' he asks, looking back at me as he keeps walking up to the third floor.

'Three,' I say automatically.

'Well that's a lie.' He smiles, actually smiles at me, like my desperation amuses him.

'Okay, I haven't fought any Officers directly, but I can help. I swear.' I catch his arm, stopping him in front of the door to the third floor and looking directly at him.

'Please,' I say, however begrudgingly.

He closes his eyes and sighs.

'If I tell you that you can come, will you stop hounding me?'

'Yes,' I say, without hesitation.

'And if I let you come,' he says, taking a step closer to me on the stairs, 'will you forgive me for last night?'

I look up at him, shocked. His expression is strained and he honestly looks apologetic

'Fine,' I murmur.

'Then you can come.'

I drop his arm, nodding, and leave to get ready.

22

Kole heads in the direction of the old base, near the river, which means heading back in the direction of Oasis. We're never going to get close enough to actually see the walls, and Kole hopes to stay far enough away that we won't be in any danger, but my heart still speeds up at the thought of it, memories jostling for attention, making me feel ill.

'You okay?' Kole is walking behind me, and I didn't even hear him coming.

'Fine,' I say, shaking my head and swallowing hard.

He blinks at me for a moment, but he doesn't ask questions. He looks away, off into the forest, and I take a deep breath, trying to pull myself back together.

'Why didn't you tell anyone about last night?' I ask, so desperate for a distraction that my mind latches onto this. This of all the things I could have said.

He has a gun in a holster at his hip, and I can see the Oasis stamp on it.

'I shouldn't have asked about it,' he says. 'It wasn't my place.'

I don't say anything. I think I'm in shock. Of all the things I thought he would say, that is not one of them.

'Everyone here has a past,' he says, 'and it's none of my business what yours is.'

'You're right,' I say. But maybe it is his business. I wonder if they knew what happened, if they knew what I did to her—

Stop.

I stop thinking of anything at all, just so I won't have to think about that.

o o o

We walk until dusk, until Kole regretfully turns us back, promising another search in the morning. He looks even more exhausted now, and I can tell by the way he's walking he's having trouble staying awake. I fall in beside him, thinking I can help keep him going by talking, keep his mind off how tired his body must be.

'How many people are missing?' I ask.

'Six,' he says, glancing over at me. 'Jay and five people stupid enough to follow him.'

'Did you let them go?'

He doesn't say anything for a long moment.

'Yes. They were going to go anyway. At least this way I could tell them how to not get themselves killed.'

'And that worked out so well,' I mutter, and he looks over at me. He looks hurt, almost. 'I'm sorry,' I mumble. 'I didn't mean it like that.'

'Yes, you did,' he says, and I can't decide if he's angry or not.

We don't talk much after that, but we make progress, and we're almost home when Kole freezes, holding a hand up to stop us all. Everyone goes perfectly still, listening.

Everything is completely silent, but Kole twitches like he can hear something we can't, and suddenly he's gone from beside me and into the trees. I barely register that I'm chasing after him before I come to a screeching stop beside him.

Kole kneels beside a girl, her dark hair spread across the forest floor, blood pouring from a wound in her shoulder and soaking into the earth beneath her. I freeze, my breath stopping in my chest, because it's Bea's blue eyes staring up at me from the girl's panic-stricken face. It's happening again. Her blood stains her hair as she watches me with the kind of fear I can only imagine you feel when you know you're going to die.

She knows she's going to die.

She can't die.

I can't let her die.

'Give me your backpack,' Kole orders, pressing his hand to the wound and talking to her in a low voice.

I haphazardly pull my pack off my shoulders, dropping it to the ground and immediately pull out a shirt and throw it at Kole, who uses it to stem the flow of blood. He gestures for me to take over, putting pressure on the wound, and I try desperately not to think about Bea bleeding out on the gravel just inside the fence of Oasis.

Mark and the others arrive through the trees, and the minute Kole sees them he starts giving orders. He slips into this different version of himself so easily that I can't help thinking this is more natural to him than he acts like it is.

'Mark, take the girls and set up a perimeter. She's been shot, so there are Officers out here somewhere.'

I go still.

'Quincy, keep talking to her. You need to keep her conscious.'

'What's your name?' I ask the girl, but my voice is shaking so badly I can barely get the words out.

'Lauren,' she whispers. 'My shoulder.' She groans.

'You're going to be fine,' I reassure her, but my fingers are sliding on the fabric of the shirt that's against her shoulder, her wound gushing blood so fast it's already bled through the cloth. Kole pulls a knife from his backpack and leaves it by my leg.

'I'll be back in one minute. Use this if you need it.' And then he's gone.

The girl's head rolls back in agony.

'Hey! Lauren, look at me.' Her dazed eyes lock back onto mine. 'Good. You need to keep looking at me. Where'd you come from?'

She opens her mouth, then shakes her head. Her eyes start to close.

'Oasis? Did you come from Oasis?' She nods. 'So did I. Did you come alone?' She nods again.

'Lauren, listen to me. Just past those trees there's a house, and we're going to bring you there, and you're going to be fine, okay?' She nods, slowly, her head lolling to the side. I can't move my hands from her shoulder, so I call her name until she looks at me again, but her eyes are distant.

'KOLE!' I'm panicking. The girl's blood is everywhere, on my hands and across her chest and on the floor, and there can't be this much blood. I hear someone shout in the distance, and if this girl wasn't in front of me right now, if this girl didn't need me right now, I would be even more terrified than I already am.

'Lauren, you have to stay awake.' I'm tempted to shake her, but I'm afraid that might make her bleed out faster.

Footsteps sound in the forest, and my heart thunders in my chest.

'We're gonna be okay.'

The footsteps keep coming and the closer they get, the more my hands shake, the more I glance at the knife beside me.

I see a flash of Officer blue between the trees and my heart sinks. I turn back to the girl, unwilling to take pressure off her wound until I have to defend us. I keep pressing my hands to her shoulder while I try to think of a way to get us out of this.

I can't move her. I'm not strong enough, but even if I was, I'm too scared of her dying to attempt it.

The footsteps are closer, and they are behind me, and I am grabbing the knife in my blood-soaked hands and launching myself at the Officer before I can even get a good look at him.

Kole catches my hand hard, forcing me to drop the knife.

'It's okay,' he says, catching both my arms and holding them at my sides, making eye contact with me, trying to calm me down. 'Breathe,' he whispers, and my lungs obediently gasp for air.

'The Officer …'

He nods. 'It's okay. He's not going to hurt anyone anymore. And he was on his own. No one else around. It's okay now.'

Kole looks over at the others. 'Mark, take the girl. We need to get her back to the house,' he instructs, but he won't let go of me.

I try to turn around to check on Lauren, afraid she's bled out in the split-second I've left her, but Kole puts his hands on either side of my face and stares down at me.

'Are you okay?' he asks deliberately, afraid I'm too delirious to even understand him.

'I'm fine,' I say, shaking my head. 'I'm fine. Is she okay?'

He doesn't say anything, just watches my face for another second, and then lets me go, picking up my bag and throwing it over his shoulder as Mark starts back towards home.

23

We reach the house in a matter of minutes, but the journey is torturous and the return is havoc. In our absence Lacey had stationed look-outs around the house, and when they see us coming, covered in blood, carrying a half-dead stranger, fear breaks out across the house.

'Kole!' Lacey shouts from the door, the colour draining from her face.

We carry the girl into the house and straight to the kitchen. Kole orders everyone out of the room, and I swipe the table clear for Mark to set Lauren down.

'She's unconscious,' I say. I think I might be going into shock, but Kole's focus on the girl is unwavering as he starts looking her over.

'I need hot water, a needle and thread. And towels,' he says calmly, but no one moves. '*NOW!*' His voice booms in the small room, shocking us into action.

I swivel around, knocking the lid off the wooden box as I pull the dented kettle from inside it, throwing it onto the top of the stove. My shaking hands knock the kettle off the stovetop twice before I can fill it properly.

'What else do you need?' I ask Kole, returning to his side once the water is heating. Lacey has gone for the towels and Mark for the needle and thread, and everyone else has disappeared, afraid of getting in his way.

'I can't see anything. There's too much blood,' he says in frustration. 'Get me a knife. I need to get her shirt away from the wound.'

One of the clean hunting knives is on the counter behind me, so I hand it to him.

'Do you know how to check a pulse?' He doesn't look at me as he asks, focused on not nicking the girl with the knife as he cuts the shirt away from her shoulder.

Lacey and Mark return while I take Lauren's limp hand to check her heart rate, trying to calm my own enough to be able to feel hers.

'It's slowing down,' I tell him, and he curses under his breath.

The kettle whistles, and I take it from the stove and pour it into a basin with some cold water for Kole to wash the wound. I throw one of the towels into it and leave it on the table beside Lauren, where Kole can easily access it without putting down the knife.

'Give me that needle,' I tell Mark, taking it from him and running it under the last of the boiling water to sterilise it.

Kole is turning the girl over, and for a second I don't understand what he's doing, until he curses again.

'The bullet's still in her. I'll try to get it out, but you have to be ready to take it from me and give me the needle. She's going to start bleeding more heavily once it's out.'

'Okay.' My voice shakes.

He cleans the blood from her shoulder so he can see what he's doing, and then he takes the knife he used to cut her shirt away from the wound, and takes a steadying breath.

I focus on the basin, the water turning pink as the blood swirls through it, and a minute later I hear him exhale. I reach out and he drops the shell into my hand, taking the basin from me and washing the wound. He reaches out for me to hand him the needle and thread, and there is a second where his eyes meet mine, and there is fear there.

'Get something clean to use as a bandage,' he orders, beginning to sew up the wound. His hands are careful and steady, but the wound is bleeding again, and I don't understand how he can do this. His hands don't shake as the needle pierces her skin, pulling the thread out the other side as blood coats everything, his hands, the needle, Lauren, the table. Yet my hands are shaking as Mark and Lacey help me rip clothes into strips to use as bandages.

When we turn around, he has the knife back in his hand, cutting the thread carefully.

'Is she going to be okay?' I ask, watching her pale face as Kole washes his hands. He takes the strips out of my hands and starts bandaging her shoulder.

'I don't know.'

It takes him a few minutes to bandage her shoulder, but once he's done we cover her in blankets and fold one under her head as a pillow.

'Go to bed,' he tells Lacey. 'You're tired.'

'But what about you?'

'I'll stay down here and keep an eye on her.' When Lacey gives him an unsure look, hovering in the doorway, he tries to brush it off. 'Don't worry about me, I'll be fine.'

'Promise?'

'I promise. Now go.'

Mark follows her up, clearly grateful to be getting out of the cramped kitchen, and we're suddenly alone. Kole leans his head back against the shut kitchen door and closes his eyes.

I don't say anything to disturb him, because there's nothing to say here that won't sound stupid and out of place.

'Do you want some tea?' he asks quietly after a few minutes, finally lifting his head and peeking out from under his eyelashes at me.

He doesn't even ask me to go to bed. I'm glad. I didn't want to have to argue with him, not tonight.

'I'll make it,' I say.

He just nods in reply, too tired to argue with me either.

24

We sit with our backs against the wall, staring at her chest rising and falling. For a long time neither of us speaks.

'Do you think she's going to be okay?' I ask eventually, and I know I've asked him before, but I can't help it.

'I don't know. I'm just hoping it didn't hit an artery. I don't think I'll be able to repair it if it has.'

'There was a lot of blood.'

'There was.'

We go silent, and I can feel Kole holding his breath so he can listen to her breathing.

'What do you think happened?' I ask him.

He draws his legs up to his chest, balances his cup on his knee.

'I don't know.' I watch him bite his lip, lost in thought. 'If she was shot, there has to be Officers in the forest somewhere. I don't trust the fact that we only found one.'

'And what does that mean for us?'

'I'm not sure. We might have to move again, but I don't want to do that if we don't absolutely have to.'

'Seriously?' I turn to face him, almost tipping over my cup in the process. 'But you only just got here.'

'Three weeks,' he says, then lets out a quiet laugh. 'It would be a record.'

'You're serious? You're actually considering picking up and taking off again? After all our work here?'

'Of course I'm serious.' He looks at me like I'm crazy. 'How would I not be serious? If there are Officers out there, we have to leave before they get a chance to find us.' His voice turns sour at the end, and I can tell he's remembering the last time they had to run.

'But what if you fought back?' I ask, setting my cup down, afraid of spilling it. 'What if you found them before they found you?'

'Quincy, that's not how this works.'

'Why not?' I ask excitedly, and I don't know if it's because I'm exhausted, but it feels like the best idea anyone's ever had. 'You could do it, I know you could.'

'And risk how many lives in the process?'

'How many lives are you risking by letting them hunt you like prey?' I ask.

I'm suddenly angry.

'Why are you letting them do this to you, Kole? You're just allowing them to take the power without question. Maybe if you just tried—'

'And end up dead, like Jay?' Kole snaps, turning to face me so suddenly, I pull back an inch. 'You think I don't know he's dead?' He catches a look on my face and laughs. It's a dry, horrible sound. 'I know he's dead. They're all dead.'

'But you went looking for them …' I feel like I'm being strangled.

'Because I'm the one who has to pretend we're going to be okay,' he says. 'That's my job. If I didn't do it, we wouldn't be alive, and not because we starved or because of Oasis. The minute you lose hope, you're as good as dead.'

'But you …' I trail off, my chest tight.

'Exactly,' he says, looking directly at me, and his eyes eat me alive.

For the rest of the night we watch her, and we don't speak.

In my entire life, I have never pitied anyone. I had to learn not to, because pitying people was dangerous. It meant you cared too much, or maybe I was just too busy pitying myself, and my situation, to think of anyone else.

But this. That look in his eyes, like he had painted his armour to look like skin but behind it, there was nothing.

I can't help pitying that.

25

I wake up and the first thing I see is Kole, asleep. The girl is on the table and I'm stiff because of the awkward way I've been sleeping. The sun is making its slow ascent into the sky, and I get to my feet slowly, trying to let Kole sleep. I press a hand to my forehead, a headache pushing against the inside of my skull as I try to steady myself.

I check the girl's pulse and it's steady. Her breathing, though a little shallow, is continuous and steady, too.

She's alive.

I almost collapse with relief.

'Wh-what? Is she okay?' Kole sits up abruptly and is on his feet before I can say anything. 'Did she make it?'

'She's okay. She's breathing. She's okay.' I sound breathless. I sound happy. I sound like I'm about to cry, or fall down, or fall off the edge of a cliff.

He moves quickly to her side, checking her pulse, her breathing, her stitches.

'I already checked. She's okay.'

'Of course, I just need to ...'

'Check for yourself? Don't you trust me?' I'm poking fun, but the joke falls flat.

There is still blood on my hands from last night, and neither of us can say we believed she'd last the night.

She lost so much blood.

We look at each other across the room, blankly. Exhaustion feels like something sitting on my back, pulling at me from all angles. Kole looks like he could sleep for a week and still be tired.

'I want to thank you,' he says suddenly.

'You don't have to thank me.'

'No, I really do. You were incredible.'

'I didn't sew up a dying girl,' I say, a little robotically.

'Can't you just take a compliment?' His laugh sounds hollow.

'I can, but I prefer the ones I actually deserve.' I turn away from him and pour myself a drink of water from the canister left against the wall.

'Well you actually deserve this one,' he says, looking at me pointedly as I hand him a drink. 'You were amazing.'

'Fine. I was amazing. Incredible. Brilliant, really. The best water boiler ever.'

'Shut up.' He throws a towel at my head, and I duck just as the door opens. The towel hits Mark in the face, and he looks around the room, extremely confused.

'I came down to check on the girl …' he says, looking over my head at Kole. 'I didn't realise you stayed up all night.'

'I wanted to keep an eye on her,' Kole says, gulping down the water I gave him in two huge swallows.

'Do you want me to watch her for a bit? You look tired.'

'I'm fine. I got better sleep than I have in a while.'

'On the floor? For three hours? With a bleeding girl on the table in front of you?' I ask, raising an eyebrow at him.

Kole flashes me a smile, and I roll my eyes. This feels weird. This feels wrong. It shouldn't happen like this.

I imagined this, the trust slowly creeping in because I said all the right things at all the right times, not because a girl nearly died in front of us, or because I happened to be there when the cracks in Kole's armour started showing.

It wasn't supposed to happen like this, but I think it just did.

26

It doesn't hit me until I get upstairs. Everyone is up and gone, hunting and fixing and mending, and I stand in the middle of the room, and my knees buckle underneath me. I stare down at my hands, the blood dried into the base of my fingernails, and I need it off. Now.

I scramble towards the basin that Lacey has laid out in the corner of the room for washing, a cracked shard of a mirror hung precariously above it, and I think this is something only Lacey would think of and I think she's pretending we're okay, like Kole does, and I think I'm going to die out here.

The water is freezing cold, but I can barely feel it as I drag my nails across my skin, trying to scrape the blood off. My hands begin to shake, and my heart is loud and insistent in my chest, and my breath just stops.

Just like that.

Just like she died.

I can't hold the memories back anymore. I've been fighting them for weeks. I've been battling against the images because if I let them in, even for one second, I know I wouldn't be able to get up again. But I'm tired.

I can't do this anymore.

The memories pour in like ice water over my head, always colder, always harsher than expected. I feel the memory of that night forcing its way over every barrier I've placed within my head, and suddenly it's all there. Every gruelling detail, playing before my eyes. I remember his face, the rage and the fear and desperation and a million other unspeakable things, and I remember her face, so terrified, and the way the dark seemed to shatter the light instead of the other way around.

The way Aaron's face twisted right before he pulled the trigger, as he transformed into something I couldn't even recognise.

Leaping off the ledge, and falling and falling until I thought I'd never stop, until I did.

The endless forest stretching before me, inviting me into my own death.

But the worst ones are of Bea. Of her body not falling, but folding. Head to chest, chest to legs, legs to knees, knees to gravel.

I can feel the decision locking into place in my mind, less like a memory and more like living through it all over again, every logical move knocking into the next. I can feel myself slipping into self-preservation like a favourite shirt, comfortingly instinctual as I place my life above hers. I feel myself turn, because all that mattered was the escape, not Aaron, not her, just the escape.

I feel hot tears burn trails down my face as my body slumps, unwinding into a pile of fragile, snapping bones, and I feel like I've been stabbed. I feel like I'm the one bleeding out, not Lauren. I feel like I'm the one who's dying.

That's all that was left. Freedom. I sacrificed everything for it, and now I have it, and what good is it to me? I've had my old problems stripped from me and replaced with this. This endless spiral of dying in one place, and dying faster in another.

All because of them. Because even when they had brought me to my knees, even when they had forced me to run for my life, they're still hunting us.

What I said to Kole last night was true. These people have let

Oasis walk all over them and even now, as they scavenge for food like animals to keep themselves alive, Oasis hunts them.

And Kole was wrong. Running isn't our only option. It can't be our only option. My hands turn to fists at my sides. I stare at my reflection in the broken mirror, and I see dark hair and pale skin and a gaunt face. But I see fire in my eyes. I see a determination there that I have never seen before. Because I've made a decision.

I am going to fight for something better, or I am going to die trying.

27

I pick myself up off the ground and walk downstairs with my heart thudding in my chest. Kole is still in the kitchen, and so are several others – Mark and Walter by the front door; Lacey standing nervously by the table; Jonas, Meredith and several others talking in low voices in the corner; Clarke standing sentry by the door, her expression unreadable. It seems like they're not really sure where they should be or what they should be doing. Kole seems so focused on Lauren that he doesn't even notice the small group congregating around the edges of the room.

I walk straight up to him, and my heart feels like it's rising in my chest, about to float away and take me with it.

'I need to talk to you,' I say, my voice strong and even. I am glad. I need him to take me seriously now, more than ever.

'What is it?' He turns to me, and though he looks distracted, there's a tone to him, a less aggressive set to his shoulders that tells of a shift in his attitude towards me.

I swallow, but I can't lose my nerve now.

'I want to fight back against the Officers.'

I have his attention now.

'Quincy.' His voice is sharp, warning. His eyes skip around the room, checking to see if they've heard me. They have.

'Kole. We need to do this.'

His lips tighten into a hard line, and he steps away from the table to stand closer to me. 'We've been over this. I'm not needlessly risking lives like that.'

'It's not needlessly risking lives. We need to do this. We have to make a move on them before they find us.'

I can feel the anger coming off him in waves as more and more people start staring at me, as if I'm speaking gibberish.

'Can we talk about this in private?' he asks, catching my arm and tugging me towards the hall. More people have arrived in for their morning meal and the room is filling up quickly.

'No,' I say firmly. 'They need to know that they have more options. We need to talk about this. All of us.'

'What do we need to talk about?' Clarke says.

I glance back at Kole, but his eyes are fixed on the floor, his arms crossed tightly over his chest as his dark hair falls onto his forehead, masking his eyes.

I turn back to Clarke.

'Lauren,' I say, pointing towards the girl asleep on the table, 'was shot—'

'You don't say.' Clarke raises her eyebrows at me sarcastically.

'By Officers,' I finish, trying to keep my voice level. 'Outside Oasis. In the forest. Which means they're out there, right now, hunting us.'

'They are always hunting us,' Meredith points out quietly.

'Because you're allowing them to,' I say, and the minute the words are out of my mouth, people start shouting.

The cacophony becomes so loud a previously frozen Kole drags me into the next room, ordering everyone to follow.

Almost everyone is here now, and the room starts to feel small as thirty pairs of accusing eyes fall directly on me.

'We need to fight back,' I state. Everyone goes silent, and I'm forced to continue. 'There isn't anything more to say. You've been hiding and running for so long, I don't think you even know what you're doing anymore. You can't keep running. If they find you, they *will* kill you.'

I make eye contact with everyone, watching different emotions race across their faces.

'Unless we fight back.'

I let those words hang in the air for a moment. Let them consider the impact of what I'm suggesting.

'I didn't think there was anything outside of Oasis. I thought I had no option but to stay in the same place, doing the same things, every single day, until Oasis found the Cure. But now I'm here. And you're here. We don't have to believe what Oasis tells us, and what Oasis has been telling us is that we can't win. We can't fight back. That all we can do is run and run and delay the inevitable. But it's not true. Genesis fights back. *We* can fight back.'

My hands are shaking. I don't know where that came from, and everyone is staring at me, blinking slowly, but no one is moving.

Jonas steps forward. 'We had a plan,' he says. 'We wait for the others, we regroup, and we find someplace safe. Someplace far from Oasis.'

'And how long do you plan to wait for them in a war zone?' I demand.

'It's not a war z—'

I point at the door, gritting my teeth so hard I'm afraid I'm going to break them.

'Why don't you try telling that to the girl laid out on the table in there? But you can't, because she's been unconscious since we *dug a bullet from her shoulder.*'

'What if we left now?' a woman says from the background. 'We could leave before they had a chance to attack again.'

'That's very easy for you to say, you don't have anyone on the Inside,' someone else snaps.

'How do you know you do anymore?' the woman retorts. 'They could all be dead by now for all we know.'

The shouts start again, the argument reaching a point where I'm tempted to run because this is too complicated and too messy and I wasn't ready for this, and I'm not ready for this, but then—

'I agree with Quincy,' someone says, their voice projected, but not shouted. Firm, but not angry.

The shouts die down, and we all turn to see Clarke at the door, eyes locked on me.

'It doesn't matter how far we run. How good we get at evading them. She's right. They're not gonna stop. Not until we're all dead.'

'You think we have a chance?' Jonas asks, disgust in his voice. 'Against them? They'd kill us before we even knew what was happening.'

'*That's what they're doing here,*' Clarke spits. 'They're killing us off one by one because they know we're not willing to fight back.'

'They're killing us off one by one because they know they're *stronger than us,*' a girl shouts, pushing her way to the front of the group. 'We need to run, now, while we still have the chance.'

'Running hasn't done us any good,' someone else shouts.

'What about our families?' a young man cries from the back. 'Are we supposed to just *abandon* them?'

'We're supposed to *survive*!'

'HEY!' Clarke yells, and again the shouts die down. 'No one's making you fight. If you want to run, run. If you want to sit here and wait for a miracle, you can do that. But I'm not ready to give up. I'll fight.' She moves to stand beside me.

'I'll fight,' Mark says, raising his arm to be seen above the heads of the others, moving through the crowd until he can stand on my side of the room.

'I will too,' someone else calls.

'And me,' says Walter.

'I'll fight!' another person calls, and another and another, until the room is split in half.

My eyes fall on Kole, hands stiff at his sides, jaw clenched as he stares at the floor. He looks up at me, his eyes burning holes into me, but when he speaks, he just sounds broken.

'I can't stop you.'

And with that, the lines are drawn.

28

Two days pass, more like heartbeats than days. The camp is suddenly split into three groups: those who think we need to stick to the old plan – wait, regroup and run; those who think we should run now, while we still have the chance; and those who are ready to fight back.

There are twelve of us now, preparing for our first mission, packing up supplies and training. The second group are doing similar, except they're not preparing for a fight – they're preparing for a journey. I don't know when they're leaving, but I do know that no one's willing to admit it's actually happening.

Mark brings me hunting, to teach me how to fire a gun at a moving target, but all I do is shoot a metre to the left of the bird I'm aiming at, scaring it and everything else in the forest into hiding.

We have guns, pieces stolen here and there and some taken from Oasis, but it's unlikely we'll have anything like what the Officers will be carrying.

We're betting our lives on the element of surprise.

'Quincy, can I talk to you?' Kole asks, dragging me from my thoughts as I stand at the door of the house, watching people prepare for our trip.

We're leaving in an hour, and we have no idea where to start looking.

'Sure,' I say, letting him lead me into an abandoned room.

He turns to face me, running his hands through his hair, trying to gather his thoughts. He looks pale and exhausted, and I know from the sound of him pacing at night that he hasn't been sleeping.

'Are you okay?' I ask, and I don't step closer or reach for him, even though something in me is telling me to, because there is too much weakness in those three words already.

'I want you to call off the mission.'

'Kole …'

'I'm serious,' he says, and his voice rises at the end. I look into his face, at the panic stained there, and I wonder what the hell is wrong with this boy. 'You need to stop them from doing this.'

'Kole, I can't. They're not doing it for me. They're doing it for themselves.'

'But they listen to you.'

'You're assigning power to me that I don't actually have, Kole. They agreed to fight with me because they already wanted to. I can't change their minds now.'

'No,' he spits. 'No, this is not how this happens.'

'Kole—'

'STOP.' His voice booms, and I take a step back. 'You don't know what it's been like. We've been fighting for our lives for years.'

'No,' I say, shaking my head. 'No you haven't. You've been running for your lives. There's a big difference.'

'You don't know what you're talking about.' He's shaking now, and he's white, the blood drained from his face.

'I know that this isn't what I escaped for. I risked my life leaving Oasis because I wanted freedom. This isn't freedom. It's just a different kind of cage.'

'You are risking those people's lives, and all you can think about is yourself.'

'They're risking their own lives, Kole, that's what you don't seem to understand. I'm not forcing them into anything.'

'But I'm responsible for them. If they die, it's on my conscience.' He falls back a step, raising a shaking hand to his face, covering his mouth like he's horrified, and I don't know what to do. I don't understand why he's acting like this, like it's killing him to watch them go.

He's not coming. He refused to come, along with a handful of others who are staying behind.

'They're not your responsibility. They can look out for themselves.' I grind my teeth in frustration at this problem that shouldn't exist in the first place. 'If everyone would just look out for themselves and stop getting caught up in each other's business, I wouldn't have to have this conversation with you.'

'It doesn't work like that.' He's talking through gritted teeth, too, his hands fisted at his sides as he tries to keep his frustration in check.

'Well maybe it should,' I shoot back, just as Walter sticks his head around the door.

'Time to go.' He grins, as if we're going on a picnic, not a manhunt.

I look back at Kole, but his face hasn't changed. He looks terrified, as if he's in physical pain.

'Look after Lauren,' I say to him. And I'm wishing I could find a way to break that invisible wall he's built around himself, get inside his head, make him see what I'm seeing.

'I will,' he says, but the wall is still there, and I feel like slapping him.

'We'll be back,' I say, then I walk out the door before he has a chance to respond.

29

The forest is cold as we march through it. I am at the front of the group, more because everyone dropped into step behind me than that I actively put myself there. Clarke is somewhere to my right, and Mark somewhere to my left, but I keep my eyes dead ahead.

Twelve. Twelve people followed me out here today, and twelve people are coming back home tonight. That's what I keep telling myself.

We've been out here for hours. I'm not sure exactly how long, but my feet ache and I'm beginning to see double. Clarke's the best tracker we have, so she leads the group as we follow, searching for any signs of life. A footprint, disturbed undergrowth, ashes, anything that could be a sign Officers have passed through.

I can't get Kole's face out of my head, the panic in every tense muscle in his body, all for these people. I glance around me, watching everyone as they watch the forest around them. They are wound tight, all flashing eyes and quick reflexes, and I wonder why he cares so much.

And then I think of Beatrice. I wonder, if I could have her back again, would I be as terrified to lose her as he seems to be of losing them? And suddenly it clicks together in my mind: he has seen so many people die, he feels he needs to hold on to the ones he has. And I can see it. I can understand it, but somehow I can't *feel* it. It's like the moment before you feel pain, when you watch the blood trickle across your skin, but you can't feel anything. When you just watch, in sick fascination, as it stains your skin red.

'Quincy?' Walter pokes me.

'Huh?' I look up at him, shaking my head as if I can shake the thoughts out of it.

He points towards Clarke, who is kneeling down three metres from me.

I pause, holding up a hand for the group to stop.

'Clarke?' I step towards her.

'They've been here,' she says, leaping to her feet. Her eyes are bright, but she won't look at me, her gaze drifting after the trail she's picked up. 'This way.'

We fall into step behind her.

o o o

We follow the trail for half an hour, so long that I'm beginning to think she's leading us on a wild goose chase, but that's when I hear it.

I whip around, holding my finger to my lips, warning the group to stay quiet. Several people adjust guns on their shoulders, adrenaline spiking as Clarke turns to us, a manic look in her eyes.

I can hear them talking. The Officers. I can't hear what they're saying, but I can hear them murmuring back and forth, and I follow the sound blindly, the rest of the team fading into the background as I creep towards the clearing.

There are six of them, sitting in a circle around a fire. We stopped a few hours ago to eat and rest, but Clarke wouldn't let me start a fire, in case they saw the smoke and used it to track us. But they don't have to worry about that. They own everything – they own us – so they don't fear being ambushed.

Until now.

I glance back, making eye contact with each person, and then nod. My hand grips the handle of my knife, the only weapon I know how to use.

I hold up three fingers, then two, then one ... and we launch.

We're on top of them before they know what's going on. They reach for their weapons, pulling guns from inside their jackets, at their ankles, laid beside them, but before they can aim at us, we've struck.

I hear guns going off around me, but I don't know if they're our weapons or theirs, I'm too focused on the Officer I've launched myself at. He half falls back over the log he was sitting on, pulling a long, thin knife from the holster at his hip. My knife catches the light of the fire as it arcs towards him, but he blocks the blow with his wrist before it can make contact.

He advances on me, pushing me back a step as I try to regain my balance. He stabs at my middle, and I barely have time to slide away from his blade before he's pulled it back, thrusting it towards me again.

He takes another step forward, and I step closer to him, missing the edge of his knife by a hair's breadth as he stabs blindly at me repeatedly.

Everything is moving too fast. I don't know what's happening, how he is moving so fast, except that I'm lashing out, my instincts taking over as I take the advantage of his last missed hit to place one of my own.

I only realise I've stabbed him in the chest when his eyes meet mine, terror freezing him for the smallest moment before he pulls his knife back and falls to the ground.

I stare at his chest, at the blood bubbling up around the knife still lodged in a downward arc in his sternum, as he gasps in vain for one more breath.

I crash into someone as I stumble backwards, spinning around, my heart beating wildly. I hold my hands up in front of myself defensively, as if it would do anything to help. But it's only Walter, an utterly terrified looking Walter, stumbling around a blood-soaked battlefield.

But as I look around, I notice the Officers are down. Every single one of them.

I look around the campsite, at the shell-shocked and bloodied people around me, and I realise something I'm not sure I'd even considered possible until this very moment.

We won.

30

The aftermath is worse than the attack itself. As their bodies grow cold, I rifle through their supplies, packing their food and their weapons into my pack to bring back to the base. I can't help seeing how much this will help.

I can't help seeing this as the difference between life and death.

And that's when I hear the shouts. Mark freezes where he stands, just a few steps away from me, and suddenly everyone in the camp is looking at each other. The shout is brittle, followed by cracking, and I take a trembling step forward, moving towards the sound. I follow it to one of the tents, pushing aside the fabric of the door to find the tent empty.

Empty other than a black radio in the corner, like the ones the Officers at the Dorms used to carry, only bigger. I duck my head into the tent and grab the radio, holding it closer to my ear as I exit the tent again, back to the circle of people standing outside.

It's quiet for a moment, and we all stand silently, hearts in our mouths as we wait. It crackles back to life, the voices rough on the other end, and static fills the line during intervals, but I can hear most of what's going on.

'Unit 32, do you copy? Unit 32?'

I look at Mark, his bright blue eyes locking onto mine as he steps closer.

'Unit 32, do you copy? We have a disturbance this side and we need back-up. Unit 32, I repeat, there's been a disturbance. The rogues have attempted escape.'

A muffled thump comes across the line, and a crash.

'Take them down, Officers!' the same voice shouts at something we can't see.

And that's when we hear it.

'COWARDS!' A new voice now, with an edge as sharp as a blade and enough rage in it to strangle a person.

Mark goes still beside me, the blood draining from his face as he looks at me, his jaw slackening.

'What?' I ask, my stomach dropping.

'Jay,' Mark breathes. 'He's alive.'

31

Kole is gone when we return.

People come swarming out of the base, faces stricken at the sight of us. We are covered in blood that is not our own, but we are alive. Twelve of us return. Injuries are minor, and as we are swallowed back inside the house, I do not pull away from the crowd.

I need to be here, in the middle, if I want them to trust me. My plan is falling to pieces in my hands, but I push it to the back of my mind.

I have to focus on this. On this crush of bodies, this tangle of arms and voices all pushing and questioning and *'Are you okay?'*, *'What happened?'*, *'Did you find them?'*

It won't last forever. I know that. But it's here now, and for now, I am one of them.

We eat a mixture of the last meat from the deer Clarke killed and the new supplies from the Officers' camp, and the room has never been so loud. While we were gone, Lauren was moved upstairs and I am told she is still breathing. I sit in the corner of the room, nursing my side as I watch them quietly. This time, it's not because I want to be apart from them that I stay in the corner, but because I want to see it, this rare elation within them.

And I wonder if I could ever feel about them the way Kole does.

o o o

That night, I can't sleep. I roll over onto my side, listening to the rustling of trees outside my window, and I keep seeing the look on his face when he realised what had happened. The sound of his body slumping to the ground as blood bubbled out from his chest echoes in my ears, and I have to stop myself from gagging.

I feel cold. Every inch of me feels ice cold, and I don't know what to do to stop this feeling crawling around inside me.

He was an Officer. He deserved to die.

But Aaron was an Officer, and if it had been him, would I have been so quick to kill him?

I can't breathe.

A loud rapping sound on my door startles me, and I groan at the pain in my side as I jump to my feet.

'Quincy!' Kole half shouts, half whispers. 'Get out here.'

I pull open the door tentatively, unsure of myself. Those others who'd stayed behind told us that he'd just walked out a few hours before we came back, that no one had seen him since.

I follow him into the kitchen. He looks pale in the moonlight streaming in the window, but not pale like he did this morning.

He's furious.

'What?' I ask, and I wonder if I should start sleeping with a knife and some combat boots if he insists on starting fights in the middle of the night.

'I need to talk to you.'

'So? Talk.'

His eyes are sharp as they meet mine, but I won't back down.

'You've attacked the Officers, you've raided their camp. You fought back. You're done now.' He says it as a statement, but I can see the doubt in his eyes as I step into the kitchen, pulling the door shut behind me.

'No. This isn't a once-off, Kole. We're doing this now, and you can't stop us.'

'So what's your plan? To spend everyday wandering around the forest, hoping to stumble across some idiot Officer patrols you can take down.'

'No.' Yes. I hadn't thought past today. I was too caught up in the fact that it actually worked to think of anything else.

'This is ridiculous, you know that, right? You're not getting anywhere. You're not actually doing anything.'

'We took out an entire patrol—'

'Do you have any idea how many more of those Oasis has? Officers are as expendable to Oasis as the Dormants are. They're nothing. That patrol was *nothing*.'

'It's not just about the Officers—'

'I swear, if you give me a lecture on morale—'

'Kole, Jay is alive.' I let the words hang in the air between us.

'What?' he says, quietly, like it might disappear if he's too loud.

'We found a radio at the camp. We heard Jay on the other end.'

'How would you know—'

'Mark recognised the voice. He's alive, Kole.'

Kole doesn't breathe. He doesn't move or do anything but stand, staring straight through me, like he can see something beyond this room.

'He's alive?' he repeats, his voice strangled.

'He's alive.'

'If you're lying—' he says, catching me by both shoulders. A gasp escapes me, the jerking motion tearing into my side, the pain lacerating through me. He releases me immediately, like I burned him.

'What's wrong with you?' he asks, his voice gruff, as if he's trying to cover up the weakness in his voice a moment ago. Like he's trying to cover up the pain that crossed his face at the mention of Jay.

'Nothing.'

'Were you hurt? Why didn't you get medical help?'

'Oh yes, I'll just run over to the nearest hospital … Oh wait.' I raise an eyebrow at him.

'You've been spending too much time with Clarke,' he scoffs, and I'm a little taken aback.

I guess he's right.

He pours water into the kettle on top of the stove then turns to me.

'Show me where you're hurt,' he demands.

'No.'

'Show me.'

'No.'

He cocks his head to the side, as if to ask if we're actually going to do this. I huff, rolling my eyes as I lift my shirt and pull away the T-shirt I'd wrapped around my middle before I went to bed, to stop the bleeding.

'God, Quincy, what the hell were you thinking?' he asks as he examines the wound. I glance down at it, only long enough to see the gash has started bleeding again.

'It's nothing.'

He looks at me, raising a single eyebrow in response.

'Sit on the table.'

I obey, but I don't spare him any complaining while I do it.

He takes the kettle off the stove and pours the hot water into the cracked basin we used for Lauren, and I start feeling cold again.

'You're not going to …'

'No. You don't need stitches. But you do need a little more than a shirt wrapped across your ribs, surprisingly.' He dips a piece of fabric into the hot water and dabs it against the wound.

I hiss, pulling away from him involuntarily. He places his hand on my other side to hold me in place, and I freeze. I'm still holding my shirt up so he can clean the wound, so his hand is directly on my waist.

I shift away, sirens going off inside my head every time the rough skin of his hands makes contact with my abdomen.

'Be careful,' I whisper.

He looks up at me, his eyes steady, his hands frozen above my waist.

'You don't have to worry about that anymore.'

'You don't know. I don't understand—' I grit my teeth, both from pain and frustration. 'I don't understand why you're all so calm about it. The gene could activate at any time, and once it does, if it's me, I'm a danger to everyone.'

'Don't quote them to me,' he says, his shoulders stiffening.

'I'm not—'

'You are,' he says, cutting me off. 'You need to stop letting them get inside your head. You're not gonna hurt me.'

I release a shaky breath, and he glances at me for a second.

'It's okay,' he whispers, focusing his attention back on the wound. 'I promise.'

For a long moment, neither of us says anything, and I'm not sure what I'm supposed to do. My heart is pounding too fast, so I focus my eyes on a random point on the wall across from me, staring at it until I can catch my breath.

'Was it a knife?'

'What?'

'The cut. Is it a knife wound?'

'Oh, yes. Yes. An Officer nicked me before I could kill him.'

His eyebrows draw down in a question, but he doesn't look up, too focused on cleaning the wound. Once he's done, he tells me to hold still, then leaves for only a moment, returning with a heap of bandages.

'From the raid,' I breathe.

His eyes lock onto mine for only a second before dropping again, and he begins to wrap the bandage around my body.

'Yes.' He releases a slow breath. 'I'm glad it went well, and I'm thankful for the supplies, but I hate putting them in danger.'

I try to ignore the feeling of his hands on my skin long enough to respond.

'They've always been in danger, Kole. It's just that this time, it's through their own choice.'

He goes quiet, and I can tell he doesn't have an argument for that.

He pulls my shirt back down over the bandages, finally letting me hop down from the table.

'Does that feel better?'

'Yes.' And it does. A lot better.

There's a short silence, and he just looks at me. I take a step away, towards the door, not fully understanding the tug in my chest at the sight of him like this, quiet and calm in the moonlight.

'Goodnight,' I say, and my hand is on the door knob when he stops me.

'Wait.' He says. 'I want—' He pauses, and I glance back at him. 'I want to help,' he says finally. 'I want to help you rescue Jay and the others.'

I am quiet for a moment, and then something like a smile crosses my lips.

'Good,' I say quietly.

We stare at each other in the half-light for another beat.

'Goodnight,' I repeat, breaking the silence.

'Goodnight.'

As I step into the cold silence of my room, closing the door behind me, I try to calm my racing heart.

32

I wake to the sound of Kole shouting. I am up and awake and out the door before I'm even fully aware of what's going on.

'Kole? Kole, what the hell is going on?'

Kole is standing outside the door, dressed, with a pack over his shoulder and a gun slung over his back.

'We're going hunting,' he says, smiling.

'What …?' I try to rub the sleep from my eyes, my heart still thundering in my chest.

'If they're alive, we need to go find them. Now.'

His sentences aren't making any sense to my foggy mind, but then Mark comes up to stand beside me, looking like he was wrestling with a bush before he came out here.

'Kole, what are you doing?' Mark asks quietly, trying to calm Kole down.

'We're going after the Officers who took Jay and the others. I was up all night thinking about it, and I know where they are. Remember the base camp they used to talk about in training?'

'What training?' I ask, confused, but he's not listening to me, distracted by all the thoughts flying through his brain.

'I know where it is, and if they have hostages, I figure that's where they're holding them.'

Mark runs a hand over his face, trying to sort through what Kole is saying, but when he looks up the hope on his face is evident.

Kole starts nodding. 'We need to go now.'

Mark stares at him for a second. 'I'll get the others,' he says, and he walks back into the house.

'We're going to find them,' Kole says, looking back at me, and I don't say anything.

∘ ∘ ∘

It takes us less than an hour to get ready and leave, but Kole stands in front of the house the entire time, restlessly pacing the length of the building. I insisted on checking on Lauren upstairs, who was conscious but only barely.

I'm not sure she's fully lucid, so I can't do anything other than make sure someone stays to keep an eye on her and hope she'll be okay until we get back.

Now that we've left and are heading into the forest, Kole is moving through the trees like hell is on his heels, his gun gripped so tightly in his hands, his knuckles are turning white.

We move further into the forest this time, travelling for so long I wonder if we'll be able to find our way back, but Kole keeps his eyes locked ahead, as if he knows exactly where he's going, and I have to trust that he does. We've been walking for hours when we hear someone shouting angrily in the distance.

Kole pauses only for a moment before taking off, leaving the rest of us to try to catch up.

I hear gunshots, but I don't slow down. I keep my eyes glued to Kole's form, a blur in the distance as he runs so fast we don't have a hope of keeping up with him. That's when we see him.

He comes crashing through the forest, a bruise marring one side of his face, his eyes widening at the sight of us. He slams straight into Mark, catching him by the shoulders as his breath comes in gasping heaves. The bruises blooming across his face make him look like deranged art, some kind of fierce sculpture of marble and granite.

Mark holds him up. 'Jay!' he shouts.

They swarm around him, asking questions so rapidly I can't discern one from another, the voices pouring over each other until it's just a rush of sound, like a waterfall. Jay tries to say something, but I don't get a chance to hear it because before I know what I'm doing, I'm grabbing the gun from the person on my left and taking after Kole, towards the sound of gunshots.

This camp is huge, set inside an enormous clearing, with tents pitched in a perfect circle, and I can see flashes of Officer blue between the tents. I duck behind a tree and aim the gun at an Officer squatting behind a tent. From the angle I've found he can't see me, but my line of sight is clear as I try to steady the gun in my hands.

The sound of gunshots starts ringing in my ears, and I can feel the others running out of the trees around me, finally emerging into the sunlight as Officers begin to fall in front of my eyes, hitting the ground as the spray of bullets disperses among them.

I try to focus, to slow my heart down, to stop the trembling of my arms as I line up my shot with the Officer in front of me. But my mind is being split in half, the images in my head not of Officers but of him.

Of Aaron. Of his humanity falling away from him so easily.

How was I so stupid?

I try to pull the trigger, but my finger slips off, and my breath is coming to me uneven and rasping as I retake my aim.

How did I not see it coming?

I try to fire again, but the bullet lodges itself in a tree about half a metre from the Officer I'm aiming at, and if it weren't for the cacophony of gunshots surrounding us, he would have seen me.

I throw the gun from me in frustration, pulling the long, thin knife from my boot as I take off, shaking the images of Aaron from my mind. I don't know where Kole is, or where the others are, or anything else, other than this feeling that's overtaken everything else.

Survival. It seems to be the only thing I'm good at.

I keep low and stay quiet around the perimeter of the camp, until I see an Officer with his back to me. I don't think. I don't hesitate. And part of me wonders why.

I plunge the dagger into his back, and only stay long enough to hear his gurgled scream and to pull the knife back out, just before I see another Officer advancing towards me.

I try to steady myself, to find my balance again, but before I can he knocks the knife from my hand, and I watch it fly from my hand, terror gripping my insides. He launches himself at me, one of the few Officers who is unarmed, and his fist connects with my face with a crack. I fall backwards, scrambling on my hands and knees towards my knife as the world swirls around me. He catches my heel before I can reach the knife and drags me back towards him, his fist crashing into my face again and again.

Blood pours into my mouth, and I cough and splutter as I try to breathe, my vision swimming as I try to shake the impact of his fists from my muddled brain.

For a moment I don't feel anything. I am suspended in half consciousness. Then I blink away the blood in my eyes enough to see the barrel of a gun and my heart stops. Because he's found a weapon, and it is pressed to my forehead and this is it.

This is how it ends. In a battle that is only half mine, bloodied and bruised with a gun to my head.

I watch as he opens his mouth to say something, but before he can get the words out a gunshot rings across the campsite and his weight falls forwards. I try to pull myself out from underneath him, but he's heavy, dead weight, and I can barely move.

A figure comes up beside me, pushing the Officer's body off me with a black boot, and when I look up, I see Jay, his hand reaching down to help me up. He pulls me to my feet, but takes a quick step backwards once I've balanced myself, grabbing my knife from the ground and handing it to me silently.

'You dropped this,' he says, gesturing towards the gun in his hand, which I now recognise as the gun I abandoned outside the camp. 'Mind if I borrow it?' There is a smile in his words but not on his face, and I nod numbly because I don't know what else to do.

He winks at me before taking off, ramming the butt of his gun into an Officer's face and shooting him in the crown of the head as the Officer falls to his knees before him.

I fall back a step, wiping the blood from my eyes as I watch the battle rage around me. There are only a few Officers left, but they keep appearing out of nowhere, bursting out of tents, bristling with guns. I watch as three Officers fall one after another, like dominoes, and look up to see Kole adjusting his aim smoothly as he takes down another and another and another, until the battlefield is cold.

It is there, hot and bloody, the fear filling the air like a physical presence, and then it is gone.

The world goes quiet, and we become still, watching each other as we wait for a next wave that will never come.

33

'Kole,' I growl, as he pushes my hair from my face to dab at the cut on my cheekbone. The water is cold, taken from water canisters and poured onto strips of cloth he found I don't know where and I don't want to know, but he insists on doing it.

'You won't do it yourself,' he murmurs dismissively, and I grit my teeth against the pain.

'How's your side?' he asks, holding my gaze.

'Better. Hurts still, but it's healing.'

'Good.' He nods, packing up the supplies.

I think about asking him where he learned to fight like that, but I hold myself back. I'll ask him later, when things have quietened down. He's more likely to give me a straight answer then.

'Kole.' A rough voice comes from behind us, and Kole swivels in his crouch, looking up to see Jay standing behind him.

'Jay,' Kole says, and his voice has turned into something I can't speak of, like pain and grief and regret and guilt and, somewhere beneath the mess, joy. He hugs him, the kind of hug that's so tight, it's mostly there to make sure the other person is real.

I am silent, and I can't help thinking of Aaron. He used to hug me like that, like he worried about me when I wasn't with him. My throat feels tight.

Kole finally releases Jay, and turns to face me.

'Jay, this is Quincy.'

'We've met.' Jay smiles at me, and his smile looks like my knife when it catches the sunlight, transfixing and violent.

'Thank you,' I blurt out, my mind forcing images into my head so fast I can't process them.

I can barely see him from my left eye, which began to swell almost immediately, but what I can see in him is dangerous. I remember Lacey saying he was reckless, and I can't help feeling she must have been right. His dark hair is cut tight to his scalp, his eyes sharp beneath his perpetually drawn down eyebrows, his thin lips curled up at the corners. He is tall and muscular, but with none of Mark's broadness. Everything about him is harsh, and something about him reminds me of the street dogs in Oasis, weatherbeaten and wary of everyone and everything. But he masks it better. Acts like he's not always ready to attack again, forever waiting for the next fight. I can't decide if I should be scared of him or not.

Kole gives us a questioning look, but lets it go.

'If it weren't for Quincy, we wouldn't have found you,' Kole says, like a confession, his words slow, a measured release.

Now it's Jay's turn to shoot Kole a questioning look.

'She wanted to fight back against the patrol Officers. It was her who led the team that found the radio that led us here, to you.'

Jay looks back at me and lets his eyes drift over me, sizing me up. Eventually another one of his knife smiles appears, and he offers me his hand.

'I guess it's me who should be saying thank you, then.'

'You were escaping anyway,' I say with a shrug. 'I was there for the Officers.'

He releases a bark of laughter and looks up at Kole as if to say, 'are you seeing this?'. Kole just closes his eyes, shaking his head like he can't believe me.

o o o

We strip the Officers' campsite of anything we might find useful and then start walking back towards the base. We won't make it back tonight, but no one wants to stay in that camp any longer than we have to.

Eventually, as the sun starts to set, we settle down in a small clearing, only wide enough for us all to lie down. The minute we sit down, Jay speaks up.

'I want to keep going,' he says.

'Jay, I am going to sleep now, and you better not try to stop me,' Mark says, pointing a threatening finger at him as he gives him a slightly mad look.

We've been up since dawn, and everyone is exhausted.

Jay laughs. 'I don't mean keep walking home. I mean with the raids. I want to keep ambushing the Officers.'

'Jay …' Kole begins, but I cut him off.

'We are. We've already taken down two. We can keep taking them down.'

'Exactly,' Jay says, sitting up straighter. 'If we take down enough, they're going to retreat back to Oasis. They have to.'

'Or they could redouble their attack and kill us all in the process.'

We ignore Kole.

'We need to regroup, first. You guys need to heal up, and we need to train more, but once we're ready, we can get back to work,' I say excitedly, timelines flashing in my mind, trying to work out how long it will take us to get back on our feet.

'Yes. Someone needs to teach you to shoot,' Jay says, seriously.

'Hey,' I murmur in protest, but I'm so tired there's nothing behind it.

Kole releases a sigh that sounds like it's coming from the depths of him. 'If you're serious,' he says, 'then I'm coming with you.'

That catches my attention.

'*Seriously?*' My voice is pitched high with surprise.

'Yes. But we are training first. You need to know how to fight. All of you.'

I meet Jay's eyes, and the excitement in them mirrors my own. Kole is our best fighter, everyone saw that today, and if we have him on our side, fighting, we might actually be able to do this.

'But,' he says firmly, 'no more random ambushes.'

He looks directly at me, and I feel something fluttering at my throat.

'If we're doing this, we need a plan.'

34

I sit across from Kole and Jay late at night, three days after the rescue. Kole is biting his lip as he bores a hole in the table with his thumbnail, a nervous gesture showing his discomfort as Jay explains his plans.

We rescued six people from the Officers' camp, including Jay, and all of them needed medical attention. The bruises on Jay's face are only now beginning to fade to a sickly greenish colour at the sides, but he doesn't seem to be bothered by it at all.

My face, on the other hand, still looks like I was hit by a truck.

'But we can use the radio to track them!' Jay argues, rolling a knife between his hands.

Lauren is awake now, but won't say a word. I spent three hours with her yesterday, trying to coax something out of her, any piece of information that might be helpful to us, but she wouldn't utter a single syllable. In the end I got frustrated and stormed out.

I don't know why, but I feel like she knows something. If she was attacked by Officers, she must know *something*.

'Or they could use the radio to track *us*. Jay, you're not thinking.' Kole sounds calm, but I can tell by the way his hands won't stop fidgeting that he's uncomfortable.

'We won't *use* it, we'll just listen to them.'

'And what if they have a tracking chip inside the device? What then?'

Jay growls, flipping the knife into the air. I pull my hands from the table, afraid of the sharp tip on that blade, making my own frustrated sound.

Kole glances up at me, cocking his head to the side.

'What are you thinking?' he asks, causing Jay to turn to me too.

'I'm thinking that that radio is the least of our worries. We need to stop going around in circles and start moving forward.'

'And what do you propose we do?' Kole asks, placing his elbows on the table as he leans forward.

'We need to start training,' I say, snatching the knife from Jay when he's not paying attention.

He gives me a curious look, but I ignore him.

'Anyone who can fight needs to be ready. We're gaining ground on them, and I'm not letting them take it back.'

Kole's face twists, and it takes me several seconds to realise he's fighting a grin.

'What?' I growl.

'Nothing.' He shakes his head, standing to get a drink of water.

'I agree with Quincy,' Jay says, looking back at me. 'We need to start moving again.'

'You're not fit to train yet, Jay,' Kole mutters, sitting back down at the table.

'I'm fine,' Jay scoffs, pulling the knife deftly from my fingers and flicking it into the air, shooting me a smile when it lands back in his hand.

'And what about the others? The people who won't fight?' Kole asks, ignoring Jay.

'I don't know,' I sigh, rubbing my hands across my face. I'm getting tired. These last few days have been exhausting, even if we haven't started training yet. The third floor was turned into an impromptu infirmary, and I've been trying to keep up with Lacey, who's been tending day and night to the survivors with the worst injuries.

My interactions with her are short and formal, and I can tell she's angry with me. Of everyone in the base who is against the rebellion, Lacey hates it the most. Other than asking me to hand her scissors or more bandages, she hasn't said a word to me since I led the first attack against the Officers.

Kole is still staring at me, waiting for an answer.

'I don't understand what their problem is,' Jay cuts in. 'You're not even making them fight with us.' The tone of his voice suggests they would be, if he could make them.

'They just want peace, Jay, not more war,' Kole says quietly, and he sounds just as tired as me when he says it.

'Well they're not going to get it,' I say, pushing away from the table, suddenly restless. 'None of us are. Not while Oasis is sending Officers out here to hunt us down.'

Kole squeezes the bridge of his nose, closing his eyes, frustration in every line of him.

'I know you're right,' he says. 'But I don't think they're going to see that.'

'It doesn't matter. We need to keep moving forward. We'll start training tomorrow morning, and if they join us, great. And if they don't ...'

'That's their loss.' Jay smiles, flipping the knife through the air again, catching the blade between two fingers. 'So that's the plan then? We start training, then systematically take out every patrol unit outside of Oasis?'

I make eye contact with Kole across the table, and he nods once.

'That's the plan.'

35

Kole wants us to train with weapons and without them, so he sets up a rota of classes. Clarke has been working on her archery, and after a little coaxing from Kole has started taking small groups out hunting in the morning to let them practise. Jay takes a training session in the morning for knife fighting, but I don't need the class, so I hang out by the door, watching them move across the clearing. I'm surprised that Jay is handling it so well, guiding a dozen people through drills calmly, nodding when people get it right, but not even reacting when they make mistakes.

'You should be training,' Kole says, coming up behind me.

'I don't need to. I know how to use a knife.'

'Yeah, that's basically what every idiot says, just before they get stabbed.'

'Did you just call me an idiot?' I ask, raising an eyebrow at him threateningly.

'*Never*,' he says, with exaggerated horror.

Did he just make a joke?

'How's Lauren?' I ask. Kole is up with her almost as much as I am, and he went up to check on her a while ago.

'She said hello to me,' he says, surveying the training session in front of us.

'And?' I ask, my heartbeat picking up.

'And that was it.' He looks back at me, shrugging. 'That was all she said.'

I bang my fist into the doorframe in frustration.

Kole disappears into the house for a moment, then comes back out, tucking two handguns into the waistband of his trousers.

'Let's go,' he says abruptly, and starts walking towards the trees.

'What are you doing?' I call after him.

'Somebody needs to teach you how to shoot,' he says, without looking back.

I glance back at the house, thinking of my first miserable attempt to learn with Mark, but the idea of being cramped in the house all day is worse than any embarrassment I might have to endure with a lesson, so I jog to catch up, following him into the trees.

Kole walks us farther west, in the opposite direction to Oasis, until we're far enough away from the camp that I can't inadvertently shoot anyone. He pulls one of the guns from his waistband and throws it to me, and I look up just in time to clumsily catch it before it hits me over the head.

'Now what?' I ask, taking the gun into my other hand.

He shrugs, cocking his head to the side.

'Shoot.'

'You?' I ask, fighting a smile.

'That tree,' he says, pointing to the thick trunk of a tree to my left.

'That's it?' I ask.

'That's it.'

'You're an awful teacher,' I mutter, turning to face the tree.

I stand with my shoulders squared, my eyes locked onto the bark of the tree. I see a blurry, dark image of Aaron's gun pressed to Bea's temple, feel the secondhand terror.

I pull the trigger, my eyes squeezing closed as the bullet skims the bark of a tree to the left of the one I was aiming at.

'See?' I say, trying to sound dismissive, but I can feel the anger bubbling up beneath my skin. 'I can't do it.'

Kole considers me carefully, his eyes skimming over me like he's analysing my every movement. I shift my stance, feeling uncomfortable, and he takes a step forward.

'Do it again,' he says.

'No,' I snap, the anger bursting to the surface. 'I hate this.'

'Exactly,' he says, and suddenly his dark eyes lock with mine, his stare so intense I want to take a step backwards, but I won't show that kind of weakness. 'That's exactly your problem. You need to stop hating it. You need to stop feeling anything for it.'

'What do you mean?'

'What did you think about? Just before you fired, what were you thinking of?'

'Nothing,' I say, too quickly. 'I wasn't thinking about anything.' I see Aaron's face in my mind, the light of the Celian City glancing off his blonde hair as he looks at me, his smile mocking.

'Well that's a lie,' he says, coming to stand beside me, pulling out his own gun and aiming at the tree. 'I don't need you to tell me what it was, but I do need you to stop thinking about it. It doesn't matter now.' He shifts his stance, releasing a slow breath as his eyes narrow on his target. 'Forget everything but the gun and the target.'

He pulls the trigger. The bullet buries itself in the centre of the tree trunk. He lets his arm fall, and turns to look at me.

'Now it's your turn.'

I shake my head, fixing my stance in determination, pulling the gun up in front of me.

He tweaks my hold on the gun, placing my thumb on the opposite side, the callouses on his fingers scraping against the skin of my hand.

'Deep breath in, deep breath out. When you feel all the air push out of you, that's when you fire,' he says, quiet now. I do as he instructs, but every time I release a breath Aaron's face appears in front of me, or worse, Bea's. He sees the expression on my face and knows what it means.

'Your emotions won't help you,' he says, looking directly at me, his hand cupping the gun beneath mine. 'Not now. And not when there's an Officer in front of you. You need to let it go. Everything, every single thought inside your head. Let it fall away from you.'

I take a better grip of the gun, closing my eyes as I inhale, feeling his hand fall away as I imagine my brain clearing, my emotions fading away.

I open my eyes, pull the trigger, feel the recoil push me back a step as the bullet lodges itself in the bark, just beside Kole's.

36

The next day, a quarter of the group leaves. Jonas and Meredith are the only ones I know personally who are leaving, but it's hard to see them go nevertheless.

'Don't go,' Lacey begs, tears streaming down her face as we stand at the front of the house, seeing them off. 'You don't have to fight either. Just stay here with us, where it's safe.'

But no one answers her, because we all know it's not. It's not safe here, and it's not safe out in the open, and it's certainly not safe raiding the Officers, but as the group of nine people walks past the clearing and into the forest, I think the fighting can't possibly be worse than this, just staring helplessly as parts of your community slowly fall away.

In the ten days that follow, we find two separate Officer encampments. The first one is small, and we take it on just with the scout group, which is me, Jay, Clarke, Walter, Mark and Kole. The other camp is bigger, and we regroup at the base, returning with the rest of the group, now sixteen people in total. Word of our raids must be getting around, however, because we got the distinct sense they were ready for us. The fight was bloody, and several of our people were injured, but the numbers were on our side, with almost twice as many of us as there were Officers, and eventually we were able to go home intact.

Lacey still won't talk to me. Although the missions are successful, we come home each time with more than a few of us injured, which means our makeshift hospital on the third floor is kept busy. After the last attack, I listened from my room as Lacey argued with Kole in the kitchen.

'We can't do this anymore,' I heard her whisper furiously. 'We can't afford people getting injured like this. It's only a matter of time before you're carrying home a dead body, and then what?'

'Lacey,' Kole murmured, trying to calm her down, 'we're getting on better now than we ever have. The supplies we're taking from the Officer camps more than cover anything we sustain during the fighting, and our food stock has been growing. We could win this, Lacey.'

'Win what?' Lacey asked, with more venom than I expect. 'Because I don't see any great prize at the end of this. They are stronger, they have more weapons, they have numbers on their side. You're winning battles, Kole, not the war.'

There was a silence then, before Kole said, 'Lacey, I know where you're coming from, but I don't want to keep running either. I don't want anyone to get hurt, but I want to provide a safe place for us. The others are convinced this is the best way to do that. I don't have a better answer, so I have to be willing to let this happen.'

Lacey sighed. 'You know I like her, Kole, but I don't like what she's doing to the group.'

'I do,' he said, and there is a firmness in his voice I didn't expect either, no trace of doubt left over from when he was fighting against me, instead of with me. 'I think she's what this group needed.'

'But when Jay was doing this, you said he was reckless. That he was a danger to us all. How is she any different?'

'Jay ran headlong into the biggest patrol we've ever seen, grief-stricken and angry. She gathered people. Made sure she was meeting the Officers on her own terms.' I heard him take a deep breath, could imagine him running his hand through his hair, desperate to keep everyone happy.

But he can't. At least *I* knew that.

'Listen,' he said softly, 'it's not perfect. But it's better than nothing. We couldn't have continued on like that forever. Running from Oasis was never going to do any good, even though I convinced myself it was our only option. But it wasn't. We always had a choice. All Quincy did was open my eyes to that.'

I heard Lacey sigh in a long, drawn-out breath.

'I want to stand by you, Kole. I want to support you. But I can't. Not this time.'

I could feel heat burning its way through me at her words. I couldn't believe her. I couldn't believe any of these people, willing to stand by, criticising us from the sidelines as we try to fight for our lives – and theirs.

The restlessness to keep moving forward has been taking me over the past few days, and no matter how much we do or how fast we work, I still can't shake the feeling that it isn't enough, that we need to do something more.

Instead I tell myself that everything is fine. That we've done more in the last few weeks than this group has done in years. I tell myself it's enough, and attempt to ignore the sick feeling in the pit of my stomach, pushing the sense of foreboding somewhere deep inside of me, where I can forget about it and it can't touch me.

37

Kole forces me to take a hand-to-hand combat session with Mark in the mornings. I tried to argue that I didn't need it, but he insisted. An hour into my first class I flop down onto the grass, groaning.

Clarke, who is sitting on the grass sharpening a knife as she watches us train, bursts out laughing. I throw her a sour look, and she grins at me.

'Hey,' Mark says, crouching down beside me. 'You okay?'

'Other than getting beaten up for an hour?' I ask, sarcasm dripping from my tone. 'Peachy.'

I'm not used to fighting with my own two hands; I had a knife in Oasis, and a person with a knife was the person in charge, and that was never questioned. But the bruises on my face from the brawl with that Officer are a testament to how different things are out here, and Kole insists we know how to defend ourselves from any position.

'You didn't do too bad,' Mark says, sitting back onto the grass as he slings his elbows around his knees.

The sun is warm against our backs, and as the first touch of spring melts the ice from the rivers and takes the edge from the wind, it feels almost too perfect out here, considering what we're training for.

'That was horrific,' I say with a shudder. 'I've never been so bad at anything in my whole life.'

'You'll catch on. Everyone finds it hard in the beginning.'

'I suppose ...' I murmur, rubbing my ribs where I took a hit. 'Couldn't you have gone a little easier, though?'

He just shakes his head, like I'm being ridiculous.

'He was going easy on you, genius.' Clarke laughs. 'You need to toughen up, that's your only problem.'

Clarke doesn't pull punches, but her snarky remarks seem to have changed from aggressive to laid-back, as though she's not actively trying to tear me down anymore.

Wonderful.

'Hey guys.' Kole lands beside me. Startled, I shove him when I realise he'd been creeping up on us. He laughs at my reaction, and I almost jump again. The sound is still a shock every time I hear it, incongruous against everything else I know about him.

'Having trouble?' he asks, handing around water to us all.

'No,' I say, just as Mark and Clarke say, 'Yes.'

Kole bursts out laughing again, and I move to get up and leave, but he drags me back down.

'Stay,' he says, trying to keep a straight face. 'I promise I won't laugh.'

'You're laughing right now!'

'Okay, I promise I won't laugh in one second.' His mouth works as he tries to stop, and I shake my head, looking out across the clearing as I drink.

The house we've been living in is mostly buried in trees, but directly around it is bare, except for the grass and weeds that have taken root in the years it's been desolate. I wonder who lived here, and I wonder why they left.

Lauren is up and moving around now, and the bullet wound is slowly healing. She's still not saying more than a few words to anyone, all of them mundane, meaningless and completely useless to us.

Kole has finally stopped laughing and is talking to Mark about the content of the training sessions for the next few days. This easy, calm version of him makes me edgy, because suddenly I don't know what to expect from him. Frowns and jabs and arguments I'm ready for, but not jokes and laughter and smiles. I don't know this Kole, and I haven't even decided if I want to.

He sees me watching him and he grins, his dark eyes sparkling in the sun. I lie down on the grass so I don't have to look at him, too confused to think straight, and close my eyes against the bright sun, letting the gentle hum of conversation wash over me.

But maybe I shouldn't push away this newfound Kole. Everyone has been changing, not just him. Suddenly people are smiling when they see me, and conversation doesn't drop off when I come near. I feel like maybe this is what it feels like to belong somewhere.

And maybe I shouldn't push that away, I think sleepily. Maybe *this is* what I was looking for when I left Oasis.

38

Kole shakes me and I try to push him off, but when I open my eyes he looks frantic, and I'm abruptly wide awake. I sit up and he grabs my hand and starts pulling me back towards the house, shouting something at me, but I can't hear him, can't hear anything but the terrifying crashing all around me, the sound of something howling in the distance.

I look over my shoulder, watching the chaos unfold behind me. Officers in blue uniforms swarm out of the trees, and the sound I was hearing was shouts and screams and gunshots and the advancing troops, pouring out of the forest endlessly.

Kole and I burst into the house, and I can't breathe. The kitchen is packed, and everyone is shouting, and I can hear people crying in the background as I feel the room closing in on top of me.

'Help Lacey get everyone upstairs!' Kole shouts into my ear, dropping my hand and grabbing a gun from under the sink. He bolts through the door before I can respond, so I turn around, scanning the room for Lacey, who is over by the stairs, guiding people up to the next floor.

'What happened?' I shout to her.

She shouts to someone behind her, then turns back to me, eyes wide with fear.

'They just appeared out of nowhere and started taking pot shots at us. This is payback,' she says, looking directly at me.

'Is everyone okay?' I shout over the noise, ignoring her.

Lacey grabs my arm and drags me upstairs. 'Quincy, we need to go! *Now!*'

I shake myself, forcing my feet to run alongside Lacey, taking the steps two at a time. Upstairs is a mess. There are people crying and arguing and shouting at each other, all piled into the room together. The minute Lacey makes it into the room she screams for everyone to be quiet in a way I didn't expect to come from her.

'Everyone get down on the ground! They can shoot through the windows!' She sounds scared, but everyone obeys her, and soon everyone has their backs to walls or is crouched on the floor.

'Check upstairs,' Lacey instructs me. I nod, sprinting up the steps and onto the third floor, where I find several of the injured sitting bolt upright, four pairs of terrified eyes staring wildly at me.

'Everyone downstairs!' I shout, helping a man up by the arm. His leg was injured in one of the raids and he still hasn't healed enough to walk on his own. I move them downstairs as fast as I can, leading the man by the arm.

There are muted sobs in the back of the room, but all anyone can actually hear is the shots being fired.

Clarke bursts into the room, a gun in her hands and a fierce expression on her face.

'Clarke,' I breathe, and I don't know how we got to a stage where I'm relieved to see Clarke's face. 'Get three others and guard the doors,' I order, and my voice doesn't shake.

'Hey.' She catches my arm before I walk out the door. 'What are you going to do?'

'I'm going to fight,' I say, looking straight into her dark eyes.

She nods, without a word, and walks straight through into the room, picking three people to defend the room with her.

I turn on my heel, sprinting downstairs and into my room for my gun and then straight for the door. I push it open, my heart thundering in my chest as sweat drips onto the back of my neck.

We haven't dealt with this before. Not this many. Not on their terms.

I slip around the side of the building, my eyes scanning for Kole and the others. They've set up posts around the house, hiding behind barrels and debris as they fire blindly at the Officers, who are constantly moving forwards and getting closer.

There has to be fifty Officers at least, breaking into units and moving together, as if they have one brain, their movements not their own. I push up against a corner, setting up the rifle behind the wall and dodging in and out, firing at the spots of blue swarming the clearing.

We should have been ready for this, I think, we should have been prepared for a counterattack, for them to do to us what we've been doing to them. I feel a white hot anger at my own stupidity as my sweaty palms slip on the cold metal of the gun. The smell of the steel enters my nose, and it calms me. I remember Kole's instructions, and wipe my mind of thoughts and emotions. I exhale slowly.

It doesn't matter.

How we got here doesn't matter.

What happens next doesn't matter.

All that matters is the gun in my hands and the targets in front of me. I fire, only watching long enough to see the Officer fall before moving my aim to the left, firing again and again and again.

Officers fall like flies all around us, but I can't see any of my friends, and it's putting me on edge.

Let it go, I tell myself sternly. I have to keep my focus.

I quickly fall into the rhythm, just like every other fight: one Officer at a time, one shot at a time. My aim is better now, a million times better, but every time I miss I struggle to keep my temper in check, frustrated with myself.

Focus.

I pick another one off, and then another.

And then I see them dragging him out, four Officers surrounding a black blur, knees scraping against the gravel as they pull him along by his arms.

Kole.

I can't feel my heart beating. I can't feel anything except the crushing weight against my chest, the air frozen in my lungs. I watch him struggle against their hold, but there are too many of them and only one of him.

Out of the corner of my eye I see a blonde head, and for the tiniest second I look away from him, watching as an Officer kicks at the back of Lacey's knees, and she drops to the ground and he's raising his gun. What the hell is she doing out here?

A gunshot sounds from my other side, and before I understand what's happening I'm bolting across the grass as my grip tightens on the gun, my mind screaming…

No.

No.

No.

Why am I doing this?

This is dangerous and stupid and idiotic and I'm going to get myself killed, but all I can see are their hands pulling and tugging at him, dragging him away from the house, away from us, and maybe I've tied too much of this new life in with him, with his existence, with his life but—

My gun goes off, sending a bullet into the back of one of the Officer's heads, and another and another, and Jay comes up behind me, helping me, and there is all of this rage, everywhere and everything and at everyone, and I cannot believe they would do this.

The Captain of the troop, whom I recognise by the markings on his left sleeve, is in front of me. He pulls up a gun, but I am faster.

I pull the trigger, and there is this huge, monstrous thing rising up inside me because this is my home and this is my life and how *dare* they ...

The Officer falls to the ground with a thud. Dead.

I spin around, the butt of my gun held against my shoulder, waiting, watching, ready, so ready, but—

Nothing.

They are gone. The clearing is littered with bodies, some of them Officers, some not. It takes me a moment to register that they have retreated. Once they saw their Captain go down, the rest fell back immediately. We are alone with the dead.

My eyes fall on a blonde head in a pool of red blood, and it's happening again. As Lacey bleeds out on the gravel I watch her hair stain red, gulping back a hysterical laugh and I come apart, piece by piece, and my gun falls to the ground and I fall after it, my knees hitting the earth with a dull thud. Something like a scream is trying to claw its way out of me. I look over, and he is on his knees, his hand covering his mouth as he looks around him, some enormous, broken thing looking out from those dark eyes, and the tears in them push the scream back inside my lungs, because the pain in my chest is nothing against the look on his face. Like this is it, like the worst thing that could have possibly happened just did. Like something crawled out of his nightmares and into the real world, tearing apart everything he loved as it went.

Like this is his fault, and it is *destroying* him.

39

Kole pulled himself together faster than I did, than I *could*. He dragged up walls behind his eyes and picked himself up off the ground, coming over and kneeling down beside me.

'You saved my life,' he said. His voice was grave, with something else underneath it, but I couldn't tell if it was just the remnants of the pain he was trying to hide or something else.

My hand was left against my gun, which was left against my leg on the grass, all the bodies around me so close, and I felt a sensation like fingers crawling up my back. I was shaking so badly I couldn't answer him. I couldn't do anything but stare straight at him, my brain chasing itself in circles.

'We need to get you inside,' he murmured. He stood up, pulled me up along with him, his arm coming around my shoulders, to hold me up or to hold me together I couldn't tell.

As we walked back inside together, I tried not to see the bodies, lying around the clearing like broken things. I tried to pretend I didn't see the ones in civilian clothes, the ones who weren't Officers. The ones with blonde hair and blue eyes and soft laughs, the ones who trusted too easily but loved more than I ever could. I tried to pretend I didn't know those were our people lying face-down in the dirt, shot to death by an attack *I* should have seen coming.

Once we are inside, Kole wraps a blanket around me, sits me down in one of the chairs. He turns quickly as someone comes crashing through the door, voice loud and insistent. And that's how it's been for the last hour. One by one they started clambering towards him, blaming him for everything that happened.

But they didn't mean it. They just needed someone to aim their anger at. Somewhere to put all of the pain filling them up until they couldn't contain it, until they couldn't keep it inside of themselves any longer. All the fear clawing its way into the gaps between their joints, locking them in place as they stare around the clearing, at all of the dead.

'There is nothing we could have done to stop this,' Kole says quietly, calmly, to another one of his accusers, but there is the smallest tremble, the slightest hitch at the end of his voice that speaks of the effect it's having on him.

'*We?*' An unfamiliar voice shouts. I look up and a man stands there, poised like he's trying to keep from attacking Kole. I've never heard a word from this man before. He keeps quiet at meals, head down, with few friends. But this attack has done something to people – or maybe, more accurately, it has undone something in them. 'We couldn't do anything, but you should have. How does this keep happening?'

I've heard those words a lot in the last hour, *How does this keep happening?*, said with varying degrees of aggression.

Lauren has come downstairs, but she's sitting in the corner, not looking at anyone, so no one looks at her.

'Victor, this is the world we live in.' Kole is a lot calmer than I would be, and I try to tune out the argument, because I can't handle listening to it anymore.

I stare at my cup, full of tea that Kole made for me when the shaking got so bad he started getting scared for me, and I pull the blanket tighter around my shoulders. The tea doesn't taste like it did the first day, and my ears are still ringing from the gunshots.

Mark comes in after checking on everyone upstairs, followed shortly by Clarke. Her eyes are bloodshot and puffy, as if she's been crying, but her mouth is set in a hard line, the look in her eyes as murderous as it's ever been. She's only in the room a moment before she turns on Victor.

'Get out,' she snarls at him, before Mark steps between them, gently reminding Victor that everyone is just trying to cope with their loss. He eventually leaves, slamming the door on his way out, but he doesn't forget to remind Kole, before he storms out, that this should never have been able to happen.

There is an eerie silence in the kitchen when he's gone. Kole collapses into the chair across from me, leaning his head against the table.

'Kole?' Mark sounds scared, but everyone sounds scared. Everything is crawling with fear.

'I'm fine,' Kole grunts, but doesn't lift his head from the table.

Mark pulls up a chair to the table, and we sit quietly, watching Kole, because despite everything, we expect him to give us an answer. A solution. *Something*.

Clarke leans her back against the door, as if to block anyone else from entering, her face completely blank.

'I don't know,' he says, as if he can read our minds. 'I don't know what to do.'

'How did they find us?' Mark looks angry. 'It's only been a matter of weeks. How could they have found us so fast when we're so far into the forest, so far from the Wall?'

'I have no idea.' Kole raises his head from the table, a desperately helpless look on his face. 'I have no idea.'

Jay comes crashing through the front door, back from a search of the perimeter.

'Nothing,' he says, throwing himself down in a chair. He is seething with anger, every muscle taut with the need for revenge.

But we've killed all we can today. Anyone who escaped is long gone by now, and those who didn't are lying outside with bullet-holes in their heads and their hearts, piled up in the middle of the clearing, waiting to be burned.

'What do we do now? Do we move again? Stay? How are we supposed to fight them when there are so many of them and a few dozen of us?' The questions come pouring out of me, and my fist hits the table, as if that's going to do anything.

Eight of our own died today. Lacey died today. And almost everyone who was fighting is injured in some way. *Lacey died today.* I can't even think the words without feeling faint, so I press my knuckles against my temples and try to push the thought from my head.

Kole looks at me, or more like through me. I can't see any solution, and I can't see how he could either, but we wait, as if still expecting him to pull something out of a magic hat.

'We need to find out how they're tracking us,' he says, which is true, but impossible.

'How?' Clarke pipes up. 'The patrols are foot-soldiers, nothing more. They probably have as little an idea why they are attacking as we do.'

'Kole,' Mark says, his tone a warning. 'No.'

'What?' I look at her, at him, at Kole, but he's just staring blankly at Mark.

'We don't have any other option,' he says wearily.

'Kole, you're going to get yourself killed,' Mark says, and I can nearly taste the fear in his voice.

Kole stares at the table, but I can see a determined set to his shoulders, like he's made his final decision. 'We lost two dozen people last month, and eight tonight. There are less than thirty of us left. This can't keep happening. We're not going to survive it. We will all be killed.'

'What are you talking about?' I demand, forcing Kole to look at me.

'It's something we talked about before,' he says with a sigh. 'We dismissed it as too dangerous, but there's a point—' he cuts himself off, grinding his teeth in frustration. 'There's a point where enough is enough,' he says with a forced calm. 'We have to go to the source. We have to infiltrate Oasis and find out how they keep finding us. That's the only way we're ever going to be safe. We need to know how they operate, how they track us, and then, how to evade them.'

'Kole …' My stomach drops, but immediately I see the sense in it. It's barely sense, but I don't see any other way forward.

Everything in Oasis has a system. A set of rules and regulations by which every element of its function runs on. And tracking us, finding us, killing us, that will be no different. But if we could find that information and use it against them, we could be safe. Really, truly safe.

'You're asking me for an answer,' he says, standing from his chair. 'I'm giving it to you. This is my answer. I'm going back to Oasis, and I'm going to find out how they keep doing this to us, and I'm going to stop them.'

40

We don't sleep that night.

They stayed in the kitchen for another hour, arguing, saying the same things over and over until they didn't mean anything. I made eye contact with Jay across the table, the only other person who wasn't saying anything, and I knew by the look in his eyes he was thinking exactly the same thing I was.

That this is our only option. That this is our best chance.

But after that, there were bodies. Bodies of people I had known. Not all of them well, not all of them like Lacey. But as Jay and Mark and Kole and some of the others dug holes in the ground, I watched from a distance, unable to come closer. They worked for hours, as if it was nothing, but it wasn't nothing. I could tell by the sweat dripping off them and the strain of their shoulders, but most of all by the glassy look in their eyes.

No one really knows how to bury someone they love. You simply stumble through the motions in the hopes of doing it right, doing them justice, all the while feeling like you're turning yourself inside out, bleeding yourself dry as you do the one thing in the world that feels totally impossible.

Back in the Outer Sector, people died all the time, and it didn't matter. Crematorium workers would turn up in white suits to bring the dead bodies away, slinging them into the back of huge trucks as if they were waste, and no one ever saw them again.

But here, it's different. It does matter. We stand above the open graves with the moon hung low in the sky, and we lower the bodies one by one into the ground. Every one of them looks off, like themselves but not like themselves. Like a mirror reflection. The line of Kole's mouth is tight, and he doesn't look anyone in the eye. Kole and Mark lay boards over the graves for now, they will fill them in later. When each grave has received its body, that's when people start talking about those who died. They talk about who they were, talk about their lives, their memories together.

I feel sick. I feel sick because as I watch thesm stand up and talk about these people they loved, I'm faced with the fact that I care about them, too.

And I let her die.

I stare at the hole in the ground where they've just laid her body, and I realise that I could have done something, and she wouldn't be there. She'd be here beside me, heartbroken and crying, but alive.

I decided that Kole's life was worth more than hers. I made that decision.

My stomach turns, and I fall backwards a step.

At Lacey's grave, Kole stands up to say something. Suddenly the world feels like it's collapsing in on top of me, and I stumble farther and farther away. A few people glance back at me, but most are too consumed in their grief to even notice.

Between one second and the next I've turned on my heel and begun running. I don't stop when I hit the tree line, I just keep going. I continue in the dark, my path illuminated only every now and again as the moon peeks through the trees. I run until I'm out of breath, then I collapse into the dirt.

This is the mess that I've made. These are the bodies I leave behind me. Bea's and now Lacey's. Their blood is on my hands, no matter how much I wish it wasn't.

I punch the ground, a scream escaping me as my tears fall onto the soil. But I'm not sad, I'm angry. I want to make a difference. I want to change this, all of it, the world we live in, the way we live, but all I seem to be doing is letting people die.

o o o

I return to the house after everyone has gone to bed, and when I step inside the front door, Kole is standing by the table, leaning the tips of his fingers against the tabletop. When I walk into the room he looks up at me, and the exhaustion in his eyes is painful.

'You need to get some sleep,' I say.

'I was just making sure you got back okay,' he says, running a hand over his face.

'I'm fine,' I whisper.

He bites his lip, watching me, but I can see he's too tired to question me.

'Go to bed, Kole.'

'Okay.'

'I'll see you in the morning.'

o o o

I wake up an hour or two later to the sound of a door closing.

There's an imprint of a number behind my eyelids.

7425.

I stand up, the sound of blood rushing in my ears as I creep outside and pull open the door to the kitchen.

7425. That's Bea's sister's serial number.

The moonlight is spilling across the kitchen floor, but it immediately recedes as Lauren closes the front door. She looks up at me, her eyes wide as saucers.

'What are you doing?' I ask, stepping into the kitchen. 'Are you okay?'

My eyes immediately jump to the wound on her shoulder, but I can't see any sign of blood.

'I needed air,' she says quietly.

I'm so shocked she's spoken to me I almost smile, but instead I just nod at her. She nods back and walks towards the door, closing it behind her before she walks back upstairs to bed.

I try to steady my breath once she's gone, but my dream is still clinging to me. Leaning my back against the wall, I slide down until I'm sitting on the floor, my hands slung around my knees. I'm thinking about Bea and her sister, about how close to her I would be if we broke into Oasis. I could find her, wherever she is, and bring her back with me. Give her a chance at a better life, out here.

Give her a chance at the life I took from Bea.

But I don't know where she is. She could be anywhere inside Oasis. But Bea said she could find her using her serial number, so maybe I can too. I know Bea was at the South Dorms, which means her file is somewhere there. If I can find her file, I'll find her family records, and that will tell me where her sister is stationed.

I stand up from the wall and begin pacing, my mind analysing and planning.

This is the thing that I can do to make up for everything else. I could save a girl's life. Isn't this what I wanted, to make a difference?

I can do this. I can find Bea's sister and bring her here. I can do it. I have to do it.

I owe it to Beatrice. I owe it to Lacey. I owe it to myself.

41

I must have fallen asleep at some point, early in the morning, because when I wake up I can hear Kole arguing with Jay in the kitchen. I get dressed as quickly as I can, but when I leave my room, there's already a small crowd in the kitchen.

'I'm not bringing you with me,' Kole says, pushing past Jay as if he's trying to ignore everyone at the same time.

'Well I'm not staying here twiddling my thumbs until you get back,' Jay says, laying a hand on Kole's chest to stop him. 'You don't get to decide if I go or not.'

'I have to make decisions for the good of the group, not what's best for me or you or anyone else. For everyone. I'm going in alone. This is the decision I've made.'

'And I respect that, but this isn't something you *can* do alone. Let me go with you.'

'We need a team,' I say, pushing by them and pouring myself a cup of water.

Everyone turns to face me at once. Clarke is there, as well as

Mark, Walter, Lacey, Jay and several others.

'You say breaking into Oasis is our only option,' I say to Kole, to all of them. 'Well if we're going in, it had better work and it had better be worth our while.'

'I'm going to find the information and—' Kole starts, but I cut across him.

'No. That's not good enough. Whatever or whoever it is that's been tracking us needs to be taken out. We can't risk doing it any other way. And we can't risk failing.'

'That's ridiculous—' Kole says, frowning at me.

'No, it's not.' I look him straight in the eye, and though he doesn't back down, he doesn't say anything else. 'If we're going to stop this, we need to kill it at the source. And for that we'll need more than just you, Kole.'

'And what are you suggesting?' Jay asks, curiosity in his tone rather than accusation.

'That we pick a small group and we go in together, find out how Oasis is hunting us, track it back to the source, end this, and come home.'

The idea, however outlandish it sounds at this particular moment, that there is a chance of a light at the end of this tunnel, makes me feel weak at the knees.

Kole looks agitated. The group takes a step back as he starts pacing, running his hands through his hair as he considers all the options. But I know he's going to come to the same conclusion that I did last night. That no matter how much he might dislike this plan, it's the only hope we have of ending this.

'Who do we bring?' he asks, and just like that, we're going.

42

We decide to leave in two days. Jay, Kole and I decide who to bring with us late one night, after everyone has gone to bed.

Clarke is an obvious choice.

Kole suggests we bring Mark, which I agree with, but if Mark comes it'll be hard to convince Walter to stay, and Walter's too much of a risk. He can be nervous and jumpy at the best of times. Besides, we need someone to look after the base while we're gone.

We talk and talk and finally it's decided: me, Kole, Jay and Clarke. A small group, small enough, hopefully, to get in undetected, but enough of us to pull it off.

Kole explains the plan to get in, using an underground water system, the same one whose outlet I used to escape. I don't say anything, and I don't question how Kole knows so much. That seems to be normal here, to know too much about something but for no one to say a word.

I guess everyone has secrets.

o o o

The next day, with the planning complete and everyone informed, we begin to prepare for the mission itself.

I'm helping Mark pack the bags we'll be bringing with us when I come across old uniforms. There are stacks of them, almost one for every person here. I lay my hands flat against the grey fabric. Lacey must have washed them, because they're all completely clean, holes sewn up with a precision I've never mastered. It's like she knew we'd need them again eventually. I wonder if she was the last one to hold them. What she was thinking as she folded them so neatly, always attempting to make this place feel less desperate, even with the smallest things, like this.

I hand the pile back to Mark, who only pauses for a moment before he moves on, continuing to pack the uniforms into separate bags, but I can tell by the slant of his shoulders he's thinking about Lacey, too.

Once we have everything packed, there's nothing left to do but train, most of it led by Kole, who never seems to stop moving anymore. It's as if he thinks he can fend off the memories if he never sleeps, never takes a break, never takes a moment to breathe.

He insists I train with Jay, so that Jay can teach me to fight properly with a knife, and I do, in the hopes of granting him a sliver of peace.

Jay's form of teaching is different, but I can see small details of Kole's style in his, making me wonder who taught him before he taught me.

'Search out the anger,' he says to me now, standing outside in the clearing and holding the practice knife Clarke whittled for him. 'Anger is cold. When you find it, let it take over. It'll stop you from caring, and that's what's going to get you in trouble.'

I mutter under my breath as I roll my own practice knife in my hand, finding a better grip.

'Let it in,' he shouts at me, circling me as we move within the clearing. 'Let the anger in. Let it make you cold. Feel it.'

I think of the irony that he is telling me to let it in while Kole told me to let it go.

'You don't have a gun in your hand,' he says, as if reading my mind. 'You have a knife. It's different. You shoot an Officer from far off, you barely feel it. With a knife, it's violent. It's up-close and personal.'

He lunges forward, and I try to duck away from him, but the wooden blade skims across my side, over the scab of my actual knife wound. I flinch.

'Let it in!' he shouts at me. 'This is what you signed up for. This is blood and guts and feeling your blade hit bone. You have to stop letting that get in the way. Your pain doesn't matter, your opponent's pain doesn't matter. All that matters is survival.'

I lunge forward, going for his abdomen, but he's out of the way and standing behind me before I know what's happening. He holds his practice knife to my neck.

'You're dead,' he whispers, then pushes me away. 'Again.'

I turn around, facing him, my heart thundering in my chest. I need to learn this. I need to be better than them, or everything is going to fall apart.

Jay lunges at me and I duck out of the way, but before I can get out of range he hooks his heel behind my foot and pulls, sending me tumbling to the ground. He moves to jump on top of me, his practice knife arcing towards me, but before it hits home I push out and roll from beneath him, finding my footing and jumping back up before he can catch me.

'Good.' He grins, and there is a predatory glee in his eyes as he comes towards me again. He stabs forward, and I jump a step back, the tip barely missing my stomach.

Pushing forward off his back foot, he thrusts the blade towards me again, and I fall back another step, and another and another as he keeps pressing forward.

'FIGHT BACK!' he shouts, but his hits are coming too fast, and I can't think, I can't bring my knife up, I can't do anything but dodge away from him. 'Let it in!'

He moves to the side and launches himself at me again, but this time, instead of taking a step back, I step forward, meeting his wooden blade with my own.

'Good.' His razor smile is back, but without hesitation he slides his blade from mine, stabbing it towards me again. I jump sideways instead of backwards, land a blow to his arm, jump back.

'*LET IT IN*!' he shouts again, still not happy, still not satisfied. 'Let it *consume* you!'

My patience snaps. Instead of looking for an opening, I lunge for him, stabbing and stabbing and stabbing as he blocks each movement, always one step ahead.

'*ARGH!*' I scream, throwing myself at him, my knife held aloft, and as he raises his blade to block me, I swivel around, flipping myself over so I am behind him, lodging my knife in his abdomen as I go.

There is a moment where we are both as still as the dead, our breaths held within us, like we're not sure what just happened. But finally he turns around. His smile is manic and happy and *hungry*, like he feeds on this energy, on the speed and force and precision.

'Exactly,' he says, and his voice sounds both breathy and excited. '*Exactly.*'

43

I wake up in the middle of the night, only a few hours before we leave for Oasis, a dream still clinging to me. I shudder as I remember it, standing up out of my makeshift bed as I try to shake off the remaining horror. I don't remember much, except that Bea was waiting for me inside Oasis.

I pace around the room, trying to clear my head, but I can't get her face out of my mind. Her image haunts me, the look on her face the moment I made the decision to run, to run no matter the cost. I swallow the bile rising in my throat and pull open my door, desperate for some kind of escape.

Kole turns to face me in sweatpants and a loose-fitting black T-shirt, his hair rumpled. I wonder if he's slept at all tonight.

'I heard you moving around,' he says.

'Sorry,' I mutter, pulling out a chair and sitting down at the table. He's making tea at the stove, and I welcome the warmth radiating from the fire. I'm coated in sweat from the nightmare, but my bones feel cold.

'It doesn't matter. It wasn't like I was asleep.' He shakes his head.

'How are you feeling?' I ask. I don't want to admit it to myself, but I'm worried about him. Ever since the attack he's begun to look progressively more strained every day, and I'm afraid he's going to snap.

'I'm okay,' he says, without any inflection.

'Are you?' My voice echoes through the room and falls flat.

He takes the nettle leaves out from beneath the sink, Lacey's concoction, the last batch she ever got to make. His hands are shaking.

'Kole ...' I stand up and move towards him, but I don't know what I think I'm going to do.

'I just want to fix it,' he whispers, his shoulders hunched over the stove.

'Kole,' I breathe. I don't know what to do. I don't know how to make him feel better. I don't know why I am so desperate to make him feel better.

When he turns around there are tears in his eyes and my heart feels like it's going to explode.

'I never wanted this. I never wanted a war. I just wanted them to leave us alone.'

'I know,' I say, and I'm not crying. I won't cry. But he looks like he's being ripped apart, and I know that feeling. I look down at his trembling hands and his face frozen in a twisted sort of horror and it feels like I'm standing in front of a mirror.

And then I do the single stupidest thing I could choose to do. The thing that every instinct in me screams not to do, the one thing the Dorms taught me to stay away from at all costs. I wrap my arms around his waist and press my face into his chest, and he pauses for a second, shocked, and then he hugs me back, too tight, like he's needed this for so long, and I wonder what I'm doing, but I can't let go.

We stand still for too long, holding too tight as the kettle whistles and the wind rattles against the shutters, and we are like two statues leaning against each other, and if one of us moves, we'll both fall, and we can't do that.

We can't afford to.

And even after we break apart, after we fill our chipped cups with hot tea and sit at the table with our knees pulled up under our chins, our hands grasp together, because I cannot let go of him, because even when I think about it he seems to see it in my eyes and hold on tighter, like he'll drown if I do. And we talk about nothing because something is too painful, and we hold on until the dawn comes, and I don't let go, not even once.

44

'*Wait!*'

We're standing in front of the building, ready to leave, when Lauren runs towards us, shouting and out of breath.

'Are you okay?' Kole asks, stepping forward, concern and a touch of panic flitting across his face.

'I want to come with you,' she gasps, her breathing fast and uneven.

We all look at one another, shocked that she's even trying. Taken aback by the desperation in her voice. She's out of breath and her arm is in a makeshift sling, why the hell does she want to risk herself like this?

'Lauren, you can't,' Kole says gently.

'No, please.' Her voice is high and reedy, and ever since she's had enough energy to get up and move around, she's been twitching, constantly edgy and restless. 'Please let me come. I promise I won't get in the way.'

'It's not about you getting in the way—'

'*Please.*' She steps closer to Kole, and her eyes are so wide and so desperate and so terrified. 'My little sister's Inside. I have to go back for her.'

Kole's eyes widen a fraction, and I can see his resolve weakening.

'Kole,' Jay warns from behind him, his eyes narrowing into slits.

'No, she can come,' Kole says all at once, and turns on his heel just like that.

'Kole, I'm not sure that's a good idea—' Clarke starts.

'No,' Kole snaps. 'I said she can come. End of discussion.'

Jay mutters something obscene under his breath, fixing the straps on his backpack.

'Let's go,' Kole grunts, and that's it.

I trail behind, watching them walk into the trees, and I wonder why they just agree with him like that. I would argue with him, but I can't help but see the similarity in her going back for her sister and me going back for Bea's sister. And though that shouldn't sway me, it does, and I keep my head down.

45

We stop only when the darkness makes it impossible to keep moving forward. Kole starts a fire in a small clearing, and we sit around it, huddling together against the cold. It's going to take four days of walking to get to the Wall, and four days to get back to the base. If it weren't for the raids we led on the Officers, we wouldn't have enough food to make it both ways.

Kole unpacks the food, handing cans across the circle, along with utensils, and we settle down to eat.

'To Oasis!' Jay yells, lifting his can up in a sarcastic toast.

'Shut up, Jay,' Clarke growls at him, elbowing him in the ribs.

Kole shakes his head beside me, eating quietly. Clarke and Jay argue for a few minutes, nothing unusual for them, though there's a lot more fire on Clarke's side than on Jay's. After a while things settle down, and I stand up and move to sit beside Lauren.

'Hi,' I say, feeling a little awkward.

'Oh, hi.' She looks around, a little confused. She hasn't really spoken to anyone since we left, and all of us are so used to silent Lauren that we didn't even question it.

I glance around to make sure no one's listening to us, but everyone is caught up listening to Jay, who's begun talking about something I can't hear from this side of the fire.

'What age is your sister?'

She looks up at me, her eyes widening a little. 'Eight,' she says quietly, looking back down at the empty can in her hand.

'Where is she?'

'In the Outer Sector somewhere. I don't know. She's probably been moved by now. I'm going to have to search for her.'

I don't respond. I suppose I should say something encouraging, but finding a Dormant child in the Outer Sector is like looking for a needle in a needle stack, and I'm not going to give her false hope.

I wonder if I shouldn't be hoping either. I wonder if I'm making a mistake, risking my life for something I'm never going to find.

But I remind myself it's not just about Bea anymore. It's bigger than her or Aaron or me or even Kole.

It's bigger than all of us.

o o o

For four days we walk. In the early mornings Jay trains me, and I'm improving so fast that I'm actually holding my own against him. Sometimes Kole trains with us, but against him I don't have a chance, and it frustrates me so much that on the third day I drop my knife and walk off into the forest, needing to get away, find a breath somewhere where I wasn't expected to be quick and smart and precise and defend myself constantly.

Lauren stays mostly quiet, and with the exception of Jay and Clarke's constant bickering, the rest of us do too.

We know what we're walking into, and none of us has the heart for anything but silence as we drown in our own minds.

PART THREE

RETURN

1

The Wall rises up above us, and we take a minute just to stare at it.

'How the—' Jay starts.

'Don't finish that sentence,' Kole cuts him off.

'—are we going to get in there?' Jay finishes, eyeing Kole.

'Not the fun way,' Kole responds wearily.

There are two water outlets in Oasis. One is a storm drain, to funnel the water out of Oasis in the case of a downpour, but the other drain is for sewage. I escaped through the water outlet, but if we followed that backwards it would land us just inside the Wall, where patrols monitor the perimeter at all times.

The sewage outlet, on the other hand, we can follow all the way into the Outer Sector.

We move along the tree line until Kole finds the spot we're going to break through, and then we sprint across the opening. The grass is wet beneath our feet, and I almost slip twice before we hit the bank, which we slide down as quickly as we can, launching ourselves into the trench, which is filled with both water and sewage.

I hear the others splutter as we wade through the mess, thigh-deep in filth as we scramble towards the outlet. I breathe through my mouth, trying not to gag as we move closer to the other bank.

The bank is steep on the far side, and it takes us forever to pull ourselves up.

'You ready?' Kole asks, looking at all of us as we face the sewage drain, which is wider than the one I broke through.

We all nod, and he goes first, crawling through the drain in a half crouch, steadying himself against the sides. We follow close behind, me, then Jay, then Clarke and Lauren.

I start to feel dizzy, and the deeper we go, the darker the drain gets, making it hard for me to orient myself as I try to keep from puking as the rancid smell enters my nose.

We move like this for what feels like hours, until finally Kole stops.

'Shh,' he whispers, holding a finger to his lips as he reaches above him, moving across a cover that I didn't even see, releasing light into the tunnel. He puts his hands either side of the opening, and then suddenly he disappears, pulling himself upwards.

I glance back at Jay for a moment, who simply nods me forwards. I catch hold of the sides, like Kole did, but before I have a chance to pull myself up, Kole catches my forearms, hoisting me up himself.

Once I'm out and on my feet I glance around, taking in our surroundings as the rest of the group are pulled up and into Oasis. We're in a short, deadend alleyway, the sun a muted orange colour just before it dips below the Wall.

Once we're all in we start moving silently through Oasis, all six of us like shadows against the buildings, moving deeper and deeper into the Outer Sector, Kole leading us. We don't speak. The streets get tighter and tighter as we go further in, the buildings closer and closer together as the architects tried to cope with the sheer quantity of Dormants that had to be housed.

I'm glancing sideways at a window, where I think I see a curtain twitching as if someone is watching us, when Kole suddenly catches my hand, pulling me in between a gap in the buildings. He pushes me up against one of the walls as I gasp, and he covers my mouth with his hand, pointing to patrols as they pass through the street we were just on, their flashlights casting harsh shadows against the walls.

His arms are placed either side of my head against the concrete, and he's holding very still, waiting for the Officers to move on, his breath huffing gently into my hair.

I swallow,

I can feel his heart beating like a jackhammer in his chest, keeping time with my own as he finally pulls back, glancing out between the buildings.

'You okay?' Kole whispers, looking back to me.

'I'm fine,' I breathe, but my hands are shaking as we step back onto the street.

The Outer Sector never really stops moving, because the power station never stops running. People's shifts differ so much that there are people who don't ever see daylight, working straight through the night and sleeping during the day.

I breathe in the familiar air as Kole gestures for us to follow him. He winds down familiar streets, keeping his head low and we follow suit, attempting to blend into the crowd as we push forward. We keep together, Kole drawing us down alleys and streets he obviously knows well, his shadowy figure moving quickly in front of us.

Something grabs my sleeve and I jerk back, shocked, but I can't move, the grip on my sleeve is too tight.

When I look back I'm faced with a vaguely familiar sight, the white-grey hair of an old man, hunched over as he holds onto me.

'I know you,' he croaks, showing the gaps in his teeth as he pulls me closer. I tug hard against him, but he's holding me in a vice-grip.

'I don't know what you're talking about,' I say, and I hate myself for the wobble in my voice.

'You're that girl—' He stops speaking as the tip of a knife presses to the skin of his throat.

'You're hallucinating,' Jay says, his knife smile snapping across his face. 'You've clearly been taking too many happy pills, old man.'

The man's hand drops from my sleeve and I pull away, my breathing fast as I push back into the shadows. Jay says something else to the old man quietly, flicking his knife back in a gesture more threatening than pushing it closer would have been, and moves back to join us. Kole shoots us a questioning glance, but keeps moving forward.

My heart is thundering in my chest, but we keep going, keep walking steadily like wind-up toys as we follow Kole down ever darker alleys, until he stops in front of a ladder leading up to a fire escape.

'This is it,' he says, and I take a steadying breath, trying to be prepared for whatever awaits us inside.

2

I catch hold of one of the cold, rusted rungs and start pulling myself up.

Kole doesn't stop for several stories, so far up that even I start to feel a little dizzy. When he does stop, he swings himself under an overhanging pipe, then knocks on the peeling paint of a blood red door. It makes me wonder. All the government regulation doors in the last eighty years are steel, not flimsy wood, which was constantly needing to be replaced.

After a few moments a barrel-chested man with a shaven head tugs the door open, only a crack, and grunts something unintelligible at Kole.

'Nails, it's me,' Kole says under his breath.

The door jerks open, and the barrel-chested man's eyes are so wide, I'm afraid they're about to fall out of his head. He has a scraggly beard, a bright orange colour that seems wildly incongruous for some reason, but I can see him grinning through it.

Nails? I think, as the man pulls Kole inside, slapping him on the back so hard it has to be painful.

'My God, Kole, I thought you were dead.'

'Not yet,' Kole says, and though his smile seems to be genuine, he seems to flinch at the man's statement. 'Nails, these are a few of my friends,' Kole says smoothly, gesturing to us, huddled outside the door.

'Come in, come in!' Nails ushers, and we all rush inside, the nip in the air somehow worse inside of Oasis. He closes the door behind us, but I can't help noticing the way he glances outside the door before he does so, like he's checking for something.

Or maybe waiting for something.

The room within is small and tight, with a beaten-up sofa pushed against the wall, the stuffing pushing out of it as the ceiling leans in on top of us, like it's eavesdropping.

'You all smell like death,' he says, pulling his head backwards with a look of disgust on his face. And we do smell bad. 'What are you doing here?'

'We're in town for a while. We need somewhere to lay low for a few days.'

Nails releases a bark of laughter so loud it's almost violent, and I jump back a step, bumping into Lauren. I pull back, murmuring an apology, but she just smiles, shaking her head.

'In town for a few days?' he asks. 'What the hell is that supposed to mean?'

'Come on, Nails,' Kole says, smiling at him across the room. 'You don't ask questions, remember?'

'I didn't ask questions,' Nails corrects him, his tone suddenly sober. 'Things change.'

Kole's eyes widen the smallest fraction, and I can see him processing the information, trying to find a new angle to approach the situation.

'But for you …' Nails concedes.

'You're a life-saver.' Kole smiles, releasing an all-too-real sigh of relief. Life-saver is a more accurate term than any of us cares to admit.

'I need you and your friends,' Nails says, glancing around at each of us, 'out of here within a few days, though. I'm not taking on any more long-terms, got it?'

'Got it.' Kole nods, his lips flattening. He's trying to calculate how long the mission will take, but he can't. There are too many variables.

'Great.' Nails grins, slapping Kole on the back again as he moves towards the back of the room, where there's another red door, this one with several locks running down the side of its peeling paint.

Once he has all of the locks undone, he pulls the door open, revealing a dark staircase leading downwards. Nails walks straight down without hesitation, and the others follow, but I pause at the threshold, unsure.

'Trust me,' Kole says from behind. 'This is our best bet.'

I look back at him, reading the sincerity on his face. Kole seems to know this guy, and trust him enough to keep us safe, and if Kole trusts him, I guess that's enough for me.

I step downwards, moving deeper into the darkness, and pray that I'm right.

3

I stop at the bottom of the stairs and Kole almost smacks into me. I'm facing a long hallway, but to my left there is an arch, which I pass under with bated breath. The room is large and open, with two ratty sofas facing each other in the middle of the floor, but that's not what has shocked me into silence.

There are people milling around the room, sitting on the sofas and talking to each other in groups. A few of them glance up as I walk in. My breath is knocked from my lungs as I look back at Kole, my eyes wide.

'Not everyone escapes,' he says. 'But that doesn't mean they're not there.'

A tall guy with white hair walks up to us, trailed by a short girl, her hair cropped close to her head, her eyes sharp as she watches us.

'This is my second-in-command, Lyonel,' Nails says. 'And this is Kerrin.'

'You can call me Ly,' the white-haired one says, shaking my hand. He seems to already know Kole, and they nod silently at each other.

The girl, Kerrin, reaches out and shakes both of our hands, but her expression doesn't change.

'Kole, you can get your people settled in one of the back rooms,' Nails says, and Kole nods. 'There are showers at the end of the hall, on your left, but they only run for three minutes at a time, so you better be quick.'

'We'll be out of your hair as fast as we can,' Kole assures him, and Nails nods at him, his smile tense.

A few moments later Kole is leading us down the hallway, stopping in front of the last door. He pulls it open, revealing a small room with mattresses lying directly on the floor. It has no windows and will barely fit all six of us, but it seems luxurious after a week of sleeping on the cold ground.

There are two showers, so I have to wait several minutes before I get to clean off, and when I do, the water is ice cold. With a lumpy bar of dark, homemade soap, I clean up as best as I can before the water shuts off.

Once we're all relatively clean and changed into our Oasis uniforms, Kole pulls us aside.

'Okay,' he says. 'We'll start moving tomorrow. Tonight just get some rest, and please,' he says, speaking slowly, 'no one get in a fight.'

'Sure thing,' Jay says, grinning, a glint in his eye.

'Ninety percent of that warning is for you, Jay, alright?'

'I'm very offended,' Jay says, a lazy smile on his face.

'I'm sure you are.' Kole drops his bags on the floor. 'I'm going to go sort out food with Nails.'

I follow Kole into the hall, and he pauses for a moment to let me catch up.

'What is up with this place?' I say, glancing around nervously.

'We're not in danger here,' he says. 'Nails set up this place as a refuge for people to stay when they're hiding from Oasis. Most of them are pretty low profile, though, unlike us.'

'Nails?'

He laughs at my expression.

'Tough as,' he explains. 'He once took out three Officers while holding back the blood from a knife wound on his side.'

I reflexively touch the wound on my own side, which has mostly healed.

'What about the girl? Kerrin. Do you know her?'

'No. She must be new. It's been a while since I was back.'

'And the other guy? The one with the white hair?'

Kole stops in the hall, turning to face me. 'Ly. Stay away from him. He's … unstable. He's an escaped Subject.'

'What?' My breath catches in my throat.

'He's twenty-five and his hair is pure white, Quincy. That didn't just happen.' Kole glances away, looking down the hall. 'Don't tell anyone I told you that,' he warns suddenly.

'I won't, I promise.' I'm still shocked. I've never heard of anyone surviving the Labs. No one survives the Labs.

'He doesn't talk much about what went on at the Labs, but from what I've heard—' Kole swallows, looking up at the ceiling before dropping his eyes back to me. 'It's not the kind of place people come back from without scars. Of every kind.'

Kole leaves me standing in the hall, trying to process everything he's told me, everything I've seen, and I wonder how I ever thought I knew what was going on around me. How I spent my entire life listening to Oasis, and never once questioned what they were telling me or *why* they were telling it to me.

o o o

I'm walking down the hall an hour later when I bump into the girl I met earlier.

'Oh, sorry,' I murmur.

'You're the one from the Dorms,' she says, her eyes searching my face.

'What?'

'The Dorms. Kole said that's where you were, before you escaped.'

'What does it matter to you?' I ask, prickling.

'It doesn't,' she says. 'But I was in the South Dorms before I met Nails. You're that girl who disappeared, aren't you?'.'

I remember Kole telling me she must be new, and a question pushes itself forward.

'When did you leave?' I ask, ignoring her question.

'About a month ago, why?'

'You didn't … there wasn't a girl there, Sophia?' I ask. Her face is blank, but we didn't know each other's names. I search my memories for the serial number. '7425. Her serial number is 7425.'

Her head starts bobbing up and down rapidly. 'Yeah, yeah, I remember a 7425. I remember, some girl turned up dead … I think it was her sister or something. But she freaked out in the middle of the yard and the guards ended up dragging her away. Her serial number was announced over the intercom the next day – we were told that she was a potential threat to Dorm security, and she was to be turned in if she did anything suspicious. It went on for weeks, telling us who she was and to turn her in.'

'She was there? In the South Dorms?' My heart feels like a caged bird in my chest, and I'm afraid it's going to pound straight through my ribs.

'Yeah,' she says, still nodding. 'She was there a month ago.'

4

I don't waste any time. I wind through the streets of Oasis towards a familiar world, towards the world where I grew up, and I don't know why, but I am not nervous. The fear I thought I would feel when I made the decision to come here is absent. Instead, I feel empty. This place doesn't mean anything anymore. Or maybe it does, just something different. Something much less powerful.

I had to sneak out past Kole and the others, but none of the people from the base seemed to care if I came or went.

The uniform feels different out here, and I'm suddenly hyper-aware of the rough fabric scratching against my skin. In there, with the others, the uniform felt like clothes, but out here it feels like an old skin, too loose and too tight at the same time. But for now it serves as a ticket and a shield, and as I blend seamlessly into the Outer Sector, I'm grateful for it.

The sun is dipping fast below the horizon, but my path is illuminated by the light of the Celian City. The Dorms are set on the fringes of the tightly packed living complexes of the Outer Sector, closer to the Wall than the other buildings. I have to cross over a short expanse of open ground first, where there are no buildings to hide between, something that I never really thought about until now.

I imagine I can feel a sniper target on my back and start walking faster, dodging the heaps of scrap metal dumped in piles along the way.

And then it comes into view. The building looks the same, even in the low light. The same grey walls, the same shuttered windows. The trees that grew up around the Dorms over the years look like they're leaning in, trying to overhear what's going on inside, just like usual. Even the broken glass from when one of the girls threw a piece of rubble through one of the windows is still scattered across the gravel.

But it looks different. Fundamentally shifted and out of place.

I stare at it, and I wait to feel something, but nothing happens. I shake my head and continue forwards, ignoring my own confusion.

I move cautiously towards the fence that loops around the Dorms, to get a better view of what I'm getting myself into. The gun that I took from Kole burns my back where I tucked it into the waist of my trousers, and I am acutely aware of the damage a weapon like that can do. And of the punishment it would incur.

I shift up to the fence as quietly as I can, keeping low to the ground as I move, concealing myself within a crop of trees. The world's gone quiet now, and my footsteps crunching against the gravel surrounding the fence sound like gunshots to me. I stare through the links in the fence as I watch the silent yard.

I wait for the patrols to cross by, their flashlights skimming the ground as I watch silently from my crouch, waiting until they've turned the corner before I move.

I push my fingers through the chainlink fence and pull myself up slowly, watching the guard-house out of the corner of my eye. I use my feet to help steady myself against the wire, but my boots keep slipping, and the wire cuts into my hands as I climb. I throw my leg over the other side of the fence, glance around briefly and jump. I land loudly and unevenly, half falling onto my side as the air is knocked from my lungs, but I don't have time to worry if they heard me.

I sprint, the stones moving under my feet as I run towards the door, caught in a constant state of falling forward, and I feel my heart beat every time my boots hit the gravel, keeping time with my movements. I throw my hands up in front of me, unable to slow my momentum as I crash into the door.

I throw my shoulder against the lock, feeling it give beneath my weight. The door cracks open, allowing me to slip through and into the Dorms. I lean my back against the door and look around carefully.

Everything is silent.

The South Dorms was the first to be built, years and years ago, before the Dormant population had grown out of hand, so the security, other than the fence and the guards, is non-existent. In some of the newer Dorms there are internal and external security cameras, night-wardens set up inside the Dorms, and all of the doors are alarmed. But in the South, there's enough fear of Officer brutality to keep the girls in line, leaving the building itself almost entirely security-free.

I scan the room, adrenaline making me jumpy, shadows jutting from the walls as if there are other things hiding in this room other than me. I slip into the hallway, my fingers skimming the walls as I move silently up the stairs, trying to keep my hands from shaking. It's too familiar. All of it is too familiar.

There are four rooms, and I start with my old one, because my feet turn that way of their own accord. I push open the door and freeze for a second, because I don't know what to do. I don't know what I'm doing. I don't know how I thought this was a good idea.

Pull yourself together, I order in my mind, frustrated with my own panic.

I move into the room, my heart in my throat as I scan for blonde heads. Every time I see one my heart almost stops, but once I creep across the floor towards them, their serial numbers prove me wrong.

She's not in the first room.

I pass through the second room with no luck, and my heart starts pounding in my chest. She's not here. She's not here, and I've risked everything to find her, and she's not even here.

I go into the third room, frantically moving through it, searching.

I pause, a white-blonde head catching my eye.

She's fast asleep, so I can't see her eyes, and her hair is a few shades lighter than Bea's, but she looks like her. A smattering of light freckles runs across the bridge of a small, sloped nose, high cheekbones barely disguised in a childishly round face. She is young, eight or nine, and slim, though not in the way Bea was.

It's her. It has to be her.

I glance down at her shoulder, my heart in my mouth, and there it is.

7425.

'Hey.' My hand reaches out of its own accord, trembling as I touch her shoulder.

Her eyes fly open, and she shrinks against the wall. And there they are. Bea's blue eyes.

'Stay away from me,' she says quietly. She's uncomfortable and angry, but not actually scared, because she thinks I'm one of the other Dorm girls.

'I know this is really scary, but you need to come with me. I need to get you out of here.'

'Who are you?' she asks, her eyes widening as she realises her mistake.

'I'm your sister's friend, and she told me that if anything happened to her, I had to come get you and bring you to a safe place.'

Lie, lie, lie, lie, my brain screams at me, but I don't have any other option.

'You're lying.'

'I'm not, I promise. Bea and I were leaving together. We were friends. She told me about you, Sophia.'

The angry look eases up on her face, allowing a tiny sparkle of hope to come through. 'You knew my sister?'

'Yeah. I knew her, but we need to go now.'

She looks like she can't make up her mind for a moment, but the truth is, any girl in this room would go with me if they thought they'd actually get out. They wouldn't really care where we were going, as long as it was away from here.

She stands up from her bed, and I move out of her way.

'You promise you knew my sister?'

'I promise.'

I can see her thinking, analysing the risk, and finally she nods.

'Okay,' she says quietly. 'I'll go with you.'

'We need to go now,' I say, catching her hand. She takes it without question, and I pull her out the door, not once glancing back.

She clings to my hand as we slip down the stairs and into the hall. The door is only pushed in since I broke the lock, and I make her wait while I check outside.

'There's no one there. Let's go!' she whispers.

'Wait,' I breathe, watching the movement in the guard-house. We hunker down against the door, the girl hidden safely behind it while I stare through the crack, and we wait for our opportunity.

'What is it?' she asks.

Two Officers are walking towards the Dorms, guns slung against their shoulders.

'Stay down,' I order, and she ducks her head lower as I pull the gun from my waistband.

My insides curl as I watch the Officers approach, and I try to remember everything Kole taught me as I raise the gun up between shaking hands.

I will not let her die.

I will not let her die.

I will not let her die.

The Officers get closer. One of them readjusts his gun, holding it out towards the door, and I'm sure they've seen the broken lock and they're coming to investigate, I know it.

I will not let her die.

I will not let her die.

I will not let her die.

The gun feels too heavy, and my breathing is coming in short, quiet gasps as I try to get ready, to prepare for whatever comes after this.

I will not let her die.

I will not let her die.

I will not let her die.

5

At the last moment the patrols pass, distracted by the arrival of two colleagues. They switch over with the two other Officers, then continue their patrol around the Dorms. I nearly drop the gun as a wave of dizziness pours over me, relief making my knees weak beneath me. I fall back against the wall beside her, my heart thudding in my chest.

'Two minutes,' I tell her, and we stay very still, waiting.

I stand back up, seeing lights bobbing around the yard, and glance out as the guards pass around the corner. I gesture for the girl's hand, taking a firm grip of her.

'Ready?' I ask.

'Ready,' she says, her eyes fierce and fiercely afraid.

We sprint without looking back. I pull her behind me, her short legs unable to keep up with me properly as I run, but we eat up the ground between us and the fence so quickly the moment barely exists, and then we are at the fence and I am climbing, glancing back to make sure she's following, and she is, but slowly, too slowly. I throw my leg over the top of the fence and lean down, catching her under her arms and pulling her up with me. I jump off the other side, feeling the seconds drain away from us as the Officers come around the other side of the Dorms, and she jumps after me, both of us landing at the same time on the hard earth.

She falls onto her knees, but I don't give her time to orientate herself. I grab her hand and begin pulling her along, using the cover of the trees for as long as I can. I've only ever been this thankful for the outcrop of trees surrounding the Dorms once before, and that was the night of the escape.

The night everything changed.

The branches of the trees cut into my arms, and the dirt is loosely packed and shifts under my boots as we run, the girl stumbling after me, but I can't stop.

I can't stop running. I can't slow down. I can't risk us getting caught.

I can't risk losing her.

I turn around, checking to make sure she's okay, and run straight into something. I stumble forward and then jump away, realising that the something was a person, a person with a dark hoodie and a gun.

My heart stops and I'm opening my mouth to scream at her to run, but a hand shoots up and catches mine.

'Quincy, stop. Quincy, it's me.' A familiar voice. I release a strangled gasp of relief.

'Kole?' I stutter. 'What are you doing here?'

'I came to find you. Are you okay?' He knocks back his hood to reveal his face in the low light, the Celian City one side of us, the moon the other. His eyes glance down at the girl, and my own eyes follow to her terrified face.

There's a pause.

'We need to get back,' he says. That's it.

'But—'

'Let's just get back, will we?' He catches my arm and drags me forward. I shake him off before falling into line behind him, confused.

6

Kole raps on the red door and a few minutes later, Ly pulls it open. His eyes flick past us to the girl, and he turns to Kole sharply.

'Don't,' Kole says, holding up a hand. 'Don't say a word.'

Ly grinds his teeth, slamming the door behind us as Kole pulls the inside door open, ushering us downstairs. I look down at the girl, shivering in her thin, grey sleep-suit, and feel a pang of regret. I should have let her get changed, or at least let her put on a jacket.

Her lips are blue, but by the expression on her face, the shivering is only half from cold. We step inside the basement, and several people glance up, giving us curious looks as we pass by.

'Where's Clarke?' Kole asks someone passing us by, and they direct us down the hall. Kole pushes open a door to a small room, where Lauren and Clarke are sitting in a circle, talking. They all look up when we walk in.

'What the …' Clarke trails off, staring wide-eyed at the girl, then at me, then at Kole, then at the girl again.

Lauren jumps up from her spot on the ground.

'Kole?' she squeaks.

'This is Sophia. Can you get blankets for her, Lauren?' I ask, ignoring Kole as I push forward, never once releasing the girl's hand.

'Uh,' Lauren blinks, licks her lips, looks around nervously. 'Yeah. Yeah, of course.'

She runs off and is back in minutes.

'Take these,' she says, handing me a stack. 'Nails is sending someone down with hot water in a minute. You look freezing!' Lauren says, picking up the girl's other hand.

I wrap two of the blankets around the girl's shoulders, then sit her down on one of the mattresses pushed against the wall. It's like the rest of the room has melted away.

'Are you okay?' I ask her in the kindest voice I can muster. Her teeth are chattering, but she nods through it.

'Is this the place?' she asks, looking around the small, cramped room.

'No,' I answer, following her eyes. She's not sure what to think of this place, and neither am I. 'The place I was talking about is outside the Wall. I'm gonna take you there soon.'

'Outside the Wall?'

'Yeah,' I smile. 'I know.'

'Is it … what's it like out there?'

'Better than what you're imagining. It'll be okay, I promise.'

She smiles at me, a slow, hesitant smile that doesn't really become anything much, but it feels like progress. 'What's your name?' she asks.

'Quincy.' I smile. 'And these people are my friends. They won't hurt you, I promise.'

Lauren comes in with a cup of hot water for Sophia, which she drinks greedily.

'I'm sorry we don't have anything better,' Lauren apologises, kneeling beside Sophia.

'Quincy,' Kole says, coming up behind me.

'What?'

'I need to talk to you.'

'About what?' I don't look at him, instead watching Sophia as she watches us.

'Quincy.' His voice sounds a warning tone.

'But Sophia needs me to stay—'

'Lauren has it covered, don't you, Lauren?'

'I can stay here,' Lauren says, nodding.

'Fine.'

I march back out through the door. I expect him to say whatever it is he needs to say in the hall so I can go back in, because I don't particularly want to talk to him right now anyway, but instead he walks down the hall and into a different room, forcing me to follow him.

'What?' I demand, closing the door behind me.

'What in the world did you think you were doing?' he asks, turning to face me.

'What do you mean?'

He runs his hands through his hair as he turns away from me.

'Why did you leave without telling me? Why did you go to the Dorms? Who the hell is that kid in there?'

'I needed to find her,' I say, as if that's an answer to all three questions.

'For future reference,' he says, coming to stand closer to me, 'I don't appreciate having to track you down in the middle of the night when you decide you want to play search and rescue.'

'I didn't ask you to follow me.' I grit my teeth, holding myself back from slapping him.

'I know you didn't. Because at least everyone else I can trust to know when they need help. With you, I always have to be watching, waiting for when you need me.'

'I don't need you to fight my battles!'

'You think I'm trying to?' he asks, with a snort of unpleasant laughter. Then he leans in close to me. 'I'm trying to keep you from getting yourself killed, you idiot.'

'Don't. You. *Dare*,' I growl, stepping closer to him.

'You need to get over your ego, Quincy.'

'I don't have an ego!'

'Oh, you don't, do you? So then explain to me how you thought that you could single-handedly break into the Dorms, which, in case you didn't notice, is crawling with Officers, and just take a girl. You don't think that was just a little bit arrogant?'

'It wasn't any of your business.'

'If you get killed, it's my business. This is exactly what I'm talking about. You think you're invincible.'

'I needed to find her. I had to.'

'You didn't have to do it on your own, Quincy, that's what I've been trying to tell you. You're not on your own anymore. You're part of a team. Start acting like it.'

He brushes past me on his way to the door, before yanking it open and slamming it closed behind him.

7

Kole calls a meeting in the common room and tells us he wants to leave once it gets dark.

'We're not here to waste time,' he says, looking at each of us. 'The longer we're here, the more chance of being caught. We leave tonight for the Inner Sector, get the information we need, and come back. We'll regroup after that and decide how to move forward. Everyone understand?'

I glance around the small group, and everyone's nodding.

Kole doesn't make eye contact with me, and when he's done explaining the plan, he goes for the door, but I catch him before he leaves.

'I wanted to say,' I grit my teeth, attempting to get this out quickly, 'that I'm sorry for leaving to get Sophia without telling anyone. And you're right, I'm part of a team. I understand that now.'

He looks away from me, and my heart drops, but when he looks back there's something in his expression, like he's trying not to smile.

'That was genuinely really hard for you, wasn't it?' he asks, shaking his head as he looks at me strangely, like he can't understand me.

'You're not angry?'

He takes a breath and shakes his head. 'No, I'm not angry. I just don't want you doing anything like that again. And it's not about me, it's about the entire group. We have to move together or we'll fall apart.'

'It won't happen again.'

'Then we're good.' He shrugs.

'Just like that? That's it?'

'That's it,' he says. 'People make mistakes. It's not fair to punish them for it forever. It doesn't make sense.'

'Okay.' I'd smile, but I'm in too much shock. 'I have to go say goodbye to Sophia.'

'Good. I'll see you later.'

'Okay,' I mumble again, moving down the hall to where Sophia's staying.

'I won't be gone long,' I promise, crouching down beside her, and I'm not sure she's aware it's a promise, but it is. I won't leave her behind.

'Okay.' She nods, but there's a slight tremble in her hand.

'Lauren is going to stay with you while I'm gone.'

She nods again. 'Just, please come back. Sometimes people say they won't be gone long and then they don't come back at all.'

I put both of my arms around her, and she shouldn't trust me this fast, she shouldn't be this ready to let people inside her walls, but it's as if the Dorms haven't touched her, as if it couldn't do to her what it did to me, and I've never been so glad for something in my life.

'I promise you,' I say, with a shaking voice, 'that I will come back. No matter what.'

'Okay,' she says, and I have to pretend she's not crying so I'll be able to leave.

I'm wiping tears from my own eyes when I meet Kole and the others upstairs.

'You okay?' he asks gently, putting his hand on my shoulder.

'Yeah,' I murmur, but I sound like I'm choking.

8

Kole, Jay, Clarke and I leave the base after dark. Jay walks beside me and Clarke and Kole trail soundlessly behind us.

I shiver, and Jay looks at me questioningly.

'I hate this place,' I whisper, glancing around at the tall, silent buildings looming over us. The streets get quieter the closer you get to the Wall separating the Inner Sector from the Outer Sector. I know from the surveillance cameras at the power station that there's another wall, one separating the Inner Sector from the Celian City, but you can't see it from out here.

'It's not much further,' he says, ushering us between two buildings running up against the Wall. The buildings get smaller near the huge gates between the Inner and Outer Sectors, and Jay finally stops in front of a small house, completely different than any other I've seen.

He kicks the door roughly.

'Damien!' he shouts, and I glance behind us, my stomach flipping.

Kole shakes his head, as if to say Jay knows what he's doing.

A tall, thin man with rust-coloured hair and a long face pulls the door open, looking around angrily. He freezes at the sight of Jay.

'You owe me a favour,' Jay states, his switchblade smile twinkling from the lights inside the house.

Thirty minutes later we are all inside the house, and Damien is walking back into the room.

'A shipment of recruits is gonna be here in an hour,' he says gruffly, slamming the door behind him.

'Wonderful.' Jay smiles.

The rest of us hang towards the back of the small building, our hands resting on our weapons as we wait with tense muscles. Jay has something on Damien, who is apparently an Officer who keeps track of what moves between the Inner and Outer Sectors. Whatever Jay has on him, it must be big for him to risk this much, and I still don't trust it. I can't imagine anything Jay has on him to be worse than what Oasis would do if they found out Damien had snuck us through, but when I glance over at Jay's relaxed posture as he lounges in a chair, I wonder.

Kole glances over at me.

'You alright?' he asks.

I'm twitching, and I can tell it's driving him mad, but I can't stop.

'I just want to get this over with.' And back to Sophia, I add inside my head.

Kole nods gravely, looking back at the Officer standing at the door.

Now all that's left is to wait.

o o o

A siren goes off, and Damien pulls open the door to the house, muttering about being right back. I turn to Jay the minute he's gone.

'This was your great plan?' I ask, anger bubbling to the surface. We've been sitting in this room for twenty minutes, and I already feel like I'm losing my mind.

'He's not going to report us,' Kole says coolly, leaning up against the wall.

'How am I supposed to believe that? He's an Officer!'

'He owes me something,' Jay says, placing his feet on the table in front of him. 'Believe me, he won't turn us in.'

I glare at him, but I'm not in a position to argue any further.

The room is small, with a low-hanging roof and squeaky wooden floorboards that don't seem as sturdy as I'd like them to be. Across the room is a small stove, in front of that a short, rectangular wooden table, on which Jay's boots rest. There are no windows, and only two doors; one leads outside, the other into what I assume to be some kind of bedroom.

It seems strange. Amid all the dirt and grime of the Outer Sector this place, although small and badly put together, verges on quaint.

Damien returns just then, and we all sit up straighter, bodies rigid with adrenaline.

'That was a shipment of Officers out to an Official building across town. They'll be back in half an hour. After that there will be one more shipment, a food truck unloading supplies at the Officer outpost across town. You better get out before it stops, though, or you'll be found out.'

'No problem,' Jay says smoothly, and I watch the Officer's eyes snag on his feet propped on top of the table, but he doesn't say anything.

'So,' he says, glancing around the room nervously. 'What do you guys want in there?'

'None of your business—' Clarke cuts in, stepping towards him in a threatening way.

'Clarke,' Kole warns, his voice as sharp as a blade.

The Officer didn't turn on the light in the house, afraid to alert anyone to our presence, and so we sit in the dark, the silence tense as we wait.

o o o

Finally, the food truck pulls up outside the gates, and Damien goes out to distract the guards long enough for us to stow away inside. Kole stands at the door, waiting to give us a signal.

'Now,' he says, and we rush out, keeping to the shadows.

The back of the truck is empty, and the entrance just a piece of fabric concealing the truck's contents, so we load up in seconds, huddling in the dark as we wait for the truck to take off.

'Be ready to move on my say so,' Kole warns us, hunkered down so close to me I can hear his shallow breathing, though I can't see anything but his outline. The truck rumbles to life as the gates screech open, and I feel us move through it, into the Inner Sector.

I haven't been on the inside since I was seven years old. I wonder silently if anything has changed, but keep my senses focused on Kole, waiting for his signal.

After a few minutes he moves to the edge of the truck bed, and we all follow. He twitches the fabric aside, glancing outside.

'On three,' he whispers, as my heart speeds up in my chest.

'One.' I move closer to the exit.

'Two.' I feel the muscles tense in my legs, ready to jump, and the impact that comes after.

'Three.' And we leap.

9

My first thought is, *Where is everyone?* My second thought is, *I remember this place.*

I thought I had forgotten it. I thought ten years of the Dorms had wiped this place from my memory, but it hasn't. Rows and rows of perfect white mansions line perfect streets. Each house has a small garden, with roses and violets and other flowers I don't know the names of, and I try to imagine that just the other side of the Wall exists the heat and grime of the tightly packed Outer Sector, where people skitter like rats across roads cluttered in scrap and garbage.

But here, there is nothing. It's like a ghost town.

'Curfew,' Kole says, suddenly close to me, and I take an involuntary step backwards. 'We need to get moving.'

I stumble after Kole, trying to keep up with the group as my eyes linger on the houses, trying to catch every detail. Eventually I have to let it go, have to forget my fascination and focus on the mission.

Kole walks rapidly down streets like he knows them well, and we follow close behind, all eyes on the surrounding area, waiting for Officers to appear out of nowhere. Kole turns down another street, one where the houses, though still the same white buildings, are larger, grander things, with bigger gardens and sleek black cars out front.

He comes to the end of the road, facing a huge mansion, more like a castle, and the first one so far that looks completely different from the others.

'Here,' he says. I don't know why this is the place, or how he knows it. He wouldn't tell me where we were going before, but I don't care. I'm drunk on adrenaline, and my heart is pounding in my ears as memories of my childhood flit behind my eyelids, never fully settling into clarity.

These are the richest houses in Oasis, enormous, gargantuan things, each housing two to three people, but with enough room to hold hundreds. I know these houses are guarded and fitted with security systems, but Kole doesn't seem bothered. He walks up the perfectly paved path to the looming oak door, taking out two long metal rods from his pockets and inserting them into the lock. I stand behind him, watching as he fiddles with the rods, and the door finally swings open.

Before I can ask Kole about the security system, he walks straight to a panel on the wall and types something into it. I step in after him, my breath knocked from my lungs at the size of the place, at the grand staircase and marble floors. It's beyond anything I've ever imagined. The others come in behind me and Clarke shuts the door behind us.

'What are you doing?' I whisper to Kole, looking over my shoulder every few seconds, making eye contact with Jay and Clarke, as if maybe they have some kind of explanation.

Why is there no one here?

'One second.' He types in something else, and the light beside the panel turns green, showing that it's been disabled.

'How did you—'

Kole holds his fingers to his lips to shush me.

Someone's coming.

Kole pulls his gun from his waistband, and puts his back up against the corner wall. I pull my knife from my boot as all four of us huddle around the corner, our hearts in our mouths. An Officer finally comes around the corner, and Kole cracks the butt of his gun against the Officer's temple before he has time to shout.

Kole crouches by the man's crumpled body, stripping him of weapons and tucking them away on himself.

'Is this how you get guns?' I say as quietly as I can. Sound bounces off these walls disconcertingly.

'There's no one in the house,' Kole tells me, stepping over the guard's body and speaking normally.

'How do you know that?'

'They only leave one guard in the house while they're away.'

'Who? Who's away? How do you know that they're away?' I can feel that Kole doesn't want me asking, but I feel like I'm drowning in omissions.

'It doesn't matter.' He brushes me off. 'Okay. I want you all searching for documents, files, papers – anything that pertains to us or other rebellions they're tracking. We don't have long, so let's get moving. There are drawers and cabinets in the living room and in the bedrooms upstairs. I'll take the office.'

Kole disappears into the back of the house, leaving me, Jay and Clarke standing in the hallway, staring at each other. Without a word, Clarke disappears upstairs. Jay and I move into the opposite room to Kole, and I'm desperately thankful for the thick curtains pulled across the huge windows, concealing us from outside view.

There are several desks and side-tables in that first room, so I start pulling out drawers, riffling through pages as quickly as I can, the sound of Jay moving through the rooms fading into the background.

Shipping documents, law notices, payment schedules, cut-backs, Subject transfer notices—

I glance back at the slip of paper that I just set down, and go back to it.

Quincy Emerson, South Outer Sector, Subject 1712.

My blood runs cold. My eyes drop to the bottom of the page, to the authorising signature, and I see a familiar name.

OP Johnson. The Oasis President. But it's not just that. I stare at the last name, my heart throbbing in my ears.

Johnson.

Aaron Johnson.

It strikes me for the first time that Aaron's full name is Aaron Johnson. For some reason, now this hits me hard. Johnson. Why have I never thought about that before? Why did I never question that?

But it couldn't be him. I grab at the other pages, searching for a full name, until I find it printed on a Law Pass.

Leroy Johnson. Leroy Johnson. Leroy Johnson.

I see it everywhere now, printed on everything. We only ever knew him as OP Johnson. I remember Aaron telling me I couldn't meet his father. It wouldn't work out, it wouldn't be possible.

'*Leroy, he wouldn't*—' he'd stuttered. '*My father wouldn't understand.*'

The memory of it cuts into me like a shard of glass. I barely registered it when he said it, but now I'm looking at that name on document after document and my insides are cold, cold, cold.

Stupid.

I should have known. I should have known it was Aaron's father. The way the Officers treated him, the authority he always radiated, not just that of an Officer but more like … more like a prince. I thought it was because of Aaron, thought that was just how Pures were treated, that I didn't know anything about that life anymore. But it wasn't. It was because of who his father was.

But that means … this is his house. I'm in Aaron's house.

I stumble out into the hall, following the path Kole took.

Aaron lives here. This is Aaron's father's house. Aaron's father is the president of Oasis.

And then I stop.

Leroy Johnson chose me as a Subject. He was the one who wanted me taken to the Labs. He was the one who started all of this. We were told it was a lottery, a blessing bestowed out of pure chance – so why was I handpicked by the OP?

By the time I find Kole in the back room, in a musty office behind a huge desk, where he is sifting through a pile of notebooks, I can't breathe. My head feels full up with loud noises that don't belong to me, chattering and screaming until I'm overwhelmed. I can't breathe.

He leaps up from his chair, his face paling.

'What happened?' he asks, but he doesn't come towards me. He doesn't move, and I can't speak, so I just hold up the Subject notice.

His brow furrows in confusion, and he moves forward to take it from me, scanning the notice quickly.

'This is why you left?' his voice sounds uneven, a note of pain somewhere buried there, and I feel my knees go weak beneath me.

'They were trying to kill me. He was trying to kill me because of Aaron.'

Something passes across Kole's face that I can't name.

I realise in a burst who that means Aaron is, or rather what that means Aaron is. Aaron is the son of the leader of Oasis, the person who has made everyone's life hell. He is part of the twisted regime that stole our freedom and called it a blessing. Suddenly I can't say anything because I can see Kole's face, his expression twisting from disbelief to realisation to disgust.

Jay rushes into the room, pale faced, his gun in his hand.

'Someone's coming,' he says hoarsely.

Kole's eyes meet mine for only the smallest second before he opens his backpack and starts piling notebooks into it, along with several other piles of paper.

'What did you find?' I ask. I'm trying to push past what's going on in my head, but I'm struggling to do something as simple as keep air moving in and out of my lungs.

'There's a mole,' he says, zipping up his backpack roughly, and suddenly he's angry.

'In the base? Someone we know?'

'Has to be. I should have known.' He brushes past me on the way to the door, panic in the way he moves, dodging corners like bullets on his way to the hall.

I run after him, my heart in my throat, and I can hear someone at the front door, and we all freeze in the hall, staring at each other.

We shouldn't have wasted so much time, I think.

I shouldn't have spent so much time on the Subject notice, I think.

We should have been faster, I think, just as the door slides open.

10

Aaron stands in the doorway, frozen. He's backlit by the streetlights outside, just a silhouette, but I would know him anywhere. It's the same tall frame and broad shoulders that have been haunting my dreams since I escaped. But we've caught him off-guard. Kole has his gun aimed at Aaron's head, and there is a stalemate.

'Get out of our way, Aaron,' Kole says quietly, too calm.

I glance sidelong at Kole, trying to swallow around the lump in my throat. Kole knows Aaron. I can tell by the way Aaron's face twists at the sight of him. You don't give that look to a stranger.

'Kole,' Jay says slowly, looking for some kind of signal, some kind of clue as to how to handle this. I can feel the others behind me, advancing on Aaron slowly.

Aaron looks past Kole, directly at me. I feel the weight of his gaze like a physical thing.

'Hello, Quincy,' he says, softly, his voice like warm honey, making everything he says sound golden and powerful.

I see Kole's shoulders tense.

My heart is firing so rapidly in my chest I'm afraid he'll hear it. I'm afraid he'll smell my fear, that he will sense that I am still afraid of him.

'Put your hands above your head.' Kole's voice is deathly cold, and Aaron turns a mocking smile on him, raising his arms at the same time.

'Yes sir, Officer,' he smiles, and he's too comfortable. It's as if he doesn't care, as if it doesn't touch him.

But then, nothing ever really touched Aaron. He was like the

Celian City, so buried in walls and barbed-wire that he couldn't find his way out even if he wanted to.

Kole takes a tentative step forward, gesturing with his hand to Clarke.

'Get the rope out of your bag,' he says calmly.

Kole takes another step towards Aaron, the gun still aimed at him as he approaches cautiously.

Aaron begins to turn around, but at the last second his hand comes down, catching Kole's, twisting the gun from his grip and sending it flying across the room. Before anyone can take a breath he catches Kole by the back of his head as he brings his leg up, cracking his kneecap into Kole's face. But before anyone else can move, Kole threads his arm under Aaron's knee, hooking his foot behind Aaron's ankle and kicking his feet from beneath him. Aaron hits the floor with a sickening crack, spine and skull hitting the marble floor one after another.

Jay and Clarke descend on Aaron in quick succession, rolling him onto his front and tying his hands behind him as Kole stumbles away, blood streaming down his face.

'Kole,' I say, reaching for him, but he shrugs me off, running his hand under his bleeding nose.

'I'm fine. Get him up.'

Clarke and Jay heave Aaron to his feet, but he just smiles, as if nothing has happened.

'Still the same, I see,' he says, as if passing judgement on Kole.

My eyes flit between Kole and Aaron as they glare at each other, but I can't read anything off them.

Kole glares, and Aaron grins back at him, but I know Aaron too well to think he doesn't hate Kole just as much as Kole hates him, it's just that Aaron doesn't show it on his face. He shows it in his posture, in his hands flexing behind his back, in the way his feet shift beneath him.

Kole picks his gun up off the floor, darting a glance around the room to make sure everyone is still here, and nods towards the door.

'Let's go,' he says.

'With him?' I ask, my throat tight as Aaron's knowing smile turns on me.

'We don't have any other option,' Kole snaps, jerking his gun towards the door. 'Let's go,' he repeats, and we file out into the half-light, dragging Aaron along with us.

11

'You know, I could just scream,' Aaron points out as we jog through the streets, paranoid glances flying around in every direction as we wait for a troop of Officers to descend upon us. But this is the Inside. They don't patrol the streets waiting for someone to step out of line. There is a curfew, and it's expected to be kept, no questions asked.

'And we could just shoot you,' Clarke snaps, pushing him forward.

As the gate comes into view we all go quiet. Kole hunkers down at the corner of one of the houses, concealed by a wall on one side and a hedge on the other, with a good view of the road in front of us. We follow him in, and we are pressed close together, and Clarke's gun is pressed to the base of Aaron's skull and I watch him as he coolly surveys the situation.

Several minutes pass, and when nothing happens I begin to get antsy. I bite my lip, buckling and unbuckling the strap on my boot with shaking hands as my eyes bounce between Kole and Aaron, Aaron and Kole, back and forth until I feel dizzy. Kole hasn't looked at Aaron since we left the OP's house, but Aaron won't stop staring holes in the side of Kole's head.

When we hear the rumble of an engine moving up the road, my hand reflexively clamps down on my knife as I shift my weight, waiting for Kole's signal. The truck, a similar one to the one we came in on, only bigger, pulls to a stop as it waits for the gates to open. Damien promised he would stall the truck long enough for us to get inside, but my heart still thumps loudly in my ears as I watch the truck roll to a full stop.

Then I see Damien stepping out of the truck, walking around the front of it and towards the guard-post. I can hear them talking from here, not well enough to know what they're saying, but Damien is gesturing wildly, pointing at himself and then at the Officer.

And this is it. Our opening.

Kole moves first, quiet as a cat across the street, and then Clarke and Jay, pulling Aaron with them. I am the last to cross over, and by the time we do Kole has helped Clarke and Jay heave Aaron into the truck.

We are very still, hardly breathing, our backs pushed up against the side of the truck as we wait for the next move. I can't stop looking at Aaron, waiting for him to do something, waiting for him to get us all killed, but he doesn't move.

The Officers return, and for a moment they move around the back of the truck, and the fabric of the entrance twitches.

But they just brushed against it, and within seconds the truck rumbles to life as the gates screech open, releasing us back into the Outer Sector.

12

We pull Aaron through the streets of the Outer Sector, and no one bats an eye. Kole catches him by the collar of his perfectly pressed shirt, holding a gun to the small of his back as we come up to Nails' house.

'Go up ahead of us,' Kole says, gesturing for us to climb. We do, Jay, then a reluctant Clarke, and then me. Kole pushes Aaron to climb ahead of him, and Clarke aims a gun at him from above.

'I'm flattered, really, but I'm not going to be getting anywhere with these,' Aaron says, gesturing to his bound hands.

'No,' Kole snaps.

'I can't climb with my hands tied together.'

'Fine.' Kole unravels the knots holding Aaron's hands together. 'Climb.'

Aaron does, with no more objection, and within a minute we are all standing together, tightly packed onto the fire escape.

Jay knocks on the door loudly, and it's pulled open by a frazzled-looking Kerrin. She falls back a step at the sight of us, and we swarm into the small, humid room.

'What's going on?' Kerrin asks, her eyes widening at the sight of Aaron, whose hands are being re-tied by Kole.

'Where's Sophia?' I ask, glancing at the door, ignoring Kerrin's question.

'She's downstairs,' she says, shaking her head in confusion.

I jog down the stairs, leaving the others behind.

I need to see her.

When I get downstairs she's standing above Lauren, who's

reading something out loud to her from one of Ly's books. My steps freeze, and for a moment I just stare at her, my breath slowing. She lifts a hand to tuck a lock of blonde hair behind her ear, and my heart feels like it's going to explode.

'Hey, Sophia,' I say, trying to sound casual as I approach.

She looks up, shaken out of her thoughts by the sound of my voice. 'Oh, you're home.' She smiles, and it tugs at me, and I don't know what's happening to me.

I can hear them coming downstairs with Aaron, and I try to block them out.

'You okay? How'd you get on while I was gone?'

'Fine.' She shrugs. 'Lauren was reading to me.'

Lauren looks up, and she blushes, smiling at me.

'Sophia,' I say, crouching down to look into her eyes. I realise now that they're not actually exactly like Bea's – they're a paler shade of blue, with flecks of gold. 'I have to do something, but I'll come find you in a bit, okay?'

'Okay.' She looks a little lost in this big room, and all I want to do is stay with her, but I need to take care of something first.

o o o

I find Jay tying Aaron to a chair in the smallest room, using it as an impromptu prison.

'I need a minute with him,' I say, trying to keep my voice even.

Jay glances up, about to open his mouth, but something in my expression stops him.

'Be quick,' he says, passing me by on the way to the door.

I don't look at Aaron until he's gone. When I do, I feel my jaw lock into place, my heart racing at the sight of him. In the harsh overhead lighting his hair doesn't look golden anymore, and I wonder if this is what he looks like through this new lens, if in our world, maybe Aaron isn't anything but a broken boy in an even more broken world.

But it's fear that's causing that tremble in my hands now, not pity.

And then he lifts his head and smiles, and his eyes are still too blue and he's still too perfect, and my resolve shudders.

'Quincy,' he says, like I'm coming home.

But I'm not, I remind myself, shaking my head.

'I'm not here to have a conversation with you,' I say as clearly as I can manage.

'Oh, you're not, are you?' He smiles, looking amused. 'What are you here for, then?'

'To tell you something.'

'Go on.' He shrugs, and it's not fair that he is tied to a chair and I am standing above him with a knife at my hip, and he's still the one who's comfortable, still the one with the power.

'I don't know what we're going to do with you,' I tell him truthfully. 'But I do know this: if you ever come near me or anyone I love again, I will kill you. Understand?'

'Not really,' he says, cocking his head to the side. 'Because I thought I was someone you loved, and besides, I've never done anything to anyone you've loved.'

The words fall in the pit of my stomach, heavy in their truth. Because I didn't love Bea, and for some reason that makes me feel guilty.

'But I suppose who you're really talking about is Kole, right?' He smiles knowingly. 'You forget that I know you. I can tell when you care about someone. Or maybe,' he says, and now his smile isn't knowing but something else entirely, something sharp and precise and cruel, 'maybe you mean that little blonde thing I saw in the pit you seem to be living in. She looks awfully like—'

His words are cut off by my knife to his throat.

'Don't you dare. *Don't you dare.*' I'm breathing heavily, and I can hear my blood pumping in my ears as my vision blurs red.

'What you always forget, Quincy,' he says, infuriatingly calm, 'is that we are all half angel, half devil. You can try to repress one side, but it's always there, lurking somewhere under your skin.' He is so close to me I can feel the warmth radiating off him, feel his breath against my cheek. 'You can pretend you are the exception, or that Kole is, but you know deep down it's not true. You can't blame me for being the only one who accepts reality.'

'I hope you rot in hell,' I spit, and sheath my knife, abruptly pulling away from him and moving for the door.

'There it is.' He grins, sounding pleased.

I should just keep going. I should ignore him, but I can't.

'*What?*'

'The devil in you was always my favourite part.'

I slam the door on my way out.

13

I go upstairs, as far from him as I can get without leaving the building. My skin crawls and I feel sick, feel the wrongness of him down to my bones. I knew he was manipulating me, watching me squirm as he poked me into a rage, and somehow I was still helpless against it.

He can still get under my skin, and it makes me feel weak.

'Quincy.' Ly appears out of nowhere, making me jump backwards, my hand automatically reaching for the knife at my hip.

'Ly, you frightened me,' I say, my voice dead.

'Why the hell is the OP's son downstairs?' he demands, and I take a step away from him.

'Ly, it's complicated—'

'You understand that he's going to get us all killed, right?'

'I'll get him out before anything happens, Ly, I swear.'

'No,' he says, and he steps very close to me. 'That's not good enough. I want you both gone. *NOW*.'

'I can't—'

'I WANT YOU OUT OF HERE,' Ly screams into my face, half raging, half hysterical, just before someone pulls him away from me, flinging him across the room.

Kole presses Ly up against the far wall, his forearm pushed against Ly's throat. He's washed his face of any residual blood from his fight with Aaron, but there's a bruise beginning to bloom across his nose, only serving as a reminder of what he's capable of.

'Kole!' I call, but he can't hear me.

'What the hell do you think you're doing?' he shouts into Ly's face, and Ly tries to pull away, but Kole has him cornered.

'She brought the OP's son—'

'We didn't have a *choice*!' Kole yells.

'She knows him,' Ly spits, wriggling against Kole's hold. 'They know each other. *She's a spy*!'

'You don't know anything about her,' Kole hisses, catching Ly's jaw in his hand and forcing Ly to look straight at him. 'And the next time you want to accuse her of being a traitor, you might want to remember who I am, and what I can do to you first.'

Kole throws Ly from him, turning away from him like he's too disgusted to make eye contact.

'Are you okay?' he asks, facing me. His tone changes like the flip of a coin, but I can hear the anger somewhere muffled beneath his concern.

'I'm fine,' I say, shaking my head. My throat feels tight. 'I'm fine.'

'Quincy, you're shaking.' And I am, and he's right, and suddenly his arms are around me, and he smells like the soap in the shower and he's so warm, almost too warm.

But I'm not shaking because I'm scared.

I pull away, pushing him away, and he looks shocked, and I feel a flash of something like anger, but it's brighter than anger, and hurts more.

'I need to talk to you,' I say quietly, trying to calm my breathing.

'Okay, but—'

'No,' I say, and I reach out, yanking open the door to the stairs. 'Now.'

14

I pull him into one of the empty bedrooms, slamming the door behind me.

'Stop,' he says, catching my arm. 'Quincy, stop. What's wrong?'

But I can't. My heart is like a jackhammer in my chest, and it wasn't until I saw him with Ly, the way he pushed him up against the wall, the way he sounded like he could snap his neck in a heartbeat, that I realised what was going on. And my mind starts piecing together a million little otherwise forgettable moments, and I don't know how I'm supposed to feel, and I'm on the other side of the room, pulling my hair away from my neck because I feel like the walls are closing in on top of me, like the world is suddenly small and tight and all around me.

'Quincy, I said *stop!*' He pulls me around to face him. 'You need to calm down. You're going to have a panic attack if you don't calm down.'

I lean over, trying to catch my breath.

'Are you okay?' he asks after a minute of silence.

'I'm fine.'

I try to take a steadying breath, but he lays a hand on my shoulder and it feels like he electrocuted me. I push away from him, my heart hammering.

'What's wrong?' he asks, and now he sounds scared.

'How did you know that was where the files you needed were going to be?' I ask, my voice trembling.

'Quincy ...'

'Just say it, Kole. Stop lying to me.'

'I've never lied to you,' he says gravely.

'Haven't you?' I ask, turning on him. 'Why do you know Aaron? How did you know how to disable the security system? What is going on with you, Kole?'

He looks at me, the muscle in his jaw ticking, and he looks like he's fighting with himself.

'Kole, tell me.'

'I grew up in that house,' he blurts.

I feel cold, I don't want to know this, but I can't afford *not* to know this.

'And Aaron?' My voice is unsteady, and I try to swallow the lump in my throat. 'How do you know him?'

'He's my brother.'

I stumble backwards, and I can't pull air into my lungs. I can't cope with this. I can't cope with all of this at once, but it was me who asked for these answers.

It was my brain that was already working this out.

'I haven't seen him in years, I swear,' Kole breaks in, interrupting my thoughts. 'I barely know him anymore.'

'And Johnson?' I croak.

'My father,' he whispers.

'Why did you leave?' I ask. Before this I assumed he left for the same reason everyone left, because Oasis was cruel and he couldn't take it anymore. I assumed he'd left to save his life. But he's from the Inside. The President's son. What reason could he possibly have for escape? He would have lived like royalty, been untouchable, just like Aaron. So what does that leave?

'Quincy.' It sounds like a prayer, a supplication.

'Why did you leave? I need to know.'

'Why did you leave, Quincy? Everyone has a history, everyone left something—'

'I left because they were going to *kill me*, Kole.'

He's pale, and his hands are shaking at his sides and I am bursting at the seams, my blood racing in my veins.

'I killed for them,' he whispers, his voice thin and desperate. He looks like he's going to throw up. 'If they needed someone to stop being a problem, I took care of it. I gave them everything I had, Quincy, but I didn't want to. You have to believe me—' He comes towards me, but I've stopped listening to him, and I stumble backwards towards the door.

No.

No. No. No. No. No.

My vision blurs, tears burning down my face as I fumble for the handle, my hands shaking too badly to catch hold of it properly.

'Quincy, *please*—' He sounds awful, like a dying person, but I am the one being strangled. His words coil themselves around my throat and pull until I can't breathe.

'*No, no, no, no, no.*'

The door flies open, finally, and I run, barrelling through halls and up the stairs and out the door, my breath ripping through me as the sounds of his calls fade away, and I disappear into the filth and the cold of the Outer Sector, and nothing ever changes, it just puts on a different mask, and the only things I can count on are me and these rotting streets.

15

I find myself back on the scrap heap on the outside of town, my knees pulled up to my chest as I look out across the Celian City. The light seems dull now, after an hour of crying. I think, after a while, I stopped crying about Kole and started crying about something much bigger and more nebulous.

Like the fact that this is the world we live in, that these are the kinds of secrets we keep from each other. It seems stupid to me to cry about something like that, something so uselessly helpless as the state of a world I have no control over.

I rest my head on my knees now that the tears are gone, and my thoughts feel muffled and clear at the same time as I breathe in the familiar air of the Outer Sector.

When I hear someone scaling the scrap pile, I know who it is without looking back.

'Hey,' Jay says, sitting down beside me.

'Hi,' I murmur, shifting to make room for him. I wait to hear what he's going to say, but he doesn't say anything.

Minutes tick by, and he doesn't say a word. I glance up at him, and he's staring out across the Celian City, hands looped casually around his knees.

'Just say it,' I tell him, every muscle in my body tense for whatever it is he's waiting to say.

'Say what?'

'Whatever it is you came out here to say.'

'Honestly, I don't know what I came out here to say.' He shrugs, still staring out over the Wall.

For a few seconds I'm shocked into silence.

'Are you sure you should be out here?' he asks.

'The Officers don't pass here. And besides, I'm—,' I glance at my shoulder, '6312 now. Quincy doesn't exist anymore.'

He seems to think that's good enough, because he doesn't say anything else for a long time.

'Where is he?' I ask. I wish I didn't have to. I wish the question wasn't burning me up from the inside out, but it is.

'To answer your real question, he's pretty ripped up,' Jay says coolly. 'But he's ripped up every time he sees a puppy get kicked, so

I wouldn't worry too much about it.'

A burst of laughter escapes me, and I slap my hand over my mouth to cover it, my eyes widening as Jay flashes me a grin.

'I've known Kole for a really, really long time, and there are two things about him I know are true,' he says, looking at me properly for the first time. 'One, that he takes everything too seriously, and two, that he's a good person.'

'Ah,' I respond, nodding my head knowingly. 'There it is.'

'There what is?'

'You trying to convince me. Do you know what he told me in there?' I ask, my voice rising.

'I know all of it,' Jay says, and there's something cold about him all of a sudden. 'I knew about it while he worked for Oasis.'

I go very, very still.

'Yeah, I did,' he says, as if challenging me to say something. 'And it killed him every moment he was doing it. But he thought he had to. He thought that he was protecting Oasis. And I guess he was.'

'You're not going to convince me he's a good person. He killed people, Jay. For *them*.'

'And he knew something was off,' he says heatedly, turning his entire body to face me. 'For a long time he knew what he was doing couldn't be right, and he kept doing it, because he didn't know anything else, he didn't know anything but serving Oasis. But he is a good person, Quincy. He's a lot better than most of us.'

'Most of us didn't murder people,' I spit.

'Are you trying to tell me that you don't have things you regret?' Jay asks, and his voice sounds caught between anger and sympathy. An image of Bea flashes up in my mind, and another, newer image. This one of Sophia, the girl whose family I stole with my own selfishness. 'We all have things we regret. And no one regrets them more than Kole.'

I don't say anything, my emotions rocketing between indignant anger and a niggling understanding that I don't want to acknowledge.

'What do you regret?' I ask Jay.

'A lot of things,' Jay says, the muscle in his jaw jumping. 'A lot of things.'

'I got a girl killed,' I tell him, and it feels like falling from a roof, like forgetting gravity for the sake of a single moment of relief.

'Got a girl killed, or killed a girl?' he asks, and he seems so unfazed, I actually have to look at him to make sure he's serious.

'Does it matter?' I ask, looking back down at my hands.

'Of course it matters.'

So I tell him. I tell him about being chosen as a Subject, I tell him about the fight at the power station, and how I was put into containment, how I was Branded. I even show him the brand on my shoulder, which isn't painful anymore, but the raised scar tissue serves as a reminder of something I never want to think about again. I tell him about the escape plan, about enlisting Bea, and about the actual escape. I tell him about Aaron finding us, about him threatening Bea.

And I tell him the choice I made, and how easy it was to put my life before hers.

He just sits there, and I can't tell if his lack of reaction is painful or calming. I need to tell someone what happened that day, if only to relieve the pain in my chest I've been carrying around ever since then, like the words are a physical presence, weighing me down.

I finish by telling him about Sophia, about how I found her as if that would make up for Bea's death, but I know now that it can't. That nothing can.

'And you really think,' he says slowly, as if he's picking his words, 'that after all of that, there's no more to Kole's story?'

'What?'

'You tell me you killed a girl, and then you tell me all of that, but you can't consider that maybe Kole has a story like that, too?'

I go quiet, staring into nothing as I think.

'We all have a story, Quincy,' he says, standing up. 'Maybe you should let him tell his.'

16

I find Kole downstairs in the store room, going over the supplies with Nails. When he sees me he freezes, his eyes widening.

'Are you okay?' he asks, unsure, his voice unsteady.

I take a deep breath, closing my eyes and tightening my hands into fists, Jay's voice replaying in my head.

'I'm ready to let you explain.'

o o o

Kole and I find an empty room, and we sit down on the floor across from each other, though Kole won't make eye contact.

He starts without any urging.

'My Father was a military man,' he says, raising his knees to his chest in a gesture I still find out of place. 'That's what I grew up with. That's what he was before he became President, and that's what he was at his core, afterwards.'

Kole doesn't look at me as he speaks.

'After he became President, he married my mother, because his advisors thought it wise to have a perfect little family for everyone else to replicate. A year after they were married, my mother became pregnant with me. My father was happy; he'd always wanted a son. But he'd been cheating on my mother, and the woman he'd been with was about to have a child of her own.'

'Aaron,' I breathe.

He glances at me, reading my expression, but quickly goes back to staring at his boots.

'Yes. When Aaron was born, his mother came to my father, asking him to take Aaron in. She thought he would have a better life with us than with her. She was Pure, but she had a job, and she didn't have anyone to look after a child while she was at work. My father wouldn't take him, though. He was afraid that if the public found out, he'd be taken out of Office. So he paid her to take care of the kid.

'I was born a few months later, early, and a little too fragile for my father's tastes. He set about toughening me up. When I was four, he bought me a knife for my birthday. My mother cried and cried but wouldn't say anything about it, because she was too afraid of him. By the time my next birthday rolled around, I was better with a knife than any man in my father's force, and my father was satisfied that he was doing the right thing by me.'

He leans forward, showing me his hands, the scars running across his knuckles and palms.

'A lot of these are from that knife. This one,' he says, showing me a particularly long, raised scar running along his palm, 'is from the day I got it. I didn't realise how sharp it was.' He shrugs, as if this is normal.

As if any of this is normal.

'Anyway,' he shakes his head, clearing away memories. 'Another year rolls by, I'm turning six, and my father comes home with Aaron. His mother had died a week earlier, and when my father's cheque to her bounced back with an acknowledgement of her death, he decided to take Aaron in, under the guise of a charity ward.

'Aaron was my antithesis. He was always angry, always ready to snap, and fiercely competitive. He was naturally better built than me, but where he beat me with strength I beat him with skill. My father started pitting us against each other, because he thought it would make us improve faster. Aaron became obsessive, but no matter how hard he worked, he was the secret shame of the family. Inside he was treated the same as all of us, but outside of our home he wasn't to be seen or heard.

'Now I'm thirteen. My skills far outweigh any of my father's Officers, and I'm better, even, than Aaron, who up until this point had been my only real challenge. As my father's focus lands solely on me, the competition he started between us becomes almost unbearable. Aaron hates me. He believes that I don't deserve any of the attention my father is giving me, and that the lack of any human affection he's receiving is entirely my fault.

'Now I'm sixteen. I've been convinced we're under national threat, that the rebels outside of Oasis are planning on burning it to the ground, with everyone inside it. I've been convinced that the only way to save the lives of everyone inside Oasis' walls is to take out the people who threaten it. So I do, and I'm good at it. I hate every second of it, and every kill makes me feel closer to losing my mind, but I still think I'm doing it to help people, so I keep doing whatever my father tells me.

'But the problem was, it never stopped. The threat never left, and the more people I took out, the more targets I was handed. I couldn't eat, couldn't sleep, because all I could see were the faces of the people I'd killed. I knew I was doing something wrong, I knew it in my bones, but I couldn't stop. I couldn't let my father down.'

He goes quiet for a moment, and I can't tell if that's it. I can't tell if he's done but I can't move my limbs, frozen in shock as I watch a range of emotions pass across his face.

He stretches out his wrist to me, and for a moment I don't realise what he's doing, until I see the tattoo on the inside of his wrist.

'Thirty-two Xs,' he says, his voice so thin I can barely hear it, but the pain I can hear. I hear that like an echo of the feeling in my chest. 'Thirty-two Xs on the inside of my left wrist, for the thirty-two people I killed while I was inside Oasis.'

I can't breathe.

'Why—' My breath won't come back to me, but I push on. 'Why did you leave?'

He closes his eyes briefly.

'I found records of a conversation my father had with the captain of a unit of Officers out west, about restarting the programme.'

I look at him, my eyebrows drawing together in confusion.

'I was the programme, Quincy. Me and Aaron. And we were successful. When I found out that they planned on doing that to other people, to other children—' He takes a shaky breath, and he looks like he's going to throw up. 'Everyone has a breaking point.'

'And that was yours?' I say, my voice a raspy whisper.

'That was mine.' The look on his face is too many different kinds of heartbroken for me to process. 'Later, once I escaped, I figured out why they needed people like me. The rebels are rising up, everywhere, not just out here. *Inside* Oasis. Sometimes inside Oasis' *elite*. And when someone with that much power was about to start spilling secrets, or if they were thought to be aiding any form of rebellion – well then, there was me and Aaron. We took care of that problem.'

And that is it. That is Kole's story, that is his history. I can't decide if Jay was right, if this was the right thing to do, because his words crash around inside me, ripping things apart and putting them back together, and I can feel things shifting inside me that I don't think I'm ready for.

I look back at Kole, and I feel like I'm looking in a mirror, and more than anything, *that's* what scares me.

17

I dream of Kole, of shadows and shattered glass and bullet casings, of shaking hands and the metallic taste of fear in the back of my throat, the sound of Sophia screaming in the back of my mind.

No.

I shoot straight upwards, my heart in my throat as I realise the screaming wasn't a dream, but Sophia, twisting in her sleep, her face tight with fear.

'Sophia. *Sophia*. Sophia!' I shake her awake, and her eyes snap open, sitting up straight as she quickly takes in the room, searching for something that's not there.

'It's okay.' I try to sound calm, but my own heart is still pounding from the sound of her screams. 'It's okay. You're safe.'

She shakes her head, closing her eyes tightly as she pulls her knees to her chest, hiding herself.

'Sophia,' I say gently, placing a hand on her knee. I take one of her tight fists in my hands. 'Sophia, you're safe now. I promise.'

'You can't promise anything,' she mutters, still shaking her head, causing strands of her pale blonde hair to come out from her ponytail, flying around her head.

'Hey.' I pull her close to me, and my voice sounds intense, even to me. 'I promise I will keep you safe.'

She pushes her face into my neck, and the sound of her crying rips my heart in half.

'Why do you care about me?' she sobs, her small fists knotted in my T-shirt.

'It's complicated.' My voice is a hiccup and a gasp, like the sound of seams ripping.

'I don't understand what's happening,' she says, sniffing.

'I know.' My voice cracks as I rub her hair. 'I know.'

o o o

An hour later she's calm again, and her tears have dried completely. I kneel down next to her, handing her the cup of water I went to get a moment ago.

'How are you feeling?' I ask, making my voice gentle.

'I'm fine,' she says, and I almost smile.

I sit down beside her, looping my arms around my knees. I insisted we were put in a room away from the others, half because of Sophia's nightmares, half because I'm paranoid.

'When did you see her last?' I ask, fiddling with the hem of my T-shirt.

'About nine months ago.'

She doesn't sound bothered by the question. I think she's already stronger than me.

'What about your parents?'

'They died when I was three, so I don't really remember them.'

'Bea was your only family?'

'Yeah. I was fostered in the Inner Sector until I was tested. Then I was put in the same Dorms as Bea. But a few months ago some girls were picking on me, and Bea tried to stop them. She got sent to the South Dorms to keep her out of trouble. I got into trouble on purpose, so they'd let me go there with her, but by the time I got there ...'

'They didn't notify you?' I ask, horrified.

'No. Not until I asked where she was when I got to the South Dorms.'

I don't have any response for her. I stay quiet, trying to imagine what that was like for her, to find out that the last of her family had been dead for weeks and no one had even thought to tell her.

That is so much more than a child should ever have to deal with.

'How old are you?' I ask, trying to change the subject.

'Ten,' she says, tilting her chin up the way Bea did when I asked her that same question before any of this started. 'Well, almost ten. It's my birthday soon.'

I laugh at her gently, and she smiles back at me.

'You can call me Sophi,' she says, yawning. 'I prefer it when people call me Sophi. That's what Bea used to call me.'

I don't respond, but I do pull her closer to me, my heart twisting in my chest.

She falls back to sleep like that, her head on my shoulder, pressed up against the corner wall, and I feel something in my chest move. It feels like watching the foundation of a huge building shift, staring in horror as the whole thing comes crumbling down. That's what it feels like. It feels like that shift, and now I'm left waiting for everything to fall apart.

'It's hard,' a voice says, a silhouette appearing at the door. 'Losing family. It's hard when you're that young.' Clarke steps into the room.

'Why are you up?' I ask quietly, trying not to wake Sophi.

'No one in this place sleeps anymore,' Clarke says. She comes down and sits across from me, her legs folded beneath her.

'Why are you here?' I ask, and she doesn't flinch. It's one of the things that I admire about Clarke, that she doesn't mind when people ask her blunt questions.

I suppose, considering how blunt she is, that you have to learn to take what you give.

'I heard her screaming,' she says, her hands reaching out as if to touch Sophi's hair, then pulling back. 'I was like her, once. I know what it's like to lose someone you love.'

'Who did you lose?' My voice is small, but this time, not for Sophi's sake. For Clarke's sake, because she doesn't speak like this to me.

Doesn't speak like this to anyone.

'Everyone,' she says, and she sounds hazy from sleeplessness, as if she wouldn't be saying all of this if exhaustion wasn't clouding her brain. 'My entire family. All in one night.'

'How?' My voice cracks.

'My parents escaped Oasis years and years ago. I grew up on the Outside. For a long time, it was safe. Escapees were few and far between, and Oasis assumed they'd die the minute they got outside. But word got back to Oasis that colonies were being set up, and that's when the raids began. Our village hadn't seen any attacks yet, only heard about them from travellers, but I went out hunting one day, and when I came back, the entire camp was ransacked. Everyone, all of them, dead, just like that. But that's what Oasis does. It takes everything from you until you don't have anything left but it.' Her tone has recovered some of its familiar edge, as if I could cut myself on her words, but suddenly she softens again. 'I had a little brother. Parents. I thought we were invincible. They taught me that we were invincible, but we weren't.'

'Can I ask you something?' I say quietly, running my hand over Sophia's hair.

'Yeah, sure,' she says, shifting uncomfortably.

'Why did you take your family's name?'

Her eyes shoot up, searching my face intently, then dropping back down to Sophia's sleeping form.

'How did you know?' Her voice is rough with emotion.

'Lacey told me,' I say quietly, trying not to let my voice shake.

'My father used to tell me stories. The old stories, from before Oasis. Of soldiers, but not soldiers – knights, he called them. If one was killed, another one would avenge him, but always with the knight's own sword.'

I am quiet and still, and Clarke looks as if she isn't talking to me anymore, but to herself. As if she's recited these words so many times, they have become a prayer in her mind.

An oath.

'Clarke was my family's name. When I take Oasis down, I'll do it with their name, like a sword.' She breathes. 'And when Oasis burns to the ground, they will know whose deaths they are paying the price for.'

18

There is a fragile calm in the base the next day, and no one says it out loud, but I can tell everyone's holding their breath, waiting for something to happen. Kole's been arguing with Nails all morning, trying to convince him to ignore what he saw yesterday. And what he saw was the OP's son being forced at gunpoint into *his* hideout.

I walk through the halls and Nails' refugees glare their angry resentment at me as I pass, and it's clear where we stand. We went from uneasy welcome to outright animosity with a single mistake.

A single, deadly mistake.

I've only seen Ly once since the incident upstairs, and the look on his face was so enraged, I immediately swerved out of his way to avoid him. Even Kerrin, who's been reasonably friendly, got up and left when I arrived in the common room this morning.

I'm sitting in that exact spot, Sophi by my side on the couch, when Kole comes into the room. His hair is standing on end like he's been running his fingers through it constantly, and his eyes are a little too wide.

Jay stands up from where he was sitting a moment ago, and I automatically follow him to where Kole stands.

'What did he say?'

'We have three days,' Kole says, the muscles in his jaw ticking. I can see him drawing into his own mind, planning.

'Three days to get rid of him?' I ask.

'Three days to get out of here entirely. All of us,' he says, looking at me for the first time. 'We need to work fast. Jay, go find Clarke, we need to figure out what we're going to do.'

I glance back at Sophi, who is flipping through the pages of an Oasis history book, and I try not to laugh at the irony of it.

'Lauren?' I say, louder, so that she can hear me from across the room.

She looks up. 'Yeah?'

'Can you keep an eye on Sophi for a bit?'

'Sure.'

I cross the room so I can speak to her without the others listening in.

'I'm sorry I keep leaving you with Sophi,' I say as quietly as I can, hoping Sophi won't overhear us. 'I just … I don't want her near this stuff.'

'No.' She shakes her head. 'I understand. It's no problem. I'm happy to do it. She reminds me of my sister.' She cuts herself short as her voice tightens at the mention of her sister.

I place my hand on her shoulder. We have three days to get out of here. Lauren might not know it yet, but unless she's willing to stay here in Oasis on her own, she's not going to see her sister. Not this time anyway.

But then I see her struggling to keep the smile on her face, her lips trembling as she fights the tears rising in her eyes, and I wonder if she does know after all.

'Go,' she says, shaking her head, blinking the tears from her eyes. 'It's fine. Go do what you have to do.'

'Thank you,' I whisper sincerely.

'Quincy?' Kole calls from the other end of the room, and when I glance back, Clarke is standing beside them, ready to go.

'Sophi, I'll just be gone for a few minutes, okay?' I murmur, walking back around the couch to face her. She nods, her blue eyes quietly assessing me. 'You don't need anything, do you?' I'm buying time. I wanted one day, one day where I could just sit with her, talk to her, get to know her.

She shakes her head, because she doesn't need anything, and Clarke coughs impatiently behind me and I'm pulled back into the reality of our situation.

If I ever want a chance to get to know her, I need to deal with this. Now.

I follow the others down to the room Nails gave them at the end of the corridor, right across from mine, and Kole pushes the door open to let us in. It's empty save for the mattresses on the floor, which Kole immediately sits down on, and then Jay across from him. I sit on Clarke's mattress and she sits beside me, and we all face Kole.

'Nails said we have three days to get out of here,' he starts, filling everyone in. 'So we need to figure out exactly what we're planning to do. Namely, we need to figure out what we're going to do with Aaron.'

'I say we interrogate him,' Jay says, pulling a knife from his boot. I wonder if it keeps him focused, rolling that blade between his hands. I've yet to have a serious discussion with him where he hasn't pulled that thing out.

'That won't work,' Kole says, leaning forward to rest his elbows against his knees.

'How do you know?' Jay demands.

Kole flashes him a cold look, and Jay's mouth snaps shut.

'We need to use him to our advantage,' Kole says, and he looks at me, his eyebrows knitting together.

'What do you mean?' I ask quietly.

'I mean, we came here to stop the attacks. There's only one way to do that, and Aaron's the only way we'll get inside.'

'You're suggesting we go inside? What? Inside the Celian City?' Clarke asks, her eyes widening.

'I'm suggesting we go after the real problem here. I'm suggesting we go after Johnson.'

'And do what with him?' she asks, incredulous. 'He's not going to be any more susceptible to torture than Aaron is.'

'I'm not suggesting we torture him. I'm suggesting we kill him,' Kole says, careful to leave any form of emotion from his voice.

'*Kill him*? How the hell are we supposed to do that? He's crawling with security.'

'You're forgetting I'm his son,' Kole says pointedly. I repress a shiver at the coldness in his voice. 'And more to the point, so is Aaron. We can use Aaron to get us inside, get us close to Johnson, and then we kill him. Johnson is the head of Oasis. Cut off the head ...' Kole shrugs. 'It's our best bet and, more importantly, it's our only option.'

Jay sits forward, his face lighting up. 'Could it work? Do you think it could actually work?'

Kole glances at me, and we stare at each other for a long moment.

'It might,' he says, his knee jumping as he stares at the floor, thinking rapidly. 'It might.'

19

I wake up in the middle of the night, unable to get back asleep again, and find myself wandering the halls of the base, my mind foggy and confused. The shadows on the walls look like wraiths, and when Kole comes up behind me, I almost jump out of my skin.

'Hey,' he says, examining my face in the dark. 'You okay?'

'Yeah, I'm fine, I'm fine.'

After we decided to use Aaron to get to Johnson, we started planning, and we didn't go to bed until late. I was only asleep for a few hours before my own tangled mind woke me yet again.

'You know you've said you're fine practically every time you're not okay, right?' His voice sounds strange, and his speech is slower than normal.

I turn away from him. I can feel the walls closing in on top of me, and thoughts start running through my mind so fast I feel dizzy, leaning out to steady myself against the wall.

What are we supposed to do with Aaron?

How am I supposed to keep Sophia safe when he's here, lurking in that room, waiting to strike?

What if we get found out?

How are we going to get out of Oasis?

What if Sophia doesn't want to leave?

What if we all end up dead before we even have a chance?

I tug my hair at the roots, ready to scream the entire building down.

I want to go back. We should never have come in the first place. I should have left the Officers alone. We should have just run away when Kole told us to.

'Quincy.' Kole comes over to me. 'Quincy, stop.'

'What? Stop what?'

'Stop panicking. I can tell when you're panicking.'

'I'm not panicking. I'm fine.'

'Hey, don't lie to me,' he says softly, reaching out and grabbing my hand. 'What is it? What's going on in your head?'

I stare down at his hands, wrapped around mine, and I should pull away, but I can't. He's warm, and I didn't realise how cold this hallway was until he took my hands.

'I don't know how much more of this we're going to be able to take,' I say slowly, the honesty sticking in my throat.

'We're going to get through this.'

'You already told me you don't believe that, that you only say it for other people's benefit. Don't lie to me.'

'I'm not.' He shakes his head, looking directly at me. 'I think now, because of you, we have a chance.'

'I didn't do anything,' I say, pulling my hands from his and turning away.

'Yes, you did,' he insists. 'You made them believe in something better. Made *me* believe in something better. That's why we're here.'

'No, it's not. We're here because of Johnson, because he won't stop until we stop him.'

'And you don't think I knew that?' he says, turning me to face him, forcing my chin up to look at him. He looks so like Aaron, and so unlike him at the same time. His hair is dark, not blonde, and his eyes are the colour of wet earth, like all the real, solid things of the world, instead of the brittle crystal blue of Aaron's, but I see the resemblance in his square jaw, in the lines of his cheekbones, the way his eyes tighten at the corners. 'I knew Johnson wouldn't stop, but I didn't want to have to face him. But I'm not afraid anymore.' His hand slips to the side of my face, and I feel myself go still. 'If you can face everything this place did to you, I can face my father.'

He's so close now that I can feel his breath on my cheek, see each individual eyelash, like black ink strokes against his skin.

'What are you doing?' I whisper, and my heart is a wild thing.

'I don't know,' he breathes, and presses his lips to mine. For a moment I am frozen. This is bad. This is weakness. This is the spaces between your ribs where the knife gets in.

But his hands are on my back, his palms burning holes into my spine, and it's as if I can feel his energy pouring into me with every touch, wave after wave of warmth and calm and it's-going-to-be-alright, something no one ever cared enough to say before him. My heart is trying to pound its way out of my chest, and I'm not sure if I can feel the ground underneath me.

I feel dizzy and upside-down, and there are stars exploding in my bloodstream, and I'm not sure if this is what it was supposed to feel like all along.

Maybe this is what it's supposed to feel like, like your heart can't take it and you can't breathe but you'd give it all up, give everything in the world up for this feeling, like dying and coming back to life over and over again.

Kole kisses me like the world is ending, because it is.

I pull away, just far enough to take a breath, and I'm glad for the low light, like a blanket covering us.

'What was that?' I ask, putting my forehead against his chest because I don't know if I can look at him, but I don't want to pull away.

'I'm sorry,' he whispers, but he wraps his arms around me, and I can hear his heart beating in his chest, and he doesn't sound sorry. He sounds like he can't breathe. He sounds like what I feel like.

'Don't apologise.' I sound too breathless, too uncontrolled. I want to step away from him, to find some semblance of sanity where he can't touch me, where his fingerprints can't set my blood on fire.

But I can't bring myself to walk away.

Instead I press closer, and he kisses the top of my head, and my feet are bare on the cold stone floor and so are his, and it's only then that I realise I must have woken him.

'You were asleep.' There is this muted kind of surprise in my voice as I look up and finally notice his ruffled hair, which stands up on his head, and the softness in the lines of his face, like he's been blurred by sleep.

'I was asleep,' he confirms, and he smiles. His real smiles are so rare that when they appear, I can't help staring at him. There is always that moment of uncertainty as it unfolds, like the full moon, when you're not really sure if it's really full, or if it's just your imagination tricking you.

'What now?' I breathe, and I can feel something coming undone inside me, something so dangerously raw and real and solid that I fear I'll never be able to let go of it.

'Now,' he says, pulling me close again, 'we rebuild the world.'

And that's not what I meant, but maybe it should have been.

20

Every spare second that I'm not helping prepare for our mission into the Celian City, I spend with Sophia. I want to know everything about her, but she doesn't seem ready to open up to me about more than the basics of how she got here, so instead I ask about Bea.

I see an array of competing emotions pass over her face – first joy, then pain, sadness, anger, and finally, solemnity. It's rarer to see this look on Sophi than it was on Bea, but it's strange when I see her doing things so similarly. Sometimes when she smiles I can't help staring at her, wondering if that's what Bea's smile would have looked like.

I never got to see Bea's smile.

'She was sick,' she says, looking down at the floor. We're sitting upstairs in the bedroom, and I shouldn't be here. Aaron is being held downstairs, but I'm desperate to spend as much time with her as I can, because I don't know what's coming next.

'What?' I feel my heart thudding in my chest, and I feel slightly dizzy. 'What did you say?'

'She was just sick. Mom and Dad were sick, and then Bea was sick. I don't know why. Some days she couldn't get out of bed. She puked a lot. She went to the hospital many times, but they couldn't help her. It was one of the old sicknesses, cancer they called it, but different. They didn't have any medicine for it.' Her voice, usually strong and clear, starts to quiver. 'I don't think they really cared if she got better.'

'I'm sorry,' I say, pulling her into a hug. I'm finding it hard to stay calm, but I don't want her to know what I'm feeling.

I don't even know what I'm feeling.

'Nobody knew. She didn't like people knowing.'

I hold onto her like a life-raft, trying desperately to breathe around the lump in my throat.

Bea's bones sticking out from beneath her shirt at the Dorms click into focus in my mind. She wasn't like the other girls, simply abused and undernourished. She was sick, and I was too caught up in what was happening to me to notice it while she was still alive.

I wonder how many things I can regret at one time.

21

The night before the mission, I go to see Aaron. I don't know why I think it's a good idea, but something in me needs to do this.

I push open the door to the room we're holding him in, and he looks up at me immediately. His eyes are a dangerous shade of blue as he watches me, and I know him well enough to know he is just about ready to snap.

I stand in front of him, a few feet away, and stare. I stare at the sweat on his brow, the way his shirt is rumpled and torn, the mess of hair on top of his head, and something in me revels in the mundanity of it, the humanness of dirt and sweat and anger that I have never seen on him before.

'What are you doing here?' he says, and it is a sad attempt at his usual charm.

'I'm here to look at you,' I say carefully, quietly, and I feel strong as I look at him. 'I am here to look at what you have become.'

'I haven't changed,' he replies, and there is a sharp note in his voice. 'But I see you have. You have friends now. People you care about, people who care about you.'

'I do,' I say, raising my chin.

'I thought I taught you better than that.'

'They are not my weakness, Aaron.'

I want to say

you are,

you were,

you are not anymore.

'That is what they've convinced you of. You're weak now. A bullet in the head of someone who is not you shouldn't kill you, Quincy. That's what I always said.'

'But it never applied to you,' I say, taking a step towards him. 'You never wanted it to apply to you. I would have died for you.'

'Exactly.' He smiles.

'But you don't matter anymore,' I whisper, taking another measured step towards him. 'That's what you were always afraid of, wasn't it? That you would cease to matter.'

His smile turns sour.

'You can pretend all you want—' he starts, but I cut him off.

'I'm not pretending,' I say coolly. 'Tomorrow we are going to use you to get to your father, and we're going to take him out. We're going to pull your world apart, and you're going to be nothing.'

'You can't *touch* me!' he growls, pulling against his ties. 'Oasis is invincible.'

And it's as if he thinks they are one and the same thing, him and Oasis, but as I watch him unravel I realise there is an end to this. Because Oasis is not invincible. It never was. The imagined Oasis in our heads was, but once that falls, so will everything else.

'From now on, you fear *me*,' I say, and slam the door behind me as I leave.

22

The next morning I say goodbye to Sophi, and in my head I make a wish: that I will never have to do this again, never leave her behind again.

I promise her a million things, that I will come back, that I will be safe, that once this is over, everything is going to be okay, and she holds me too tight, and I never want to let her go. The tears streaming down my face make me out to be the liar I am.

Because I don't know if I'll come back, or if I'll be safe, or if everything will be okay after this. I don't know anything anymore but the fire in the pit of my stomach that won't let me stop until I've fixed this.

I swear to her that I will build her a better world and that – though just as impossible to guarantee – is not a lie.

I will build her a world where she can be safe, or I will die trying.

23

We untie Aaron and give him a change of clothes, the best clothes Nails has available, because we can't have him walking into the Celian City looking like he's been held hostage for two days. Once he's ready, Kole presses a gun to his back and forces him up the stairs and out the door, into the Outer Sector.

Jay left late last night and returned early this morning with three Officer uniforms for us to change into. No one asks where he got them, so neither do I, but there's a stain on the collar that looks too much like blood to think about for too long.

When I put it on this morning, I couldn't help shivering. The fabric is different from the stuff I wore in the Dorms, but it still feels wrong. The weight of the belt on my hips feels traitorous, and I had to swallow the feelings bubbling up in my chest before they made me do something stupid.

Kole walks past Nails in the hall, pushing Aaron ahead of him, and nods at Nails as he passes.

'One more day,' he says, and Nails just shakes his head, walking away.

We are taking as few people as possible, so Kole, Jay and I are the only ones going in with Aaron. It took a lot of convincing to get Clarke to stay, but Kole said we were already risking it with the three of us and Aaron, and she eventually agreed.

As we come towards the gates separating the Outer Sector from the Inner Sector, several guards step forward, and my heart starts beating too fast, so fast I'm afraid they'll hear it, or see my pulse at my throat and realise something is going on.

'ID,' the first Officer says, but he sounds bored, and my breath comes a little easier.

'I don't have my ID with me, but I'm Aaron Johnson, and they're all with me,' he says, gesturing towards us.

The Officer's eyes widen, and he murmurs something to the second Officer, who hasn't yet said anything. The second Officer jogs back to the guard-post by the gate, and returns a moment later, slightly pale, and nods to the first.

'Okay, Sir,' he says. 'We can get you transport, if you'd like?' There's a slight warble to his voice, but other than that he's been trained out of showing fear, and his face is expressionless.

'A vehicle into the Celian City, Officer,' Aaron replies, smiling, patting the Officer on the shoulder patronisingly. 'Everything's under control.'

A moment later a transport vehicle pulls up beside us, and we are loaded on.

And I think, it can't be this easy.

And I think, it shouldn't be this easy.

And I think, it's not going to be this easy.

24

The Founding Towers are even more beautiful up close. We are dropped off in the very centre of Oasis, and I stare at the world I've spent my whole life dreaming about. The Towers shoot up into the sky like shafts of light, so bright I shouldn't be able to look directly at them, but I can. That's the magic of the Celian City. It looks like it's made of glass, but it's not; it looks like it should be transparent, but it's not. Aaron told me that you can see everything from inside the Towers, but no one can see you.

Kole and Jay walk so close to Aaron they're practically standing on his heels, waiting for him to bolt, for him to do something.

For him to get us killed.

We walk up to the entrance of the Justice Tower, and there is so much security here I think I can actually *feel* them watching us, waiting for some kind of slip-up.

But with Aaron at our side no one blinks as we walk through the sliding doors and into the lobby, a huge high-ceilinged room filled with people walking back and forth in front of the doors, all of them with something to do and somewhere to be and there's this stifling, buzzing sound of voices and machines moving and phones ringing and I already feel the panic rising in my chest.

Kole places his hand on my shoulder for just a second, silently reminding me to breathe.

Aaron walks up to reception, flashing a smile.

'I'd like to see my father, please.'

The woman behind the desk looks up, a little dazed.

'The OP is in a meeting at the moment, but I can—'

'It's really quite urgent.' He smiles wider. 'I'm sure you understand.'

She swallows, smiling back at him.

'Take the elevator to the eighty-fifth floor. He's in room B13.'

'Thank you,' Aaron says, smiling again.

We follow him to the bank of elevators and wait for an empty one before getting in. I've never been in an elevator before, and when it starts moving I jerk forward, my arms flying out to catch myself on the smooth steel siding. I steady myself, placing a hand to my chest as I wait. There's a dial above the door, counting down the floors until we get to the top, and we all stare up at it, Kole's hand wrapped tightly around Aaron's left arm as we rise slowly.

My heart is loud in my ears as we finally come to a stop, the door sliding open in front of us to reveal Oasis laid out before us, stretching out to the very ends of the Wall, and from here, from the sky, it does look like a paradise, with the Outer Sector clutching to its edges like a desperate parasite.

And it's then, as we stare out at the world with wide eyes, that they appear in the sides of our vision like shadows, poised to attack.

25

The walls of the containment room are steel grey, and light pours in on top of me, disorienting me.

When the Officers launched at us, we had only one-tenth of a second to think, and it wasn't long enough. There were so many of them, dozens and dozens of blue uniforms and the glint of their guns all around us as they pulled us apart. As they dragged me away I only had long enough to see Jay's head hit the floor, blood pouring from his leg as Kole was pulled backwards, blur of rage and desperation as he screamed after us, Aaron standing above it all, a grin on his face.

'YOU DIDN'T THINK I'D ACTUALLY LET YOU WIN, DID YOU?' he roars, both frantic and enraged and maniacally joyful, and it made my skin crawl.

As I stand in the containment room, I do the only thing I can think of and start screaming. My voice echoes off the walls and comes crashing back to me, and I scream. My throat is raw and painful, and I scream. I keep screaming, my fists banging against the steel door until they're numb, but it never opens.

Panic starts warping me from the inside out, and my brain concocts a million different images of a bullet through Kole's brain until I can't take it anymore.

'Aaron!' I try to roar, but my voice is hoarse from the screaming, and it comes out as what it is: a plea. At this moment in time I'd do anything to get out of this room, to find Kole and Jay and save them.

I wonder how this happens. How one day you wake up and suddenly there are people who mean more to you than your own life.

I slump to the floor, and desperation fades into bone-deep exhaustion as I realise that this is it. That the accumulation of all the bloodshed and lives lost to keep us safe is just a broken girl in an empty room, with no way to escape.

No way to escape? *There's always a way to escape.* Aaron's own words sound inside my head, and I look around and up.

I look up and I see that the light pouring into the room is from panels in the ceiling, and every second panel is made of some kind of tile. I stand up, my heart leaping in my chest, and jump. The tips of my fingers hit against the tile, which turns out not to be a tile at all but some kind of painted wooden panel. It shifts beneath my hand, just the tiniest fraction, up and down for a second. And then it hits me: this isn't an actual containment chamber, it's just some left-over meeting room too small for the OP and his senators.

I leap again, this time pushing all of my force into the jump, and the panel moves over an inch. I jump again and again and again and again, until the panel is halfway over. I shake out my hands, my heartbeat sounding in my ears like a drum, and I leap, high enough that the tips of my fingers catch the rim before I fall back down.

I hit the ground and curse in frustration, but the next time I leap, I get a grip on the edge and begin pulling upwards. My muscles scream at me, and my arms shake and shake until I think I'm going to fall again, just before I get my elbows over the side, hoisting the rest of my body up after me.

My breath comes in huge heaving gasps, and my arms feel weak, but I'm up. I glance around, trying to see in the low light. Wires from the lights coat the floor beneath me, and there are steel shafts running between panels, I assume holding up the ceiling.

I begin moving along the rafters, balancing precariously as my eyes snap down to the flimsy wooden panels below me. If I lose my balance and fall onto one of those, I'll go straight through them.

The rafters continue on, then take a sharp turn to the left, facing directly into a grate. I pause, my hands gripping a wooden shaft as I squat, staring in through what looks like an air-vent.

I pull experimentally at the grate, which comes away with an upwards tug. I place it gently on top of one of the panels, praying they won't give way under its weight, and wriggle inside the vent. It's tight, but not too tight for me to crawl through on my stomach, using my arms to pull me along. I feel as if it's getting tighter the deeper I go, but I know it's not.

Eventually I come to another grate, the vent coming to an abrupt dead-end. I pull on it, but it's fastened from the outside, not from in here. With a growl of frustration I push at it, but it doesn't budge.

I stop for a second, trying to gather my thoughts, then sit up as far as I can, shoving me legs underneath me. For a second I don't know if I'll be able to turn completely, but eventually I manoeuvre myself around, my feet towards the grate and my head at the opposite side.

I place my hands on either side of the metal vent, take a deep, steadying breath, and kick. The grate comes loose, clattering to whatever floor exists on the other side, and I jump feet first after it.

I land in a crouch, straightening as I look around, my breath frozen in my lungs as I try to understand what I'm seeing.

26

I don't understand. I don't know what I'm supposed to be seeing. The walls are lined with computers, not like the ones at the power station, old and half falling apart, but sleek silver things, information flowing across screens so quickly I can't read it.

But my eyes won't pull away from a line of vials, hundreds of them, lined in carts, the label burned into my mind forever.

Gene X51 Suppression Serum.

I feel myself slipping, the room swimming around me as I stumble forward.

The Cure.

My shaking hands pull at the vials, and I'm trembling so badly I can barely hold it in my hand, the perfect glass container, holding everything.

Everything.

This is everything. This is freedom. This tiny thing, clear serum in a glass vial, is what I have spent my entire life waiting for.

The door behind me flies open, and the vial is dropped, smashing against the floor as I search the room for a weapon before I realise who he is.

And then I realise who he is.

'*Johnson.*' My voice comes like a growl, like a hiss, like a self-indulgent exhalation of pure hatred.

'Quincy Emerson,' he says, an old name from a bygone time, when I was Pure – when I had a right to my identity.

If he looks shocked to see me, he doesn't show it. My first thought is he looks like Aaron; my second thought is a reluctant admission: he looks like Kole. He has their height, their military posture, and their sharp jaw. But his eyes are all Aaron, pale blue flashes of light, like lightning, but colder. And his hair is Kole's dark brown to the point of black, but his is greying at the temples. He's wearing an expensive blue suit, fitted perfectly to his body, made for him.

'I was coming to visit you,' he says, each word slow and warm, reminding me of Aaron's honey-sweet timbre. 'And when I didn't find you where you were supposed to be, well, I had a suspicion you'd find yourself somewhere you don't belong.'

'What's this?' I ask, gesturing my head towards the vials, towards the computers.

'The Cure,' he says. He doesn't blink.

I can feel my breathing speed up, my blood burning in my veins as I try to fight the urge to kill him right now, right this second.

I hear Kole's voice in my head. *Your emotions won't help you. Not now. And not when there's an Officer in front of you. You need to let it go. Everything, every single thought inside of your head. Let it fall away from you.*

I steady myself, slowing my breathing back to normal, and I take one short, measured step towards him.

'How long has this been here?'

'Since before I took over,' he says slowly, closing the button on the front of his blue suit calmly.

I try to process this information, form a new question, but I can't think straight.

'But they're looking for it. Oasis is looking for the Cure.' It sounds ridiculous even as it exits my mouth.

He chuckles slowly, taking a step towards me, his smile mocking. Off camera he looks older, more human.

More mortal.

'You are more naive than I thought, Miss Emerson. We've had the Cure for decades. Did you really think it would take us this long to find it?'

I take a stumbling step backwards as he continues to advance on me, quietly threatening.

'Why is it here then?' I ask, trying to keep the doubt from my voice.

I can't show him weakness. Kole said earlier that's what he wants, to see how he can play with you, make you feel what he wants you to feel.

'Of course it is here, why wouldn't it be? We need the Cure. To keep us safe. Oasis' motto is peace for all; the Cure is peace.' His tone almost self-deprecating as he repeats another Oasis slogan, one that's printed on almost every broadcast about the Cure.

'But … ' My mind is muffled, dealing with too many things at once, and I pull back, pressing my fists to my temples as a headache bursts through my skull.

Johnson takes another step towards me, and I drop my hands from my face and look at him.

'No,' I growl. 'Stop. Don't you dare come any closer.' My breathing is ragged. 'If you have the Cure and you say you need it, then what are you using it for?'

'You,' he says, cocking his head to the side. 'You and everyone like you.'

My heart drops as realisation hits me, knocking the breath from my lungs.

'You already used it,' I whisper, and he smiles, like a proud parent watching their child walk for the first time. 'You've been using it all along. We're already Cured.' My voice rises, the computers beeping around us like a round of sarcastic applause.

'It seems to me,' he says, taking another slow step towards me, 'that none of your kind are really that bright.'

My lip rises in a snarl, but he just smiles.

'First, you think you can escape Oasis merely by leaving the confines of the Wall. Then you let us plant a mole within your ranks, as easy as the press of a button. It really is pathetic, how easily you believe people. It seems a bullet in the shoulder is all you people need to trust a complete stranger.'

I feel like I've been punched in the stomach, and he can tell. I know he can tell because as I feel the blood drain from my face, another perfect smile spreads across his.

'*Lauren?*' My voice sounds high and wavering to me in this echoey chamber.

'Miss Tate, yes. She really is very devoted to Oasis, don't you think?'

I can't speak. Can't breathe. I imagine Sophia at the base with Lauren. I left her with Lauren.

'And now this,' he says, gesturing to the Cure. 'All this time, and you never figured it out. Of course we have the Cure. We couldn't have an actual threat hanging over our heads.'

'But why? Why would you hide it? They would have *worshipped* you for finding it.'

He opens his hands out in front of himself, as if in presentation. 'They already worship me.' He smiles, his blue eyes flashing in the overhead lights.

Jay said anger felt cold, like losing all the feeling in your entire body at once, but if that's true, this is not anger. I lunge at him, my vision blurring red as I go for his throat. Every other thought is gone, evaporating into thin air the moment he opened his mouth and said those four words, words I should have known were coming all along.

And then I am staring down the barrel of a gun.

'Ah ah ah,' he tuts, the same vacant smile on his face now that I've seen every single day of my life, on billboards and posters and in Oasis video-casts.

My eyes drill into his, and I wonder for a brief moment how I never realised who Aaron really was.

Those are Aaron's eyes staring back at me.

'You coward,' I spit, and I cannot pour one-tenth of the venom I feel into those two words.

'Not a coward, Miss Emerson. Merely a strategist.'

27

The sound of a gunshot echoes through the building, and the world stops. Everything is in slow motion, and my heart beats in time with his name.

Kole.

Kole.

Kole.

But I see Johnson's head twist towards the door, and I see the weakness in his grip, and before I know what I'm doing I'm disarming him, flipping the gun over in my hand and aiming it at him, before he has a chance to look back at me.

When he does, he smiles, a smile that sends a shudder down my spine, freezes my blood in my veins, but I keep my hands steady.

Let it fall away from you. I hear Kole's voice echo in my mind. *It won't help you now.*

I move backwards towards the door, the gun still aimed at his head.

I reach behind me, pulling the door open with one hand, keeping the gun on Johnson as I slip through the door.

But he just keeps staring at me, that perfect, blank smile plastered on his face.

'You can't win,' he says, before I close the door, not raising his voice in the slightest. 'This battle is nothing to us, do you understand? Nothing. You do not exist.'

I slam the door, sliding the lock shut behind me.

He'll be out of that room in minutes, but all I can think of now is that gunshot, the sound still ringing in my ears as I take off down the hall. I don't know if I'm even going in the right direction, but I can't waste time trying to decide which route to take.

My boots pound against the celian floors as I pump my arms at my sides, pushing myself to go faster, faster, faster, because I don't know who shot that gun or who they shot it at, but Kole and Jay are in this building somewhere and I need to find them.

I take a corner sharply, almost ploughing into the far wall, but when I see what's at the end of the hall I stop dead.

Aaron holds Kole against the wall on the left of the hall, a gun pressed to Kole's temple, so close to him their faces are practically touching.

'Aaron,' my voice comes out shaky, because I cannot mask this fear. Not this time. Not when it is this. Not when it is Kole.

Kole's eyes lock with mine, a mix of terror and relief exploding across his face.

'Quincy, run.' His voice is a plea, as desperate as my need to get him away from Aaron.

I see it unfolding inside my head: Aaron's patience snapping, the sound of the trigger being pulled back, the next sound, the one that follows that, like everything beginning and ending in one heartbeat.

'Aaron,' I say slowly, taking another step towards them. Aaron doesn't move a muscle, and I am intensely aware of the Officers who are no doubt on their way towards us right now.

'Aaron, you don't want to do this.'

'Shut up,' he hisses. He's shaking almost as badly as I am, and his finger twitches across the trigger. 'You don't know what I want. No one cares what I want. It's what Kole wants that matters. It's what *you* want.' He drives the gun into Kole's temple, and Kole's eyes widen. 'He deserves this.'

'Aaron, no, he doesn't. He doesn't deserve any of this. Johnson is the problem.'

'Johnson is my *father*.'

'Johnson is a monster, Aaron.'

'Shut up, shut up!' he screams, the gun shaking against Kole's temple as his voice rises. Kole doesn't move. 'Johnson is the only family I have.'

'I am your family,' Kole says, and his voice is soft, but it only seems to enrage Aaron further.

'You are nothing to me. You took everything. You took my house and my life and my father. You took *everything*.'

'I didn't want it, Aaron. I didn't want any of it. I would have given it to you in a heartbeat, but I couldn't.' Panic is entering Kole's voice, and my own fear is feeding off the sound.

'You're lying,' Aaron says, but his voice is quiet, doubtful.

'No, I'm not. I didn't want it. I don't know why Johnson chose me. I never asked for any of it.'

'I just wanted him to see me. To see that I was the best. I *was* the best.'

'But you don't need him anymore,' Kole whispers, lifting his hands to move the gun from his head. 'You don't need any of this.'

'No,' Aaron gasps, as if he's coming back to life, pressing the gun closer to Kole's temple. '*No.* You're a liar. He said you would do this. You're just trying to turn me against him. You won't turn me against him.'

'Aaron, he's not a good person. You can't listen to anything he says.'

'I was better than you,' Aaron rambles. He's not listening to us anymore. 'I did everything he wanted me to. I was better than you before, and I was better than you when you left, but he could never look past your loss, so I went straight back to being ignored. Do you know what that's like? *Do you?*'

I can't breathe. I can see him, I can feel the change in the air as his focus shifts, back to Kole, back to rage, back to the trigger of that gun. I see his face twist, watch him turn into that same monster who shot Bea, and as I hear the Officers' footsteps pound up the stairs behind me, I am faced with the same decision I was faced with that day: run, or fight.

And I feel that cold overtake me. I feel my emotions fall away, just as Kole said, like water off my skin.

I raise the gun, take my aim, feel the familiarity of my stance as I prepare for the recoil, and I inhale slowly, my finger falling against the trigger.

I fire.

I am pushed back by the force of it, stronger than what I am used to, but my eyes do not leave him for one second as his body drops like a stone in the ocean.

And he's dead. Like that, like the flick of a light switch, there and then suddenly not.

Killed by his own father's gun.

28

I fall back against the wall, and there is a high-pitched sound coming out of my chest, clawing its way out of my mouth. I'm trying not to scream, but the blood pooling around him is spreading so quickly and I can't breathe.

'Quincy.' Kole's voice is an attempt at calm, a forced smoothness with a hiccup at the end. His breath is cool on my neck, and I don't know how he ended up beside me. 'Quincy, we need to go.' I know we do, I think, but I can't get the words out. I can already hear them. 'Quincy, now.'

His voice is not calm anymore, or soothing or quiet. It is urgent, but not panicked, as he slips into this other him, the one who was built around the real Kole, the one who was taught efficiency first, the mission above all else.

He pulls me up by my arms and starts running towards the exit, towards the next level, and my body bursts into movement as my mind lags behind.

I don't look at his body when we pass. I tighten my hand around Kole's and close my eyes and run.

Kole slips down a hallway, pulling me after him, and I fight to keep up. His strides are longer than mine, and he knows the hallways well. I can tell by the way he turns on a dime, dragging me left, then right, then left again, until we come towards a staircase and come face-to-face with a troop of Officers.

My heart lurches in my chest at the sight of them, but Kole flips us around, sprinting in the opposite direction. The celian halls zip past us, but I can't concentrate on anything but keeping my feet underneath me as Kole speeds up, faster and faster until I can't breathe.

They are coming from every corner. I can hear them behind us, the sound of their boots against the ground in time with my heartbeat. We come around a corner, only to be faced with another oncoming troop, and before I can catch my breath, Kole pulls me sideways, into a small, dark room, and starts mashing buttons on the wall.

'Come on, come on, *come on!*' Desperation makes his voice unsteady, but I can see them coming already.

There are more than I could have imagined, as if every Officer in the Celian City has crashed in on top of us, but before they make it inside, in the second between being caught and being free, the doors hiss closed.

The room jolts, and I reach out, catching the wall and Kole's arm at the same time.

'It's okay,' he breathes, pulling me into his arms. 'It's just the elevator moving.'

'But they're downstairs.' Our heaving breath mixes in the small room, and I grip the front of his shirt, pressing my face into his sternum. 'They're downstairs,' I whisper.

'We'll get out,' he whispers back, and I feel him lift his head, watching the seconds tick by on the timer above us. 'We just need to get out of the City, and we'll be fine.' He sounds strong, but it doesn't mask the doubt in his voice.

'No.' My breath hitches. 'No. They have every Officer in Oasis looking for us. We'll never make it out together.' I close my eyes against his shirt, even though he can't see me.

He goes still, every muscle in his body frozen.

'Kole, Lauren is the mole.'

'Quincy,' he says slowly, and I can tell he's ignoring me.

'Lauren is the one responsible for the attack on the base, but there were more, before her, so there has to be another mole.'

'Quincy.' His breathing is suddenly uneven. 'Quincy, look at me.'

'I don't even know how many there are. There could be several. But you need to find *her* before something else happens.'

I refuse to look up at him, so he pushes my chin upwards, forcing me to, but my eyes just drift to the dial above the door, counting down the floors.

Thirty floors. Ground: zero.

'Quincy. We're getting out of here. Together.'

'No, we're not. Your only chance is to get out while I distract them.' I swallow the pain in my chest, forcing it down for his sake.

'I'm not leaving without you.' He sounds angry now, and he pushes me back far enough to look at me directly in the face. 'No.' He can see the look on my face. '*No.*'

'Find Jay, and get Sophia out of Oasis. Get her away from Lauren. I need to know that she's safe, do you hear me? Then you find Genesis, and you run, understand? *Run.*'

'Yes, but you're coming *with* me.'

'Jay said he escaped an elevator through the roof once. Can you do that?' I look above us, at the panels on the roof, and I know he can.

'Quincy, I'm not leaving you.'

I place my hands on either side of his face, and somehow the shaking has stopped. The fear has been sucked out of me, and all that is left is this determination. I'm going to save him, and he's going to get Sophi to safety.

I hope Bea can see me now.

'I'll find you,' I tell him, leaving my forehead against his. His dark brown eyes are wide, and even if I am not afraid, he is. 'I'll get out, eventually, and I'll find you. I promise.'

'No, Quincy. *No*, I can't—'

'I need to know she's safe. I need to know *you're* safe.'

'Please don't do this.' His voice is a rough whisper as he closes his eyes, pulling me closer, as if he can stop everything outside of those doors if he hopes hard enough.

But that is not the world we live in. We live within chaos and destruction, a world we neither asked for nor created.

'You're faster than me, and you know this building. If I distract them, it'll give you time to get away. If I try to come with you, we'll both end up dead.' I take a steadying breath. 'This way we have a chance, at least.'

I'm only glad that in our world, this exists too, these stolen moments of peace. We were left with this last consolation, that the connections we form are not destroyed by pain but strengthened by it.

'Go.' I close my eyes so I don't have to see him leave. I feel him press his lips to mine, and that's the only promise I need from him.

Because that is a promise he cannot break.

And then I feel him go, like a coldness, there and then not, just like Aaron.

But I will find Kole again. No matter what I have to do, or who I have to go through, I will find him, and I will rebuild our world from the ashes we were left.

The elevator stops, halting suddenly as the doors slide open, and I hear them before I see them, the stomping of a hundred boots as they prepare to take me down.

They don't know it yet, but this time, I'm taking them down with me.

Gill Books
Hume Avenue
Park West
Dublin 12
www.gillbooks.ie

Gill Books is an imprint of M.H. Gill & Co.

978 07171 6923 8

Edited by Rachel Pierce at Verba Editing House
Designed by www.grahamthew.ie
Typesetting by O'K Graphic Design, Dublin
Printed by CPI Group (UK) Ltd, Croydon, CRO 4YY

This book is typeset in 11/17 pt Plantin
Section heads in Neutra text bold

The paper used in this book comes from the wood pulp of managed forests. For
every tree felled, at least one tree is planted, thereby renewing natural resources.

A CIP catalogue record for this book is available from the British Library.

5 4 3 2 1